CAFÉ ASSASSIN

by

Michael Stewart

Bluemoose

Copyright © Michael Stewart 2015

First published in 2015 by
Bluemoose Books Ltd
25 Sackville Street
Hebden Bridge
West Yorkshire
HX7 7DJ

www.bluemoosebooks.com

British Library Cataloguing-in-Publication data
A catalogue record for this book is available from the British Library

Paperback ISBN 978-1-910422-05-2

Printed and bound in the UK by Short Run Press

One man's blood
is another man's stain.
Jim Greenhalf

For Lisa and Carter

PUT OUT YOUR FIRES

How many ways had I thought about killing you, Andrew? And now I was coming for you. I was standing in a queue, waiting. The guard was staring at me. I could feel the acid of fear and hate burning through my insides. Twenty-two years of fear. Twenty-two years of hate. I was sandwiched between a man with a mullet and a woman with a butterfly tattoo, and the guard was staring at me. I was gripped with dread. He was Saint Peter holding the keys to the gate.

He did not say good morning. Instead, he thrust a scratched black tray in my direction. I'm sure you would have got a very different reaction, Andrew: a 'please' and a 'thank you' – perhaps he would have even called you 'sir'. No one has ever called me 'sir'. Ever. I emptied my pockets. First money, then keys, followed by a packet of tobacco, a lighter and some cigarette papers. He picked up the papers and examined a tear in the card with suspicion.

I didn't have any filters, I said.

Why was I explaining myself to him? I emptied the rest of my pockets. The final item was a knife. Not just any knife – but *the* knife. Yes, I forgot about the knife: *Liv's* knife, *your* knife. *My* knife.

How could I forget about the knife? I'm sure you're wondering, Andrew. I'd had it for twenty-two years. The guard reached into the tray and took out the knife. He held it between his massive thumb and index finger, making it look tiny, almost like a toy, certainly not a threat.

You can't take this in, he said.

You know its dimensions, probably not even three inches long. He used his other hand to open out the tools, first the bottle opener and then the nail file. Then he turned it over and pulled out the blade. He let the blade glimmer in the harsh light.

You know how that knife can injure. You were there that evening when I received it as a gift. As I recall, you were the one who stuck the knife in, Andrew. You'll remember the wound gushing with blood. Two towels wrapped around my hand, the blood dripping red all over Liv's cream carpet. The blood dripping into the milk jug, fresh shock on Liv's face.

I'm going to have to take this off you. You'll need to fill this in.

The guard handed me a form and a disposable pen.

You'll have to write to the courts to get it back.

Why can't you put it behind reception and then I can get it when I leave? I said. An obvious point, I thought.

Because we don't do that, he said.

But the reception is just there, I said, pointing to the counter.

You have to make a request in writing to the court manager. It's all in there, he said and handed me an information sheet. Behind me the queue was lengthening and I could tell he was becoming hot and agitated. Good, I thought, let him roast.

I persisted. When can I get it back?

It's all in there, he said.

I folded up the form and put it in my pocket. I stepped through the metal detector. It went off and immediately I panicked. My palms were sweating and my legs weak. Stay calm, you've done nothing wrong. Another guard frisked me. I held up my arms and he worked around my body.

Turn round, he said, and frisked me from behind.

It was the assumption of guilt. I was a crook. He was looking for a weapon but it was just my belt. I went over to the listings in the corner, looking for your name: Andrew Honour. I always liked your name, in contrast to my own which, still to this day, I despise. It seemed to be a name that was going places. A name with promise. But I couldn't find your name on any of the lists.

There were clocks everywhere. I imagine the walls of hell are lined not with vents gushing fire and brimstone but instead with an array of timepieces. I watched them tick. I waited.

At 10am I was looking for you in Court One. A woman in her forties was crying, her mascara running down her face in inky rivulets. It was the woman I'd seen in the queue with the butterfly tattoo. The man with the mullet was hugging her as he ushered her in to the court. I sat down in the public seating area. Four men and a woman in black gowns and wigs were standing at the front clutching files tied with ribbons. One of the men was on crutches. They looked like a gathering of hooded crows. I scanned their faces. None of them looked like you, Andrew, as I imagined you after twenty-two years. The same age as me, forty. Fat? Bald? Grey? It didn't matter. I'd know you as soon as I saw you.

What happened? said the woman in a wig and gown to the man in a wig and gown on crutches, gasping in mock-horror.

Skiing, he said, and mimed the action of skiing with the crutches, scrunching his face up in what he clearly felt was an amusing way.

Oh no! You poor thing, she said.

The woman with the butterfly tattoo was sitting down now, still crying. The mulleted man was still trying to console her. The judge entered, we stood up. He sat down, we sat down. I wonder why these people never get shot. It would be easy to do, wouldn't it? All the fuss over security at the door and yet they walk out of the building unguarded – almost asking for a bullet.

Are you Jamie Turnbull? the clerk to the court said to the man in the dock. For a moment, I thought he was addressing me. I wanted to stand up, plead my innocence and tell him he had the wrong man.

I am, said the man in the dock.

A guilty plea for dangerous driving. Dangerous driving – I almost laughed. That's not a crime. That's just over-excitement. The judge seemed impatient, even though they'd only just started. Probably anticipating lunch in one of the fine eateries that surrounded the courts.

I was wondering whether other barristers would be involved. What was the best thing to do, sit tight and wait for you, or move around and risk missing you? It was a dilemma. I decided to sit it out. What would I do when I saw your face? Would I be able to resist putting my hands round your throat and squeezing the life out of you?

Jamie was imprisoned for nine months. Next was a robbery. The boy standing in the dock barely looked eighteen. He'd gone up to a student and asked him for the time, then he'd grabbed his phone and punched him in the face. The student ran away, but this lad, who caught up with him, dragged him to the ground and then kicked him repeatedly in the face. In the face, Andrew, in the fucking face.

He was given eighteen months in a young offenders'. I left the room and walked across the hallway to Court Two. Perhaps this was where I'd find you, Andrew.

Vinnie Howell, commercial burglary. Vinnie was a smackhead but he'd been off opiates for three months, according to his legal representative, who also wanted it known that Mr Howell had served queen and country in the armed forces. I scrutinised the barristers in their archaic raiment. They were not familiar. Surely a man cannot change beyond recognition? Had I changed? I still had the same build, though I supposed I'd filled out a bit – I hadn't overdone the weight-training but still, it showed: thirteen stone. Waist: 32. Chest: 46. Neck: 16. No grey hair. No receding hairline. Forgive me, Andrew, for rubbing it in.

Vinnie Howell was fined and given community service. He seemed relieved, the tightness around his shoulders eased. The expression on his face was one of defiance. He had a tattoo on his arm, I couldn't make out what it was. He pointed to it and stared at the judge with even greater defiance.

Next up was another smackhead; the one after him also a smackhead. What was the judge's drug of choice? Port? Cuban Cigars? Brandy? Champagne? Vintage wine? Cocaine?

You were not there, Andrew. I stood up again and left the room, making my way to Court Three. Another commercial burglary. Another smackhead. It was 10.57 and still no sign of you. I went to the next court, Court Four.

This time I thought I saw you, but it was hard to tell from where I was. It was your profile. The same straight nose and weak chin. But there was too much reflection from the screen separating the barristers from the public. I saw my own outline projected onto the glass like a ghost. I could see the court beyond but it was hard to make out the faces, just the wigs and black gowns.

Perhaps you liked wearing the costume, Andrew, in the same way some people enjoy fancy dress parties, or dressing up as the opposite sex. The barrister spoke. He had a Belfast accent. It wasn't you. Bollocks.

How many times had I thought about killing you? How many ways? Killing you was the easy part: knife, rope, gun, poison, a staged accident. Perhaps the most satisfying would be to kill you with my own hands and watch you gasp your last breath. There were no end of ways. The difficult part would be getting rid of the evidence. I could dig a grave and bury you deep in the earth, let the worms feast on your flesh. I could use acid to dissolve your corpse. I could feed you to the pigs – apparently they leave only the hair and teeth. I would then burn the hair and grind your teeth into a fine powder. There would be nothing left of you. No trace whatsoever. But some time ago now, I cooked up a better plan.

I was feeling queasy. I hadn't found you and I didn't want to give up on you, but I was finding it hard to breathe. My chest was constricting, nausea building. There were another seven courts to go, but I was not going to get round them in an hour. I could come back another day. It wasn't as though I had anything else to do. I went downstairs and out the door.

I stood near the entrance of the courts, breathing deeply. I leaned against the concrete wall. I was trembling, lightheaded, as though I could pass out at any moment. I needed a cigarette. I used up the last of my tobacco as I rolled one and lit it. What now? I sat on a wall on the other side of the road and waited. I read the form I'd been given by the guard. To get my knife back I would need to make a request within twenty-eight days. I put the form in my pocket.

After a while, they started to come out of the building: the men in pinstripe suits pulling cases on wheels, the cases filled with gowns and wigs and bundles of files tied with ribbons. They all had short hair, they were all well groomed. But none of them were you.

Then I saw you. I couldn't quite believe my eyes. Was it? Yes, it was – it *was* you. And you were walking towards me, pulling your case. Hair thinner and greyer, face fuller. You were wearing glasses and you had a paunch, more jowly, your neck thicker, but it was unmistakably you. I pulled my hood up, moving back into the shadows. Out of the two of us, you'd aged the worst. The extra weight around your cheeks had made your cheekbones lose definition and your weak chin was weakened further by the flab beneath. The beer belly didn't suit you at all. You didn't have enough muscle on your shoulders to carry it off – it turned you into a pear. I was by far the superior specimen. And that knowledge filled me with joy.

I waited for you to pass, then followed some distance behind, up the road. We walked a quarter of a mile. At one point you turned around, but you didn't recognise me. Why would you? I was just another man in jeans and a hoodie – one of the invisible people. A shadow.

Eventually you arrived at your chambers, climbed the steps at the entrance and disappeared inside. I waited for you. What now? How long would you be in there? Perhaps that was you done for the day. Would you go straight home? Would you have a game of golf? Surely not golf. Please don't let him be a golf player, or someone with a yacht, I prayed to a dead god. It must have been nearly an hour before you reappeared. You made your way to a Jaguar and drove off.

A car. I should have thought of that. I was convinced you'd take the train. I'd pictured you in first class, reading *The Telegraph* or hunched over case notes, with a servant pouring another espresso. I should have driven across in my dead dad's car, but after all this time there was no sense in rushing things. I would go back to my new flat and write to the court. I would get my knife back. The main thing was, I'd found you.

||

The next day I did a hundred press-ups, a hundred sit-ups and five minutes of shadowboxing. I showered and dressed, had toast and scrambled eggs, half a cup of black coffee. When I got to the job centre it was already busy with those signing on and those making fresh claims. I sat on one of the newer-looking chairs.

It was all new to me, my first time in a job centre. They used to call it the dole office, or the DHSS. Now it was called 'jobcentreplus'. A single lowercase word with 'job' and 'plus' in white and 'centre' in yellow with a background of verdant green, to make it appear fresh and wholesome, a living thing – it was certainly thriving.

A voice, crackly with interference, announced the next claimant.

Nicholas Smith.

I stood up with more forms to fill in, boxes to tick, walking over to the illuminated desk.

It's Nick, I said.

I'm sorry?

The woman was facing a computer screen. She was dressed neatly and was tapping away at the keyboard.

Please, call me Nick.

For the first time she looked at me. Her eyes gave nothing away. She wasn't bad looking. Medium-length straight brown hair, probably in her late twenties. Her low-cut neckline was just on the right side of respectable, so that your eye was tempted, yet at the same time you blamed yourself for looking.

Have you filled in the forms?

Most of them.

She took the forms from me and started to leaf through them, ticking some of the boxes in the 'to be completed by staff only' columns.

What do you do?

Do?

Was this to be an existential enquiry? I wondered.

What is your normal employment?

Oh, I see. I'd anticipated this question, rehearsed my response in my mind many times, but still it jolted me. I shrugged, Whatever's going. I smiled at her but she frowned.

Office work or manual work?

I don't mind.

Any qualifications? She turned back to her screen.

It's all there, I said, pointing to the form. She read on.

So you've got two degrees, one in English and one in Combined Social Sciences?

Yes.

From the Open University?

That's right.

She looked at me again, as though searching for something. I smiled back. Was I more acceptable to her now she knew I was educated? Perhaps I was more qualified than she was and she resented this.

Do you own any land abroad?

Let me think ... No.

Do you collect a war widow's pension?

I leaned back, not in a cocky way, I hoped, but an endearing one. I smiled again.

Well? she said.

I mean, what do you think?

She tapped something into the machine.

Are you a share fisherman?

A what?

A share fisherman.

9

I'd never heard of a share fisherman.

You don't own your own boat?

Correct.

Look, it may seem like a silly question but I have to ask it.

That was the nature of her employment: to incuriously ask strangers farcical questions. She tapped away for some time. I looked around. The room was still full but quiet, like a library without the books.

How much are you prepared to work for?

I turned to the woman again, Money? I don't know. What's normal?

She glanced at me once more. Perhaps my question had seemed sarcastic but that wasn't my intention. I attempted a smile but she had already turned away.

I meant the minimum ... per hour.

I was surprised by this question. I'd expected them to dictate this. I don't know really. How about ten pounds?

The woman seemed vexed. She pinched the top of her nose. You'll severely limit your ability to find work.

I sat back in the plastic chair and recalculated the sum. How about a fiver an hour? How does that sound?

The woman turned from the computer and confronted me across the table. The minimum wage is set at £5.93 per hour for workers aged twenty-one and over.

How about £5.93 then?

She tapped again at the keys and then hit the return button. You've not filled in some of the information regarding your previous employment.

I'd been preparing for this. I'd rehearsed my answer and was playing it over and over in my head.

You did the first two years of a fitting apprenticeship at a motor factory.

Yes.

But that was twenty-two years ago.

Yes.

Well, what have you been doing for twenty-two years?

I felt tired. The invented scenario in my head was still playing. Several years abroad, working in Spain in a bar, café work in Amsterdam, picking grapes in France, then years of self-employment as a handyman, but it all went out of my head and I just came out with it.

I've been in prison.

For twenty-two years?

Sort of, yes. One way or another.

What for?

It's complicated.

Go on ...

I looked at her.

Yes?

Murder.

She stopped tapping at the keyboard and looked away from her screen. She turned to me. She didn't say anything, just looked at me and narrowed her eyes, as if I was something she was trying to read from far away. Did she perhaps think I was joking? She raised her eyebrows, staring at me with renewed interest. Not horror, or even fear, just curiosity.

Don't suppose there's anything on your system for murderers, is there?

Outside the sky was bright grey. The air in the job centre had been dry and sterile and I was thirsty. It was only ten o'clock but early enough for the pubs to be open. One of the noticeable differences. You might think that I would have been more at sea in this new world, given the length of time I had been away. But you get to watch a lot of television inside and there are new people coming in all the time, so I was prepared for most of the changes I encountered. But pubs opening at eight in the morning was not something that had occurred to me. It was a welcome novelty. I bought a newspaper, rolling tobacco and more Rizlas. I walked through the city centre.

It was March, cold but crisp, clean on my skin. I'd shaved a few hours ago and the chill tickled my cheeks. I walked beneath the inner ring road, via the subway. I skipped over a rivulet of piss intersecting my path. The air was tangy. It wasn't a particularly salubrious scene or indeed an inviting one, but this was freedom and, although freedom stank of piss and incarceration stank of piss, this piss still smelled sweeter than prison cell piss.

The landlord was just opening up. He nodded 'hello' as I approached the bar. A plump and friendly barmaid served me a pint. I sized her up. It was good to gaze on a real woman and not the uniformed simulacra of womanhood the female screws represented. I sat in the corner. There were already a few postmen at the bar and some old alkies in flat caps and oil-stained overcoats. I drank from my glass and, for a moment, I felt normal.

Beer is the one thing you can't get inside. Some prisoners attempt to brew their own beverage. The preferred method is to use orange juice, sugar and cream crackers (for the yeast content). The result is a very unpalatable, albeit lethal, 'poteen' style concoction. You can easily acquire skunk, crack, smack, Valium, Mogadon, Subbies, any drug you like, but a pint of real ale ... I'd fixated on it many times. I would close my eyes and I'd be there at the bar, some curvaceous barmaid with plenty of cleavage pulling the pump. The froth flowing over her hand, like some cheesy beer advert. A pathetic male fantasy, but the sort that's necessary when you're banged up and clinging to the fine threads of your sanity.

I took hold of the glass and consumed the beer in four sups. I went back for a refill. How do the purveyors of alcoholic beverages view their clientele? With pity, scorn, disdain? Rarely with affection. But they should reassess this relationship, for what they sell is all the goodness of the world. That pint of beer tasted to me of laughter and innocence. It was golden and glowing with life. Like an eighteen-year-old girl dancing and singing, spinning round, her hair bouncing, her eyes sparkling.

I was thinking of Liv. A mess of black hair down over her shoulders, smoke-grey eyes, framed by thick black eyeliner. Curves, calves, clavicles.

The TV was on in the corner. Twenty-four hour news. Bombs, tanks, Libya. Gaddafi railing against foreign imperialism. He looked confused. A few months ago he'd been laughing and drinking champagne with the very people that were now dropping bombs on his head. You've got to watch that. Your enemy is the man standing next to you, smiling. Your enemy is the man who pats you on your back and says, well done, mate. Your enemy is neatly dressed in a charcoal suit, a plain tie and a crisp white shirt.

The footage changed. Cuts. Cuts in spending. Police, the arts, the NHS. No one escaping the axe except the bankers and the barristers. There was an anonymous suit trying to justify funding the arts by explaining how it feeds the economy. I can tell you how to justify it. You justify it like this: first, picture a man locked inside a white concrete box, with a bright light in his eyes, with no sense of hope. Picture this pitiful creature lying on his bed, repeating a line of poetry over and over again. Why is he doing this? He's doing this to feel human. He is doing this to feel connected to something outside of his own hell. He is doing this because if he doesn't the water will pour in and he will drown.

Rising crime, rising unemployment. An old man in a flat cap nursing a half, turned to me. It's like the eighties all over again, he said and stared at the screen.

There was a band on the radio sounding just like *The Pixies*. He was right, the eighties all over again, and I was transported in my mind to *that* club on *that* night.

You were at the bar, Andrew, and I was dancing with Liv on the floor. She was wearing the red and blue polka dot dress with the white collar, which made her look both chaste and filthy at the same time. It was *The Pixies* song, 'Debaser'. And I was singing along, 'I want to grow up to be, be a debaser'. Liv

13

was joining in. 'DEEE-BASER!' The whole club was moving to the manic beat. Her eyes were sparkling, her hair was shining, her skin was glowing. I was careful not to get too close to her. I kept looking to where you were standing by the bar, but you were busy chatting to someone. It was meant to be just me and you. Our last night out before you went to King's College to study law. A goodbye blowout. But we were predictable. We were eighteen and there was only one club we went to, and that happened to be the same club that everyone else in our social circle also went to.

The Hacienda was for estate scallies in designer tat and over-styled haircuts, or middle-class students pretending to be estate scallies in designer tat and over-styled haircuts. I always hated Kicker boots and baggy jeans. I hated those over-sized long sleeved T-shirts with a smiley face and 'aceeeeeed!' printed across the chest. We would look at the queue of clones outside and go next door instead, down the stairs, following the fog from the smoke machine, following the bass from the sound system, submerging into the comforting dark of The Venue.

We'd shared a small bottle of Southern Comfort on the bus. We'd had a couple of pints in the Britons Protection, and now we were coming up on a pill. We weren't very experienced in the world of illicit pharmaceuticals and this was, if I remember correctly, only our fifth or sixth time. We were starting to feel the music tingle and the warm feeling spread right to the tips of our fingers. I couldn't take my eyes off your girlfriend. I wanted to touch her skin. I wanted to kiss her flesh. Euphoria, wave after wave. Over and over. The eighties, cuts, cuts, cuts, Gaddafi, Gaddafi, Gaddafi, Ecstasy, Ecstasy, Ecstasy.

I sat back, warm in the memory, warm in the glow from the second beer. I looked back to the old man. He was staring at the TV. Two postmen were chatting in the corner. I looked over at the barmaid, taking a steaming glass from the washer and placing it on the shelf above her, enjoying watching her arm stretch up and her cleavage rise above her top. I rolled a cigarette, put it to my lips and lit it.

Immediately, the landlord rushed over and grabbed it off me. It wasn't 1989, Andrew, it was 2011, and smoking in public houses was outlawed. You could smoke in prison but not in pubs. You could smoke in the bar of the Houses of Parliament but not in pubs. Prisoners and politicians. Criminals and crooks. Only the damned are given licence. You can smoke all you like in hell. I looked over to the door. The door was open. It was something I kept having to remind myself. The door was open, it wasn't locked.

I stayed for one more drink. I wanted to bask in this state of having found you. I surreptitiously glanced at the barmaid's supple body and glistening flesh. I imagined her with no clothes on. Desire is both wonderful and terrible: it charges you with hope, it chokes you with despair.

I spent the rest of the day wandering round the city, mesmerised by all that was new and immersed in the life around me. Back at my newly rented flat I made myself a coffee and sat at the Formica table. The floor was in terrible condition and a new patch on the ceiling indicated that there had been a leak. I listened to the deafening hum of the fridge. Why was it so loud? I turned on the radio to block out the sound and listened to it for a few hours. I rolled a spliff and smoked it down to the roach. Dark outside but it wasn't late. Probably no later than ten o'clock. A bit stoned, a bit pissed. Just the radio for company. I decided to go for a walk.

It was dark and cold. I wandered down each narrow snicket, passing the backs of people's houses. As I wandered, I could peer into their lives. There was a couple, their kids probably already tucked up warm in bed. She was in a bathrobe, he was in tracksuit bottoms and vest. They were snuggled up together on their sofa, staring at the screen that lit up the room and made their faces glow.

I passed a house with a conservatory. In the living room, a man slumped in an armchair was watching a large plasma. In the conservatory, a woman slumped in an armchair was watching a smaller plasma. They were like a diminishing reflection of each other. Their wedding album on the shelf, unopened, collecting dust. Down another snicket, different houses, different windows, same images. Through a ginnel, terraced houses, kitchens.

I stopped to watch a man at his kitchen window, washing up. He placed a white plate in the sink and scrubbed at it with a green and yellow sponge. It was a simple action, but it captured my attention. He took another plate, removed the grease and made it clean. I could see the dignity of being alive, being free, independent. I watched as he took each item of crockery, submerging it in the foaming water, cleaning it with a sponge and then stacking it on the plastic drainer. He took a towel and wiped his hands, carefully dabbing between his fingers and the edges of his nails. The job was done. He seemed satisfied.

A woman entered the room and walked up behind him, putting her arms around his waist. He turned to her and they embraced. This image of them entwined was framed in the window, backlit by the kitchen light. I watched them until they broke off from their embrace and left the room, switching off the light as they went, creating a black screen. I couldn't get the image out of my head. My whole body ached. I felt sick with longing.

I came to the main road. I could see something skulk in the distance. It looked like a fox, slinking across, but as it got closer I could tell that it was a dog. Startled, it ran into the road. A car screeched round the corner, clipping the dog, sending it flying up and onto the pavement. A dull thud as it hit the flags. The car drove off, the driver perhaps unaware of what he had done. I chased after the car, but it had gone. I went back to the dog.

It lay in a heap on the pavement, eyes looking scared. It wasn't wearing a collar. There was blood pouring from its back leg. I picked it up – it wasn't heavy – and carried it back to the flat. I laid it out on a blanket. It was a male. I examined him. He didn't seem to mind. He let me feel him all over, as I checked for broken bones.

He seemed unharmed apart from his back leg. I bathed it with a cloth and warm water. It wasn't broken but there was a deep cut that revealed the bone beneath. I cleaned the wound and bandaged it with a clean rag. I looked in his eyes again. Trust.

Are you hungry?

I took two cereal bowls from the cupboard above the sink, filled one with water and emptied a tin of tuna into the other. I took them over to where he was lying but he didn't show any interest. He was probably too exhausted to eat, or in too much pain. I propped his head with a pillow and put some of the fish onto my palm. He fed from my hand. I kept doing this until all the tuna was gone. Then I took the pillow away and let him lie back on the blanket. It was hard to tell his age, but he wasn't old. He was slim, with plenty of muscle under his hair. He had done a lot of running away. I felt scabs along his back. He'd done a lot of fighting.

There's a good boy.

He needed a name. He looked like a fox so I called him Reynard. Ray for short.

I stroked him, There you go Ray, you'll soon feel better.

He'd only just met me but it was there already. Trust. It's something you lose over time. Bit by bit you lose it and then there's nothing left, is there, Andrew? It was important that this dog didn't lose it. Trust.

Outside the wind was blowing refuse around. A can clattered down the street. I closed my eyes and in my mind I was clutching a pestle and mortar. I was making a powder by grinding your teeth.

You are playing pool with a man who murdered his best friend with a hammer. His name is Philip Heggerty. You are in Gartree prison in Leicestershire. This is your final spell of incarceration. You are surrounded by killers: religious killers, contract killers, domestic killers, binge killers, nice killers, rich killers, poor killers, police killers. You have been to see the senior forensic psychologist, Stephanie Simpson. She has really helped you come to terms with what you have done. You just wanted to thank her now you have been given the all clear. You are old mates these days.

You have just seven-balled Shaun Gibbs who killed a woman by strangling her, a woman he had only just met in a kebab house. He followed her to the park, murdered her, then handed himself in. He is autistic and finishing off a degree in pure mathematics. Everything you do is being watched and everything you do is being judged. But it no longer matters. You smile at a closed circuit camera.

You have been in prison longer than you have been out of prison. There is a certain amount of respect for you now. You're a veteran. You have your own cell. It is a small room but you are allowed to put up posters. You have covered the walls with pictures of dead poets. Only the back wall is still bare. You are not allowed to put posters up on the back wall in case you do a 'Shawshank'. You have a budgie called Baudelaire which you keep in a cage. Sometimes you let Baudelaire out of the cage so that he is free within your cage.

You were given a tariff, a minimum number of years you have to spend in prison before you will be considered for parole. You were given this tariff a long time ago and you are nearly at the point of being eligible for early release. You like thinking about this. You can see the time ticking down in your skull. You can see yourself walking down a city road. You know exactly where you are going. You know exactly who you want to see. You picture this person in your mind. But this is replaced by another image. An image you don't want to see.

Instead, you concentrate on the yellow and the red balls. You like the yellow and the red balls. You like the way the green baize of the table offsets the colours of the balls and intensifies their hues. You like the white ball, isolated and yet at the centre of everything. You focus on the black ball. The black ball unnerves you. It is like you. Inside of you is a black ball. The black ball inside you is a secret. The secret is black and hard and densely packed.

You have read somewhere that pool balls used to be made of celluloid and could explode at any moment. Celluloid is a volatile substance. Your secret is made of celluloid.

In Gartree, prisoners are only locked in their cells overnight and at lunch times. During the day you are expected to keep yourself busy with education, exercise, or work. You are even paid for your work, and you can spend this money on luxuries, such as CDs, books, or treats for Baudelaire. It is not a tough prison, despite being full of murderers.

You have decided to do the rest of your time on your own. No more complications. You are over that now. You can beat it by yourself. You pocket one of your reds and snooker Philip behind another. You watch Philip pot the white ball by mistake, giving you two shots again. But you are not going to pot the black ball. You are going to let Philip win this game because, unlike Shaun, you understand what Philip Heggerty did.

|||

An old fucked Ford, a few hundred quid, a battered guitar and a rusty tool box. That was all he left me when he died. The old fucker. The old fucker hadn't worked for years. Council house. No family, no friends. Just a few old winos down the local for company. You'll remember that he was a plumber by trade, self-employed, had his own van with his name and number on. But he was done for drink-driving and lost his licence. Don't know if we ever talked about the ins and outs of it. I remember you calling for me, standing in the back yard, afraid to come in, or knocking on the front door so quietly I could barely hear you.

He'd sit at the dining table massaging his temples, staring off into the distance. You didn't dare enter the room when he was like that. Neither did I. Best to stay well clear. The drinking got to be a real problem. By the time of my trial he was rarely sober. The only thing that would wake him up was a boot in his bollocks.

As I grew taller than him and he grew more inebriated, the tables turned. I was no longer afraid of him. I looked down on this mess of a human being. But now his money, his guitar, his toolbox and his car were my only possessions. The car hadn't been driven for months. He'd won it in a bet a few years before he died. No tax, no insurance, no MOT. It took me the best part of the morning to get the engine going. Two years as an apprentice fitter in a motor factory. Some of those skills were still there. Eventually the pistons turned over and it choked into action, just like my old man used to do.

Did you know that they let me out to go to his funeral? A rare moment of compassion. There was no one there I recognised.

Just a few blokes from the boozers he frequented. I didn't introduce myself. In and out. It was over in twenty minutes. I scattered the ashes over the cricket pitch where he used to play as a lad. He was captain of his team back then. Bit of an athlete.

I stopped to get petrol. Probably had just under a hundred quid left. I was worried about what I'd do when it ran out. There was no hope of a job. Not a conventional one, at any rate. I put twenty quid of petrol in the tank. I had no idea how far outside of Leeds you lived. I imagined you in a leafy suburb, or in the countryside. Perhaps on the outskirts of a picturesque village or hamlet. There would be a community centre with activities for children and pensioners: Pilates classes, story-time, zumba. A charming summer fete with a hook-a-duck and a guess-the-weight competition. Hanging baskets full of flowers. You wouldn't be an active community member, but you would give a large donation to the centre twice a year.

I pulled up outside your chambers and waited. I put the radio on. There was someone singing about having open arms for broken hearts. I was hungry – I hadn't eaten since yesterday but it was important to watch every penny. I'd given the last piece of bread to Ray that morning. He was still weak. I left him on the rug licking his leg. Over and over, licking and licking.

It was two o'clock when you came out of your chambers dressed in a different pinstripe suit from the one I'd seen you in two days ago. I watched you walk over to your Jag, deactivate the locking mechanism with your electronic key fob, open the driver's door and get in. You got out again, nonchalantly removing a parking ticket from your windscreen. You started the engine without a single splutter and then you were off, with me following behind.

I made sure to maintain a safe distance between us, letting one car in between to act as a shield. You drove out of Leeds, up Woodhouse Lane, towards Otley. I nearly lost you at the mini-roundabout when you took the bypass to the left, in the direction of Ilkley. You drove through the centre of Ilkley, past café bars and restaurants, wine merchants and antique shops, then up a long tree-lined lane, until at last you slowed down without indicating left, and pulled up outside a pair of gold-coloured gates attached to two huge white pillars.

The gates opened without you needing to get out of your car. You drove across a gravel driveway to a triple garage. The garage building looked old – seventeenth century. Bigger than my old man's council house. You parked the car and walked round the garage, out of sight. I waited for half an hour then got out of my car. Your house was quite unassuming from the front, but as I approached the wall round the back I could see this was misleading.

In fact, your home was a palace. The garden reached out with views of the moors stretching as far as the eye could see. I checked that no one could see me, then I climbed over the wall and slunk through the orchard. Had Liv aged as badly as you, Andrew? It would make things easier. I could go back and forget about your wife. Find some nice do-gooder with a thing for murderers on matchfinder.com.

I was close to your house now. I looked through your conservatory, observing your sofa, a dining table and six chairs. I wanted to get closer but it was too risky. I was well concealed behind a thick green bush which grew around an oak tree. I waited. Then the door opened. I saw her hair first. The same flash of black, albeit shorter, neater than it used to be. She bent down to put on some garden shoes and picked up a wicker basket.

She walked across the gravel path very close to the bush where I was crouching. I held my breath. There was a herb garden just past my den and she bent down to collect some. She was wearing a white gypsy top and as she bent down her black hair cascaded and her cleavage came into view. My heart raced and my stomach churned. I was a forty-year-old man. I was an eighteen-year-old boy. It was 2011. It was 1989.

I knew then that I wouldn't be using internet dating facilities. Twenty-two years I'd been waiting. And now I was going to take what was mine. I wanted everything you had: your car, your house, your kids, your wife. I wanted your life.

I sat and I watched. Hours went by. Cars drove past, returning from work. The sky darkened, the street lights brightened, the stars appeared. I watched you eat your evening meal. You seemed to take no pleasure from the food in front of you but you reached greedily for your wine glass. You didn't have much to say to each other and neither of you smiled. You cleared the table in the dining room. Liv was in the living room on the phone. The telly was on but there was a mute symbol in the corner of the screen.

I walked round to your study. There you were, sitting with a glass of red wine, the bottle almost empty by your side. The table was strewn with legal papers. You were holding a black notebook and a pencil, skimming through the documents, scribbling in the book. You looked tired. You looked old.

On the wall by the window was a poster-sized photograph in a gilded frame. I got as close as I could to it. The picture was of you and your family. You were in a park. Your two children were in the foreground. The boy was about ten, and looked like you, the same weak chin. The girl looked to be about fourteen. She had jet black hair and silver eyes. I was shocked to see how much she resembled Liv. You were holding hands with Liv and you were smiling at the camera. You looked a bit slimmer, and I guessed the photograph was taken a few years before.

I stared at the photograph for a long time, at the smiling faces, at the happy family, and I felt sick with envy. I walked to the car. I put the radio on. An old reggae record was playing: you win at poker but I've got the joker.

I headed back to my squalid flat. I stopped off at an all-night garage on the way, to buy a tin of value-brand hotdog sausages, and when I got back to the car it wouldn't start. I flipped up the bonnet and had a look. I couldn't see anything in the dim

23

light and I couldn't call anyone. Perhaps in daylight I would be able to fix it, but I couldn't stay there for the night. First thing in the morning the garage would have to tow it off their forecourt. Life without money or legitimacy, I was discovering, was a constant succession of obstacles. There was nothing I could do but abandon it and walk the eight miles. I resigned myself to the fact that I'd never see the car again.

I arrived at the flat over two hours later, carrying the tin of value-brand hotdogs. I put the radio on and made a mug of tea. Ray tried to get up to greet me but he was still in pain and weak. I went over to him and stroked him. It's ok, boy, it's ok. You rest up.

I opened up the tin and we shared them between us. One sausage for Ray, one for me, until they were all gone. I realised that Ray was the only companion I had on earth, although there were plenty waiting for me in hell. The radio was playing some Cramps wannabes and I was back with Liv. You were still at the bar. We were drinking Newcastle Brown Ale, not because we particularly liked the taste of it, but it was what some of the more hardcore clientele were drinking and we wanted to be acknowledged as more hardcore. It was colloquially known as a 'bottle of dog' and we thought it rather cool to go to the bar and ask for 'two dogs' – at least *you* did, Andrew.

I never told you this, but I used to wince at your attempts to get in with the proper punks and goths, as you would think of them. Liv was dancing to The Cramps and smiling at me. They played two Cramps songs that evening, back-to-back. 'Can Your Pussy Do the Dog?' was mixed in with 'What's Inside A Girl', so that as one song finished the other kicked in. The guitar sounded demented and the drum was frenetic. The crowd was bouncing up and down. I didn't like The Cramps, but I knew that Liv was a massive fan so I kept my feelings to myself. But, as I let myself get carried by their rhythm, I found I was enjoying it. Liv was shaking her black messed-up hair to the music. Her eyes were heavily kohled. She looked like she'd landed from another planet. I watched her dance, lost in the moment.

Before I knew it I was enjoying the song and dancing along to it. By the time I'd made my way over to Liv, I was no longer pretending to like The Cramps, I had actually decided I genuinely and wholeheartedly liked them. What's wrong with a bit of rockabilly goth? I was willing to do anything for her. Then she was taking my hand and leading me to a dark corner by the fire escape. I remember Liv looking round to make sure there was no one about, that you were not about, then she pulled me towards her and kissed me. She pressed herself hard against me. My head was spinning, my knees weak. I knew I had to have her. I kissed her in return like it was the last two minutes on Earth. My hands through her hair, my hands on her neck, my hands on her back, my hands all over her. I couldn't get enough.

I was back in my flat, on the floor, stroking a stray dog. It was midnight but I wasn't tired and didn't want to sleep. I wanted to breathe in the night, to fill my lungs with it. The door was open, I kept having to remind myself of that, it wasn't locked.

So, out into the night I went, past the little houses, down the roads, the lanes, the streets. Through snickets, ginnels. Most of the curtains were closed. People were in bed. I was looking for the couple in the kitchen, frozen in that moment of embrace. But the blinds were shut, the lights were out, and they were both in bed, curled up like two cats, warm and soft. Warm and happy. Sleeping, dreaming happy dreams. I lay down on the pavement and placed my cheek against the damp stone.

||||

The next day I went to the pub. I yearned for human contact. Deep down, I longed for a friend. I thought of Keyop, but forced the memory back. There were two pubs close by. The nearest was The Royal Park, which also appeared to be the most likely to have a lax view of the law. Inside it was capacious, with room for three pool tables and a number of flashing machines.

It was about four o'clock. There were students sitting in clusters and what looked to be more serious drinkers gathered round the bar. I got talking to the barman. I needed a job, I told him, cash in hand. But they had all the staff they needed. There was a man in his thirties sitting on a stool by the bar. He had a clump of yellow straw-like hair and there were white streaks on his blue jeans and on his sweatshirt.

He looked up from his pint. He sized me up. Can you drive? he said.

Yeah, I can drive.

He explained that he needed a driver. He was a joiner, but he mainly assembled PVC conservatories. His name was Steve. He'd been banned from driving – caught three times over the limit. He'd received a hefty fine and a two-year ban. It was obvious from his tone that he had no affection for the law. I explained that the same fate had befallen the old fucker, my old man.

Is that what you call him? The old fucker?

Well, technically he's the *dead* old fucker now.

I like you, he said. You're all right. You look like you can shift some weight too. I could do with a cunt like you. When can you start?

He gave me directions to his lock-up where he kept his van and his tools and said to meet him there at six-thirty the following morning. He bought me a pint to seal the deal. I was unsure about him, but he agreed to pay me a fiver an hour and murderers can't be choosers.

The minimum wage is five ninety-three, I said.

Do you want this cunting job, or not?

We shook on it.

You have done labouring work before, right?

Course I have, I lied.

It was a white Transit. We loaded it up with tools and materials. Lots of tubes of silicone filler. I drove us both to the factory where they made the frames. I loaded up the van while Steve enjoyed a hot mug of tea and a Regal with one of the workmen. They sat chatting, laughing and smoking as I toiled away. Then we drove to the other side of town to the factory where they made the glass. Again, Steve enjoyed a cigarette and, this time, a mug of coffee, while I did the work. He sat chatting and laughing and smoking while I loaded up the glass into a special frame bolted to the side of the van. I had to wait while Steve regaled the man with a story about 'banging' a 'bird' in a factory canteen after closing time.

Next stop the builder's yard, where Steve had another mug of coffee with another man. More tales of comic conquests, much merriment all round. I was given the task of loading the van with five bags of coarse. The first bag I shifted with some effort. It was made harder by the fact I'd parked the van ten yards away, but shifting it now would draw attention to my mistake. The second bag was harder and I had to really concentrate, making sure I didn't drop the bag and spill the load. I placed it in the van just in time.

Hot sweat trickled down my back. I took a breather before attempting the third bag. I tried to lift it but it wouldn't shift. All those years in the gym, but they hadn't prepared me for this. I didn't want to look a fool in front of Steve and this man. I took a deep breath and used all the strength in me to lift the bag to the van. I looked around. He was still talking to the owner of the builder's yard. My arms and hands were shaking. I couldn't make a fist. Come on, pull yourself together.

We went to a housing estate in Morley. Steve had hired a cement mixer. He started on the frames. But first he told me how to make up the mix. Half aggregate, half sand and cement. Only the half that was sand and cement needed to be twice as much sand as cement. He asked me if I understood and I nodded. Inside my head was whirring. I was never good with numbers. How much water?

What the fuck are you doing, you daft cunt?

He was standing right behind me smoking a Regal.

What's wrong?

He told me I'd put too much coarse in and I would have to let it down with more sand and cement. I filled a wheelbarrow with the gloop and took it round the back to the conservatory.

Tip it in there, cuntyballs, he said, pointing to the area where he wanted it, with the stub of his cigarette.

I did as I was told. 'Cuntyballs' was his term of endearment. Even affection. I hefted another wheelbarrow full of the mix. Back and forth. Barrow after barrow, mix after mix. Until there was enough to cover the floor a few inches. I felt dizzy. Each time I filled up the wheelbarrow I put a bit less mix in. I was struggling to push it. The load was getting lighter but my perception of it was that it was getting heavier and heavier. I was down to just half a barrow of mix and still struggling with that. I was at the point of collapse.

Fill the fucker to the top, he said. We'll be here all fucking night.

I dropped us back at the lock-up. I could hardly walk. There were no thoughts in my head. I didn't even think about you, Andrew. I felt like I'd been lobotomised.

Fancy a pint? he said, oblivious to my pain. To him this was just a normal day.

All I could think about was a hot bath, sinking my aching limbs into the steamy water and letting the heat penetrate to my bones. I staggered back to the flat and made a mug of strong tea. Ray tried to get up to greet me, but he was still frail. We were both in a bad way. I went over to his bed, collapsed on the floor next to him and stroked his head. It's ok boy, it's ok. I filled a bath with hot water and sparked up a spliff. I clambered into the tub, feeling every muscle in my body throb.

I was fucked. Then I was stoned. Then I was fucked. I lay there until the water around me was cold. I started to shiver but I was too fatigued to crawl out. I shivered some more. Eventually I climbed out, wrapped myself in towels and collapsed on the bed. I'd done nine hours' work. The first nine hours of real work in twenty-two years. Nine hours lifting bags of coarse. Nine hours mixing. Nine hours barrowing. Forty-five quid. I wondered how much you were earning, what rate per hour you charged, Andrew. Not five pound an hour, that's for sure.

Five o'clock. I was coming round from my skunk-induced stupor and I registered a growing thirst. I would go out for a pint. Then I thought about Steve. He would still be there no doubt. Steve Taylor he was called, joiner and conservatory assembler, and I couldn't face conversation with him and didn't have the energy to walk to the pub further on. I closed my eyes and I was back there. That night. 1989.

We better go back, Liv said, Before he notices we've gone. She gave me one last kiss. Her lips were so soft. We headed back to the dance floor. You were making your way across with three bottles of dog, a big beaming smile on your face, oblivious to the act of betrayal that had just been perpetrated.

There you go, and you handed me mine and then you handed Liv hers.

Then you smacked your bottle on top of mine so that my beer came spurting out. I put my mouth over the top of the bottle and guzzled the excess liquid. It was a regular trick we played on each other. No malice in it. We danced and drank to a succession of songs: Freak Scene, I Want The One I Can't Have, I Wanna Be Adored, I Wanna Be Your Dog.

You said that you wanted to be adored. Really? I said. I want to be a dog. What I really wanted to say was, I want the one I can't have.

Come on, you said, Let's leave the girls to it. This place closes at two. Let's go to The Top Cat.

The Top Cat. The biggest dive in Manchester. Open all hours, open to all comers, open to all sinners. If only we had stayed in The Venue that night, got on the last night bus at two-thirty with the rest of them as planned, still loved up from a ten pound pill. If only.

I went over to Ray's bed and I lay down on the floor with him. I want, I want, I want. And all I could think of was fucking your wife, and fucking you over. I wanted everything.

I need vengeance like a tired man needs a bath.

Ray gave me a blank look.

||||

The second day of work wasn't as heavy. The ten hours' sleep had gone some way to repairing the damage of the day before. We were on the roof, waterproofing, going through lots of silicone tubes. It was my job to fetch them. It was my job to get Steve a bacon butty and a Styrofoam cup of coffee for breakfast. It was my job to get him twenty Regal and a Mars Bar at ten o'clock. It was my job to get him a BLT, the *Sun* and a can of cherry coke at twelve. It was my job to get him a can of Iron Bru and a bag of Chilli Heatwave Doritos at two o'clock. At three-thirty we were done. I drove us back to the lock-up. School girls were sauntering up the street.

Slow down, Steve said, and wound down the window. He waited until he was level with them then shouted, Fancy a shag? and laughed. They shouted abuse at him. One shouted 'perv', another shouted 'paedo'. I tried not to get their attention. I smiled benignly back when he grinned my way. One man's fool is another man's boss.

I dropped him back at the lock-up. Fancy a pint? he said.

Got a few errands, Steve, I said. I'll see you in there in half an hour.

I went over to the post office and wrote out a card to place in the window. Found: dog that looks like fox. Ring ... then I realised I had no phone. I told the woman I'd be back. I called in at a general store and picked up a twenty pound phone and SIM card. I bought a ten pound pay-as-you-go and inserted the SIM but it needed charging. I went back to the post office and finished the card – putting in my new number. I now had less than a tenner to my name.

I went back to the flat. As I opened the door, Ray managed to get to his feet and hobble to me. I made a big fuss of him. He was obviously in a lot of pain, but he wasn't soft. I gave him half a tin of dog food and I watched him eat it all up. I stroked him and poured him a fresh bowl of water. I won't be long, I said, and shut the door behind me. The pub was quiet. It was Wednesday. Another two days of work before I would have money. Then Saturday. That was when I planned to go back. I had to think it through.

What you having? Steve said. He was at the bar, chatting up the barmaid. A married man with two kids, chatting up anything in a skirt.

I'll get my own, I said. I don't have enough to get you one back.

Shut up, you daft cunt, he said, and bought a round.

The barmaid poured our drinks and went to the till.

Very fuckable, Steve said, under his breath, and winked. I'd fuck her all night. I'd tie a knot in it.

It was more than likely that Liv would be going somewhere at some point on Saturday. Best not to bump into her outside her house. That would give the game away. 'Bump' into her somewhere there was every likelihood I'd be passing. Get there early.

Fancy a bit do you? This was Steve, talking to the barmaid.

She was young, probably a student, and a worthy adversary. She looked him up and down. Not with you, she said. I was impressed by the efficiency of this retort. She was not fazed by his come-on. She clearly felt he was unworthy of her attention.

You've not seen my secret weapon, he said. They both looked at his crotch.

I've left my microscope at home, she said. Steve looked taken aback.

Well it's only six inches, but some women like it that wide.

She just shook her head at this, realising that she wouldn't shake him off with insults. She was probably thinking what I was, that this bloke was a massive twat. It occurred to me that she might be casting me in the same light. Did she think I was like him because I was drinking with him? I flashed her an apologetic 'I'm-not-with-this-prick' look. She smiled.

I had a pint. I had a pint. I had a pint. I had another pint. All bought by Steve. Steve tried again with the barmaid. This time she told him to fuck off. Talking his language. Steve fucked off – back to the wife and two kids. I went back too. Ray didn't quite bound across, he was still limping, but he was in good spirits. He lay down and let me inspect him. The wound seemed to be healing. I gave him the rest of the tin, then made myself some beans on toast. I saved Ray the crusts.

It started to rain. I picked up my dead dad's fucked guitar and strummed a few old blues numbers. I strummed some Dylan. First, It's Alright Ma then Sad-Eyed Lady of the Lowlands. But I couldn't get to the end of that one. It was the line about eyes like smoke. Twenty-two years was a long time to wait. It felt like I'd been hollowed out. Her eyes like moonlight. Her magazine husband (that's you, Andrew – although you were too porcine to really fit that description), her magazine children, her magazine house, her magazine life. It was also *your* magazine children and *your* magazine house. *Your* magazine life. And I wanted it for myself. All of it.

Water was dripping from the damaged ceiling. Drip-drip. I found a bucket and put it over the wet spot. Plink-plink. I played three of my own songs. The drips were my drum. Then the bucket was full and I had to empty it. Not drip-drip now, not even plink-plink, but a steady stream pouring from the ceiling. I dug out the landlord's number and rang it.

What the fuck are you ringing me at this time for?

It wasn't even nine o'clock.

It's an emergency, I said and told him about the leak. He said I'd have to wait until tomorrow. I built up a spliff. I emptied the bucket again. I rang up the landlord, explaining the water was now gushing in. He told me it was a bad line and hung up. I went to bed. When I woke up very early in the morning the carpet was sopping wet. I lifted Ray onto the bed. The rain had stopped but the flat was a flood plain. I rang up the landlord.

What the fuck you ringing me at this time?

It was six o'clock. I tried to tell him about the flood damage, but he said the line was breaking up and next it went dead. I gave Ray half a tin of dog food. I let him eat it off the bed. Fuck the landlord. I went to the lock-up, picked up Steve. It was a new job today, another conservatory. Over an hour to load up the van. Steve smoked and drank coffee with a bloke in white overalls, while I did the loading. Why have a dog and bark yourself?

When we got to Guiseley we had to ask for directions. We found them eventually, on the outskirts of the town, a semi-detached retired couple. He was creosoting the shed, she was doing some gardening. She stopped to make us a drink. She brought me a tea and Steve a coffee. Happy families. At three o'clock Steve said, Let's call it a day.

I drove us back to the lock-up. Fancy a beer? Steve said.

Skint.

I'll buy you a pint, you daft cunt.

I said I'd see him in there. I wanted to check on Ray. As I closed the door behind me he came rushing over, tail wagging. Still limping, but he wasn't limping quite as badly and he was able to put some of his weight on his injured leg. I lifted him onto the bed. The rain was pouring through the ceiling. I rang the landlord. It went to voicemail. I left a message. I gave Ray half a tin and went to The Royal. Steve was at the bar, chatting to the barmaid. He bought me a beer. I sat on the stool beside him.

You're all right you, he said, after some time. Bit of a shit driver, but we can't have everything. He laughed and patted me on the back. In his own way, he was trying to pay me a compliment. He wasn't all bad. I told him about the flat and about the dog.

You daft twat, what you take in a stray for?

The barmaid overheard us talking about the state of the flat and the leaking ceiling.

There's a guy drinks in here who's after a lodger, she said.

That right?

Yeah, lives just up the road in one of the back-to-backs. Richard he's called.

When does he come in?

Every night just before eleven. Three pints of cider and three Bells chasers. He's a bit of a character, she said and raised her eyebrows.

Steve bought me another beer. I listened to another tale of one of his conquests. He fucked this lass, he fucked that lass, he fucked these two lasses together, on and on. Mr Fuckface: Fucker of the Year.

Then I was back there. 1989. You were urging me on, Andrew. The Top Cat was open all night. It was almost two. The bar staff were already telling people to drink up. Fifteen more minutes with Liv, I wanted to adore, I wanted to adore, I wanted to adore, but you wanted to go before the crowd. It was, after all, your last blowout. You were off to university the next day, down South, to start your new life. I wouldn't be seeing you until you came back at Christmas. A big deal. It was almost incomprehensible to me then, that you would move away from the north, away from your family, away from your friends who had meant everything to you. It was important that we made your send-off special – a night to remember. I think we can both agree that we certainly did that.

I made an excuse, said I needed the toilet. Liv was coming out of the ladies.

I've got to go, I told her. You sure you don't want to come with us?

Best not, she said. Sharing a taxi with Helen and Jill. Then she put her arms round me and whispered in my ear, I chose the wrong one, she said. Wham. Like that. Blood banging. Head fucked. She chose the wrong one, Andrew.

I wanted her. But you were my best mate, Andrew. I had known you since I was three. We went to the same nursery, the same primary school, the same comprehensive. What the fuck was I doing? So I walked away from Liv and out of the club with you. I gave Liv one last look, physically wrenched, as though there was an invisible thread between me and Liv, and there was no slack in it. I thought I might topple over, but I kept on walking behind you, up the stairs and out into the cold night. Along Whitworth street, through Piccadilly Gardens, towards Oldham Street.

We soon arrived at the Top Cat club, Manchester's secret all-night boozer. Home to pimps, crooks, druggies, alkies and gangsters. I knew why you wanted to go there. One last bender. One last mad one. One last flirt with the underworld before you spent the rest of your life on the other side, on the right side of the law. For you there was something final about that evening which gave your motivation mettle. I had no real stomach for it, but the pill was still working, I was still buzzing, happy to go along with your plan, for you – to please you.

Next, we were on the dance floor, dancing to an unfamiliar tune and eyeing up the women. You were dancing like you always danced: like a dizzy vicar. You got chatting with a man who I didn't like the look of. He was wearing a black three-piece suit, a black shirt and a black tie. He had a shaven head, an earring and a beard. He was leaning into you, whispering in your ear. You were nodding. Then you were both laughing. When I next looked over where you were, you were both walking off. I knew you were up to something.

I went to the bar. I didn't need anything alcoholic to drink, there was no point. It wouldn't have any effect, the pill the stronger poison. I bought a lime and soda. Then you were back, walking over to me, grinning. You gave me a nudge. You'd got something for the send-off, you said. You'd scored a gram of coke. Why not, I thought, it seemed right we should push the boat out. We went to the gents, found a cubicle and locked

36

ourselves in. You chopped two lines on the cistern lid and we hoovered them up. I felt an instant numbing of my nose and then a euphoric rush. It mixed well with the pills, propping up their waning powers. You chopped two more. They went down nicely. We felt indomitable.

Dancing. Lights. Smoke machine. Strobes. Flashing. Men, women. Back to the bog. Another two lines. It's four o'clock. Both buzzing to fuck. Chatting, laughing. Flirting with some girls. Having a banging time. Music thumping. Smoking. Thumping. Buzzing. Another line. Five o'clock. You chatting up a girl. A bloke watching you. Ugly bloke. Staring.

Let's go, I said, coming round a bit. Let's go before the rest.

Ok, you said. But what's the rush?

I nudged you. The bloke was staring. Staring a hole right through you, Andrew. You shrugged it off but I persuaded you to leave. You were never any good at fighting, but nor did you have the coward's ability to second-sense danger and scram. We were outside, waiting for a taxi. There was no one around.

I need a piss, I said.

I ducked behind a wall and pissed long and hard. I walked back to where we'd been standing. You were on the ground, the bloke from the club on top of you, punching you in the face.

I run across, grabbing the bloke by his shirt, throwing him around. He's swinging punches with no great accuracy. I duck a few with ease. Then he's swinging another punch and I'm getting him on the floor. Punching, punching, punching. He tries to get up. Grabbing my leg. Kicking, kicking, kicking. Boot, boot, boot. Blood on his face. Blood. I don't remember the detail. I think I went looking for a phone to call an ambulance. Next thing I remember is you with your head on his chest, listening for his heart. You looking at me. Shock. Run, you're saying. Come on. You're running. Away. I'm standing. Blood. Over the man. My heart racing. Adrenalin pumping. Frozen. One man, then a woman. To the spot. Then more. Accusing. Shake my head. Shouting. Two blokes holding me. You're going nowhere, pal. Going nowhere. Nowhere. Sirens. Lights. Police. I'm asked. Speechless. Questions. Can't think straight. Can't think. Bundled. The van. Into the back. The doors. Shut. Black.

One for the road? It was Steve's voice bringing me back. It was 2011. Steve ordered one more pint and tried to cop off with the barmaid one more time. Then he went home to his wife, home to his kids. Eight o'clock. I found a corner and sat down at a table. I watched people come, watched people go. I watched couples laugh, watched couples kiss. I thought about Saturday, about you and Liv, your house, your family, your life. I rolled a fag, put it in my mouth. I was about to light it, but it was 2011, not 1989. Something's Gotten Hold of My Heart, was on the jukebox. A jukebox which contained only mp3 files, no vinyl. Fool's Gold on the Jukebox. 2011. 1989.

At five minutes to eleven, he walked in. I knew it was him because he ordered a pint of cider and a Bells chaser just as the barmaid had said. He sat in a darkened corner opposite my own. He looked like John Peel, only smaller, slighter, balder. I stood up, a little unsteady on my feet, and walked over.

Mind if I join you? I said.

He looked around. Plenty of other spaces but he just shrugged. Sure, why not.

I pulled out a stool from under the table and sat down facing him. Barmaid said you were after a lodger.

Maybe. It depends. I've had lodgers before. I like lodgers but I like my own company.

His voice was a whisper. I had to lean in to listen to what he was saying. We were almost touching. He must have been about fifty. Black shoes, black jeans, black shirt, white beard, three ciders and three chasers.

We went to his house, a back-to-back terrace three streets up the hill from the pub. It was run down, full of dust and cobwebs, but everything in its place. A grey sofa, a grey armchair, two mud-coloured cushions. There was a stack of M magazines lined up by the side. He had an old fashioned cathode ray tube

TV covered in dust in the corner. It would soon be obsolete, the analogue signal was due to be switched off later in the year. Blu-Tacked to the top of the TV was a plastic model of Chewbacca – about three inches in height. Along the bookshelf, there was another plastic model, this time of Yoda.

You're a Star Wars fan then?

He looked confused. No, he said.

The kitchen was also grey and drab. There was a lingering smell of fried fish. No fridge, just a few shelves with items of food neatly stacked. A large wicker bowl where he kept vegetables: three potatoes, a bulb of garlic, a green pepper, two carrots and a mooli radish. The cooker looked like something from the seventies, a white enamelled design with a grill above the hob.

I'll clear a shelf for you. Is one shelf enough?

Without a fridge there was no point in buying in bulk. There was no kettle. He boiled water in a pan. He showed me how to light the gas hob. It involved allowing the gas to flow for ten seconds and then lighting it so that there was a small explosion. The grill was a similar technique, only it required you to place your hand to the back of the contraption so when the small explosion occurred, it singed the hairs on the back of your arm. I noticed his scarred arms were kept bald.

We went up the narrow, steep, uncarpeted staircase, avoiding cobwebs heavy with dust, and into my room – a decent size and empty apart from a shop manikin painted pillar box red.

It's not furnished, he said. Have you got your own furniture?

Neither of us mentioned the manikin.

I'll be ok.

I live mainly up in the attic, he said, pointing to the ceiling. He'd got a lot of recording equipment up there, he said, as if that explained it. He was a keyboard player. I told him I played guitar.

It's seventy a week.

What about the bond? I said.

He didn't want a bond. He wasn't your average landlord. He wasn't your average house owner. Or even your average weirdo.

I've not got any money at the moment.

Pay me when you get some.

I've got a dog, I said.

I like dogs, he said. I like dogs more than I like people.

You are no longer under section. They have dismissed you from Health Care. You have beaten your illness. You have beaten the subbies, but you haven't beaten the dope. You need something to hush the noise in your head. You take some silver foil and cover the mouth of the bottle. You perforate the silver foil with a needle. You pack the silver foil bowl. You take the bucket filled three-quarters full with water. You sink the bottle into the water so that the mouth of the bottle is poking out. You light the bowl. You draw the bottle up from the water, watching the clear plastic bottle fill with two litres of pure white smoke. You want to replace the thoughts in your head, with two litres of pure white smoke. You remove the silver bowl and empty your lungs. You put your mouth over the bottle and sink the bottle back down into the bucket, forcing the pure white smoke into your lungs. You collapse on the concrete floor, clinging on, trying not to fall off. This is what you have to do to forget. But you can't forgive. Not the man who put you in here, and not yourself.

卌|

Friday. The knife arrived from the courts in a brown envelope.
I'd completed four days' graft. My muscles were aching,
my hands were cracked and calloused, my nails chipped, but
mentally I felt fresh. I felt awake, alive and ready. We finished
off the old couple's conservatory and we were given a cup of
tea and some biscuits. Sitting down to eat the biscuits, I noted
their wedding photo in a frame. She was shining in a white
dress. He was dapper in a three-piece suit, bright blue tie and
a white carnation in the lapel. They were both smiling, their
whole lives ahead of them, and now they had reached the end
of that journey – a PVC conservatory.

Back at the pub, Steve bought the first round in and took
a bundle of notes out of his pocket. I'd never seen so much
money. He counted out the tenners on the bar. Four days graft.
Nine hours a day. Nearly two hundred quid. I thanked him as
I put the bundle of notes in my pocket. It was pathetic how
grateful I felt. I'd earned thirty pounds a week as an apprentice
in 1989 – the bundle of notes in my pocket was the most money
I'd ever had. We went outside.

Have a proper fag you daft twat, he said, and offered me a
Regal.

I'm all right, I said, and smoked a roll-up.

We were approached by a man in a torn Harrington jacket.
He had a carrier bag full of meat. Steve told him to fuck off, but
I bought a roast chicken off him, and some sausages.

I finished my drink and went back to Richard's place. He was
in the attic recording. I had an early start in the morning and I
wanted to be alert. I had no idea what sort of habits Liv kept. I

didn't want to take any risks. I carried Ray outside to the park. He hobbled around, enjoying the grass and the undergrowth. He sniffed about and then pissed, struggling to cock his leg. He sniffed round a tree and pissed again. I sat on a bench and waited for him to shit but he just hobbled across and put his head on my knee. I carried him back.

I took two plates and divided the chicken in half. The flesh fell away from the bones and I made two heaps. I poured a glass of water for me and a bowl for Ray. I gave one of the plates to Ray. I sat on the floor next to Ray as there was no furniture and ate my chicken. Then I played my dead dad's fucked guitar. I found that if I didn't do something to take my mind out of itself it soon began to turn over the same subjects. Time. All of the plundered time – time you had stolen from me.

If I didn't distract my mind, the hate would seep in and the anger would build. But I didn't want to hate, I didn't want to be angry, because then you had won. You had won control over my mind and I couldn't let that happen. Or rather, I did want to hate, I wanted to use the hate, I wanted it to be pure and clean. I wanted to be in complete control of it. So that I owned it and it was *my* hate, not yours. I needed to shape it, to refine it, so that it shined like polished steel. It was a discipline that required a great deal of effort. I was singing and playing in order to strengthen my resolve, to make me mentally stronger, so that I could beat you.

I put the guitar down, took a deep breath, emptied my mind of you and tried again. I played for a few minutes but it was no good. Time. You had snatched over half my life from me. The magnitude of the theft overwhelmed me and I found I was gasping for air, my brain reeling, almost passing out with the wrong kind of anger and hate. I carried the dog outside and watched him empty his bowels. I watched him deliver the steaming faecal matter into the gutter, and I thought of you, Andrew.

Saturday. The alarm on my phone woke me at six. I took Ray to the park. It was 2011 now, not 1989, so I took a bag out and scooped up the shit, posted it in the 'dog waste only' box. I got back to the house and did a hundred press-ups, a hundred sit-ups and five minutes of shadowboxing. I had a shower in the strange, sickly pink bath. I was careful to clean and dry my feet before putting them straight into my shoes so they didn't touch the floor, which was covered in a mouldy carpet.

Richard used an old pig bristle toothbrush that had worn down to just a few stubbled patches. The soap was caked in curly hairs. At least I wasn't sharing a cell with him. At least I didn't have to smell his shit when he emptied his bowels into a bucket or listen to the wet slapping of his masturbating. Or hear him cry into his pillow after.

What to wear? Shirt or T-shirt? Jeans or trousers? Shoes or trainers? I decided on shoes with jeans and a black T-shirt, long sleeved, that I hoped showed off my toned physique without looking like that was the intention. I combed my hair then scruffed it up a bit. I caught the ten to seven bus to Ilkley, via Otley. When I got to Ilkley it was just gone half seven. I walked up the leafy street to your house. I found a secluded spot about twenty yards away and perched on a wall under a tree and waited. And waited.

Half eight. A paper boy was struggling with the weekend papers. Every house had at least one, some had more. Big fat broadsheets with twenty sections on everything from fashion, family and housing to holidays and sport. It took him the best part of half an hour just to deliver the papers on this street. He disappeared. Nothing. A few cars. A woman with a pram. Half nine. The wind picked up and I zipped my jacket to the top, pulling my collar high around my neck. I rolled a cigarette. Smoked it. I watched a woman jogging down the street in lycra, a music player strapped to her arm. Ten o'clock. A man left the house opposite, got into his car and drove off. No sign of life. Ten-thirty, still nothing.

I was about to roll another cigarette when out she came. She was wearing tight black jeans, white ballet shoes, black and white striped top and a leather jacket. Her hair was tied up loosely so that strands dangled across her face. She carried a hessian bag. She looked younger than her age. I felt my stomach turn over.

I made sure I kept in the shadows, keeping a good fifty yards behind her. She walked into town. She bought fresh bread, bacon, half a dozen eggs, milk, butter, orange juice. She stopped to talk to another woman who looked about five or six years older. I could tell from Liv's body language that she wanted to end the conversation and carry on shopping but the woman carried on talking and talking. Liv kept smiling and nodding, looking for her excuse.

Now would be a good time, I thought. I could tap her on the shoulder. She'd be glad to get away from the other woman and completely shocked to see me. But happy. Would she be happy or just shocked? Perhaps she'd be too shocked and she'd feel awkward, even embarrassed. She'd want to know what I was doing in Ilkley. I'd say I was just shopping. But then she'd ask me where I was living now. I'd say, near Hyde Park, and she'd look puzzled. That's a long way to come to go shopping, she'd say, and I'd feel I was in the dock being accused of something.

The longer I stood and watched her with the woman the more I became convinced my plan would fail. Why would I be in Ilkley on a Saturday morning, shopping? Why wouldn't I be in Leeds, which I could walk to in half an hour from where I lived? Or why wouldn't I use the local shops? What did Ilkley have that I couldn't get locally or in Leeds? I looked around. I was standing near a fancy tearoom.

Liv was walking back up the lane now, away from the tearoom, back home with her bounty, a baguette poking out of the hessian bag. Saturday morning breakfast, a magazine breakfast, with her magazine husband and her magazine children in her magazine house. And now it was too late. We

45

were too far from the centre of town, too much of a residential area, even less reason for me to be here, following her home. Even more reason for her to be suspicious, creeped out perhaps. I was the last person she would want to see. If she wanted to see me she would have come to see me inside. But she didn't want to see me. I slowed down, watching her stroll along, fading away, further and further. Then she was gone.

I caught the bus back. I took Ray to the park. I bought a bottle of vodka. I drank the bottle of vodka. Just like the old fucker. Chip off the old block. Just like my dead old fucker of a dad. Two peas in a pod. And I curled up on my sleeping bag with Ray and tried and tried to block it all out. But I couldn't. I couldn't block out twenty-two years. I couldn't block out the stark furnishings of the cell or the harsh light. I couldn't block out the stink of another man's shit. Or the stench of bleach and burning foil. I couldn't block out the feeling of self-hate. I couldn't block out your face. What was I thinking? How could someone like me be a success. I was one of life's losers. Nothing I could do would ever amount to anything.

I knew I couldn't have the life I wanted. It was impossible, everything was against it. I wanted to die. I thought about my own death. How would I do it? Overdose, noose, bridge, a trip to the coast? I would swallow a jar of Valium. I would construct a noose like the one we built for Madman Marz. I would jump from the top of a multi-storey car park. I would fill my pockets with rocks and wade into the ocean. So many ways. But then I thought about you. I did have something to live for. I would make you suffer, Andrew.

It was six o'clock in the evening. I fed Ray then took him out. I didn't carry him this time and he hobbled along beside me. He was putting more weight down on his bad leg, getting stronger. I took him to The Royal. I bought me a Peroni and Ray a Pepperami. Another Peroni. Another Pepperami. I hadn't seen the barmaid before, she wasn't the one who told Steve to fuck off, but she was cute. Another student perhaps. She started asking me about Ray.

He looks just like a fox.

Yeah, I know, I said.

Another Peroni. Another Pepperami. Telephone was on the jukebox, Eyes Wide Shut, Blind Faith, Let it Rain, Bring the Light. I sat down in my corner, fuzzy from the beer. A man was there. Had he been there before or had he just approached? Everything was becoming blurred. He said his name was Howler. He reminded me of someone, but I couldn't think who. He was drunk, but so was I. Another drunk. He had a tattoo of a parachute with wings and a crown on his lower arm.

That's a nice dog, he said.

It's not mine.

Whose is it?

I explained how I came to be looking after him. How no one had rung my phone.

Well it sounds like he's your dog now. Looks a bit like a fox.

Yeah, I know.

I pointed to his tattoo, You been in the Paras then?

Twenty years.

You must have liked it.

We talked and drank. First year, I was being bullied by this officer – made my life a misery that cunt. So one night when all the other cunts were down the pub and he was asleep, I poured petrol all over his bed sheets. Then I held a lighter in front of his face. I whispered in the cunt's ear, 'wake up'. He opened his eyes and I said, 'can you smell anything?' and he nodded. 'It's petrol', I said to him, 'it's all over your bed.' Then I lit the lighter. I said, 'You're one second from death. You ever talk to me or even look at me again and I'll come back for that second.'

And that worked did it?

He nodded.

I bought us lagers and whiskey chasers. He seemed a bit of a nutter, but again, I was in no position to judge.

So what is it you do now then?

Window cleaner. I was out of work for a long time. Got into a bit of a state. I found it really hard coming out after twenty years.

Tell me about it, I was thinking.

I got into drugs.

Oh yeah, what drugs?

Anything I could get my hands on. Then I got into smack.

Right.

You ever tried it?

Yeah.

He bought us lagers and chasers. We chatted some more about the Paras. I remembered where I knew him from. The sunken cheeks. The defiant eyes. The tattoo. From that day in court. He was Vinnie Howell – commercial burglary. I realised what he had meant when he pointed at his tattoo and stared at the judge. I bought us lagers and chasers. It was nine o'clock.

Here, he said, Cop for this.

He took out a white pill. He picked up a flyer from the bar, folded it in half and put the pill inside. He took his pint glass and crushed the pill with the thick base of the glass. He folded back the flyer and inspected his work. It had crumbled but there were still some lumps. He covered it up again and crushed again, this time grinding the bottom of his glass. He repeated the process until he'd ground the pill into a fine white powder. He took another flyer and rolled it up.

What is it? I said. Even though I knew exactly what it was.

Subutex.

As I'd thought: opiates. That was all I needed.

I don't know, I said. I've stayed away from opiates for a long time.

We can just have half each. Don't worry about it, I'll look after yer, make sure you get home safe.

Perhaps if I hadn't been so drunk, I might have been able to resist. Perhaps if I didn't need to get your face out of my head so much, perhaps if I wasn't yearning for a state of calm, free from anger and hate, I would have found it easier to resist. Opiates, the destroyer of pain. The despoiler of memories. The conqueror of desire. I looked around, to make sure the barmaid couldn't see what we were doing. She was off round the other side of the bar collecting glasses. The flesh is weak. I took the card tube and snorted half the powder. It was a clean, sharp hit. I passed the tube back. He took it off me and snorted his half. A wave of euphoria. A wave of nausea – opiate waves. Talking, talking. About this, about that. It was eleven o'clock and he was talking about his childhood.

I was orphaned at eight.

Why's that then?

My dad was a cunt.

He shrugged, as though that was the final word on the matter, then started up again.

I came downstairs one night. Him and my mum were at it. He was beating her. She was on the floor in the kitchen and he was kicking her in the gut. Something flipped. I picked up a knife and stuck it in his back.

Fuck.

Thing was, my mum rang the police. He was dead, and she said she'd done it.

Why she say that?

She didn't want to get me in the shit.

What happened to her?

She got six years. I was fourteen when she came out. I put her in there. Me. He stared into his glass.

But you were just looking after your mum. She was looking after you.

He went quiet for a bit. Lost. I closed my eyes. A wave of euphoria. Steeped. I opened them again. He was crushing up another pill. We did half each. It was one o'clock. There we were, two murderers chewing the fat, two murderers drinking whiskey chasers and snorting Subutex.

Don't worry, he said. I'll look after yer. I'll see you right. Make sure you get home.

He did most of the talking. He'd had a bad time of it. No doubt about it. But something told me he was making some of it up. Perhaps not.

Tell me a story, he said.

So I did.

There was this man, I said, And this woman.

Go on, he said. I like it so far.

The man really wanted to fuck the woman. The woman was married with kids. Nice house, lots of money, perfect life. He didn't just want to fuck the woman, he wanted more. He knew if he didn't have the whole lot he would never be happy.

So what did he do?

Well, the thing was, she was happy. He had a think about it. He had no right to take her happiness away from her. He tried to see her as just an object. Something he needed to reach his end goal. But he couldn't stand the thought of making her sad.

So what did he do?

He didn't do anything. He just got on with his life.

He nodded. He sat back thinking about what I'd said. He nodded again. That's a shit story, he said. It started off all right but you need to change the ending.

I nodded. He was chatting away again. I was trying to focus on what he was saying, but I kept zoning out.

You ever get in trouble, you just come to me. Sorted. Like that. Any cunt you need sorting. To me it's a walk in the park. It's dealt with. Happy days.

I was nodding my head, barely clinging on to the conversational threads. Each time I closed my eyes, a wave of bliss. It was gone three in the morning when I finally got back to the house. I had a spliff and collapsed on the sleeping bag with Ray.

It was noon when I came round. Face wet with cold sweat. Jangled. Smackhead jangled. It took me everything I'd got to open up a tin of dog food for Ray and make myself a mug of tea. I sat up, my back against the wall, the newly bought TV on. Watching real people fail. Watching real people cry. Watching real people expose themselves to the viewer.

I closed my eyes. Waves of euphoria. Gouched out. Came round. Watched TV. Closed my eyes. Waves of euphoria. Gouched out. Came round. It was four o'clock before I could face the idea of taking Ray out for a piss and a shit. He must have been bursting by now. I got to my feet, feeling fragile, and put on my coat.

We went to the park. He was still limping but not as badly. I was still jangling, though feeling a bit better. I could feel the heat of the sun on my face. There were too many people around. We walked into the wood. I sat down on a fallen tree. I felt weak again, as though I were about to topple over. I watched a female blackbird collecting bits of dried grass to line her nest. There was a blue tit in a tree singing his heart out, trying to attract a mate. I saw a woman walking towards me, her dog off its lead but walking by her side. The dog bounded across when it saw Ray. It rolled over to expose its genitals. It was a she.

Ray sniffed the genitals. She was just a puppy but very distinctive looking. Almost white fur. I stroked her. Soft white fur, strong boned. Plenty of muscle even at this age. Plenty of hair around her muzzle, which was almost golden. She had bright green eyes. Human eyes.

The woman was close to me now. She had the same black hair as Liv, but she had it cropped short. She was probably in her mid-thirties. Not bad looking. She stopped to watch the dogs.

That's a striking dog, I said. What breed is she?

She's an Italian Spinone.

Never heard of one of them.

No, they're not that common.

Amazing eyes. You never see green eyes on a dog. They're normally brown or amber, I said.

She's just getting used to other dogs. All still new to her.

She's very placid for a puppy.

That's one of their characteristics, she said. They're good with kids.

You got kids then?

Just the one.

She smiled, a beautiful crooked smile. Her eyes were green like her dog's. She said goodbye and walked off. The leaves were starting to sprout on the trees, the sun dappled the path. The air was rich with bird song. I sat there thinking: Nick, you need to get Andrew out of your head, you need to forget about Liv. You can't have any of it, it's madness to torture yourself with the thought of it. Night and day. When you're awake, when you're asleep.

And then I could see it clearly. Nothing good could ever come of this desire for another man's wife and another man's life. The past was the past. After twenty-two years of incarceration, I was no use to anyone. Here I was, with post-smack jangles, no friends, no money, no prospects, just a lot of soiled baggage. There was no magazine life for me, just the continual filth of my own history. I was like a slug, leaving a trail of slime over the leaves of a plant, only satisfied when it has destroyed the petals and the plant has withered. It stops. From today.

卌 ||

Have a proper fag you daft cunt, he said and offered me a Regal.

I'm all right, I said, and smoked a roll-up.

I thought about the week. Monday to Friday. Six o'clock starts. Meeting at the lock-up. Loading up the van, driving to the builder's yard, loading up the van. Driving to the factory. Loading up the van. Buying bacon butties. Buying cups of tea. Going to the job. Unloading the van. Building a conservatory. Making plastic windows fit snug. Buying fish and chips. Buying cans of Fanta. Buying Iron Bru. Filling in the gaps with silicone. Driving back. Slowing down for school girls. Steve asking for blowjobs. Dumping the van at the lock-up. Going to the pub.

I was earning my own keep. I was getting stronger and fitter, building up my stamina. A few pints every night in the Royal. Steve eyeing up the barmaid. Steve coming on to the barmaid. Steve getting the knock back. Steve going home to his wife and two kids.

Steve the sexist, the racist, the homophobe. Steve the hardworking, hard drinking, family man, Steve the shit hot pool player. Steve the Black Eyed Peas fan. He was a simple man but he wasn't without his contradictions. In a strange way, I was growing to like something about him.

We were outside the pub. He was counting out the money. Five days' work. £225. Even more than I'd had last time. This was now the most I'd ever been paid in my life. I rolled it up and pocketed it, again slightly ashamed by my own gratitude. Five days. Every day a struggle. The hate spilling over, trying to tamp it down. But now it was the weekend and I was going to get hammered and forget about you, Andrew. We went back inside. I bought Steve a pint of Stella. We went for another smoke.

So what the fuck were you doing before?

Eh?

For a job?

It had only taken him two weeks to show any curiosity. No one could accuse Steve of being nosey. Unless you had a pair of tits, you didn't exist.

You know, this and that. I did a lot of travelling.

He took one look at me, You've been inside, haven't you?

How did he know? What had I said or done to give the game away? Steve was such a paradox. He knew nothing. He knew everything.

Eh? I said, and tried to look puzzled.

Listen, I don't give a flying fuckeroo, have another Peroni.

We went back inside. I was safe. Steve had a Stella, I had a Peroni. Steve understood prisoners were casualties. For the second time I felt disgraced by my own gratitude. But it wasn't as though I'd anyone else to drink with. I'd spent an evening with a smackhead, drinking lager and chasers and snorting subbies. I'd met but rarely seen Richard. He was either upstairs in the attic recording or upstairs in the attic sleeping, or upstairs in the attic doing whatever else he did. Like it or not, the only friend I had was this grinning shark, Steve, who didn't give a shit about anything other than fucking, drinking and making money. What does a shark think about? Eating and moving. Nothing else makes any sense. A shark never stops grinning.

Saturday morning. I walked into town with Ray. I had some money in my pocket – time I bought some new clothes. I couldn't keep wearing the same two pairs of jeans. They were covered in silicone sealant in any case. I needed a new wardrobe. I left Ray outside while I went into a clothes shop. Cherry red Doc Martens, lumberjack shirts, cable knit cardigans. 2011. 1989. 1989. 2011.

I settled for a pair of black jeans and a couple of long sleeve shirts, one crimson, one green. I was trying to pull off the looking-forty-feeling-eighteen look. It was another warm day and we found a café with seats outside. I ordered a full breakfast, giving the sausages and the bacon to Ray. I reflected on how attached I had become to him already. I returned to Richard's house laden with my goods.

As usual there was no sign of Richard, just the lingering stench of fried fish. I changed into the black jeans and the green shirt. I looked at my reflection in the full-length mirror attached to the wall. I immediately felt more human. I also felt like I was a part of 2011. I took Ray to the park. I bought a paper on the way and it was very pleasant just sitting there watching the dog walkers, the skateboarders, the runners, the mums with prams, the dads with footballs. Ray was happy sniffing around, greeting every dog with a sniff of their arse.

Then I saw her, the woman from the week before with the Italian Spinone. My immediate thought was, you're not ready for her. But then I took a deep breath. Plunge into the pool. I stared at nothing in particular in the newspaper.

Oh hi, it's you again, she said.

I put the paper down, pretending I'd only just noticed her. Hi. Nice day.

Your dog's leg seems better.

We both watched as Ray fussed around her puppy. Her puppy rolled over. Ray pushed his snout in and sniffed greedily. I felt a little embarrassed by his candour, as if my dog was violating her dog.

Have you taken him to the vet?

Er … no, I've not.

You should do, get him x-rayed.

Yes, I'll do that.

I was stuck for something to say. We watched the dogs run around each other. All the time I was racking my brains, for something to talk about.

So does your fella never take her out for a walk? I managed at last.

How do you know I'm with someone? She raised her eyebrows.

I don't, just that you mentioned you had a kid. I just assumed.

Actually, I've just kicked him out.

Got the dog as a substitute? I said.

She laughed. It was a good laugh – unaffected. I joined in. It was going well.

Easier to house train, I said.

You're not kidding. And they don't come home at three in the morning and set the frying pan on fire.

Conversation. I needed more conversation. But before I could think of anything to say, she was leaving.

Right, well, it was nice talking to you.

You too.

She was edging away. I had to say something before it was too late.

Do you fancy going out for a drink?

She seemed shocked. I'd pushed it too far, come on too strong.

Not now, maybe some other time? I said.

But then she smiled. Ok, she said. Just like that.

Ha! How easy that had been. I amazed myself at how calm I'd appeared. Perhaps I was more normal than I thought. I wasn't a freak, I was someone a good-looking, intelligent woman wanted to have a drink with. We arranged a day – Monday. We arranged somewhere in town – a bar. I pretended to know it. We swapped mobile phone numbers. We swapped names. Her name was Ramona. I liked that name. I thought about the Dylan song, To Ramona, and a line from the song: the flowers of the city. Then she was gone. I sat back on the bench, smiling. You've done it, Nick. You've done it. It may not seem such a big deal to you, Andrew, but in my mind I had just run a marathon on one leg.

I was still smiling when I got home. But by the time I'd made me and Ray beans on toast, I was having doubts. Twenty-two years. I had a lot of catching up to do. The world of dating felt as remote as a distant planet. I'd seen documentaries on TV about men giving women multiple orgasms. Rock stars having eight hour tantric sex. Is that what you had to do now? I closed my eyes. I tried to imagine undressing Ramona but already her face was vague. I could picture her hair but I couldn't really hold a full image of her. Then, out of nowhere, I was back to that night. My hands all over Liv. Her hands all over me. Kissing, lips, tongues.

I met Richard down The Royal. In his black jeans, black T-shirt, black jumper, black shoes, bald head and white beard. He had a knife in a scabbard on his belt. He had his wallet in a security pouch he kept under his jumper, so that when he went to the bar he had to forage underneath to find some cash, making it obvious to any onlooker where he kept his money, rendering the security pouch redundant.

So, you play guitar? he whispered when he returned with two nearly full pints of cider, having spilt an inch of each on the pub's carpet.

It's more just fooling around, I said.

I was listening to you the other night. You were really good.

Thanks. What sort of music do you play then? I never hear you up there.

I've got it all sound-proofed. I had this problem with a neighbour a few years ago so I invested in some refurbishments. It's all state of the art. I've got a lot of ethnic instruments too.

Really, what like?

He shrugged, All sorts. Sitars, pan pipes. I've got a dulcimer from Kentucky and an alto balalaika from Magadan – would you like to come and have a look?

Maybe.

So what is it you do?

Between jobs at the moment, I said. Just doing some casual work. Driving, labouring, stuff like that. How about you?

I used to work in IT. I took a voluntary severance package about ten years ago.

And you've never worked since?

I er … like to stay clear of the rat race. It's all going to come tumbling down any day soon as far as I can work out. Don't you think?

I don't know.

It may sound small-minded of me, but I didn't really care. What I cared about was preventing my own little world from tumbling down.

Well, I mean, really, it's not sustainable, is it?

What?

Global capitalism. I think what we need in its place is an economy based on the free trading of skills for the greater good.

How would that work?

Let's say, there's a man who keeps chickens and you want some eggs. You could go round and sing him a song in exchange for half a dozen eggs.

And you think that Western civilisation could sustain itself that way?

Sure, why not?

An interesting bloke, but perhaps not all there. He'd taken too much acid in the seventies maybe. Not everyone gets along with acid. It wasn't popular inside. Acid takes you on a journey into yourself. The last place you want to travel when you are doing time. His eyes darted around as he talked. He reminded me of a dormouse. I thought of my old French teacher Miss Mulrennan, but pushed the thought away. I didn't need any more dark thoughts.

What is it you want to do? he said.

I want to set up my own business.

What sort of business?

I've had this idea for quite a while. Sort of a private members' club.

A gentleman's club?

More a sort of bohemian art space. Live music, comedy, cabaret – whatever really. Just a really free space, where everyone can be themselves.

Sounds good. I could help you with the PA if you like.

We had another drink and then went back to the house. He built a spliff and showed me the attic. It was a lot bigger than I'd thought and lined with undulating foam that looked like egg trays. He had a lot of electrical equipment up there, an array of instruments, a bed, a TV. His shelves were crammed with books and CDs. There was a big silk purple bedspread with a tree embroidered on it covering one wall.

It's from India. The Tree of Life, he said.

Have you been there then?

I have yes, I spent six months over there.

You must have liked it.

He was sitting on his bed. I was sitting in a rocking chair.

At first, the total poverty of the place gets to you. There are so many people, kids, begging. You're swarmed everywhere you go. I saw a dead baby floating down the Ganges.

Really?

It's quite common. Children under two years. They get released into the river. They escape the cycle of reincarnation and go straight to the afterlife ... He went quiet for a while, but then carried on. It's such a colourful place. Everyone seems happy. You don't see that many miserable people. Even the beggars are cheerful. This man came up to me and said, with really good English, 'I'm a collector of coins and I'm collecting English coins, I don't suppose you have any do you.' I thought that was very enterprising.

I laughed. It was a good story. It was certainly better than asking for twenty pence for a cup of tea.

So when you setting up this club?

I shook my head as I passed back the spliff. I need to find an investor.

It's not a good time for financial ventures.

I looked over to the tree of life. I looked at the brightly coloured bird at the top of the tree with a golden crest on its head. It was stretching out its wings and looking down on everything. There were birds perched on the ends of the branches. There were ripe fruits hanging from the boughs. There were animals grazing at the base of the tree. I imagined your limp carcass swinging from a rope, but it didn't fit the picture. I had another use for you.

I know someone who can help me out.

Help you out with what? he said.

Turning a thought into a thing.

And there you go, Andrew, I decided there and then to go ahead with the business. All those years in prison, thinking it through. I owed it to the tree of life. I could make it happen. I could be a success too. Perhaps I could even be better than you. I could be that brightly coloured bird.

You are climbing the walls. You are eating the furniture. You are rolling across the ceiling. You are crazy. You like being crazy. Crazy is free. You feel such relief. You don't have to keep it together any more. You are surrounded by crazy people. You like the crazy people. They are funny. You are funny.

You don't know what they have given you, but it's good stuff. You hope they will give you some more. You are talking to a crazy person. You know he is a crazy person because he says crazy things. He asks you if you want to put your dick up his arse. You don't want to put your dick up his arse. Will you tell them? Will you make them go away? Will you? His pupils are dilated. There is froth in the corners of his mouth.

You look away and when you look back he has pulled his hood over his face. He is wearing a parka with a snorkel hood. You can't see his face, just a black hole where his features should be. It is an abyss. You try not to fall into it. He is making a weird animal noise that makes you want to laugh. 'Keek, brrrmf', 'Keek, brrrmf', 'Keek, brrrmf'.

The man is Madman Marz. You laugh hysterically. You can't stop laughing. You feel your spine ice over and dread like wet sand is falling on top of you. Burying you. The abyss is pulling you into its centre. You try to fight but it is too strong. You cling on to the arms of your chair. You grit your teeth. But it pulls you into it. You are choking on wet sand.

卌 |||

Monday morning. Monday lunch. Monday afternoon. I waited until we were sitting down. Steve was stuffing his face.

I need some time off, I said.

What for?

A friend of mine. He died last night.

When's the funeral?

Wednesday.

That's quick, he said. Though he didn't seem suspicious.

He's a Muslim.

He gave me a sideways look and shook his head.

What the fuck am I going to do without a driver?

We were working in Armley, just down the road from the prison. I'd been confined there briefly. It looked like a castle in a Hammer Horror film. Inside it was even worse. Thinking about it put a shiver down my spine. The job didn't really need two people. I was only needed for about three hours a day, the rest of the time I was gofer. Steve was a man of constant appetites. No sooner had he scoffed a 'grab bag' of really cheesy Wotsits, he was wanting a tube of sour cream and onion Pringles. No sooner had he drained the tube, he was sending me off to gofer a packet of tangfastic Haribo sweets.

I can't help it, Steve.

Only one excuse for not turning up for work – and that's your *own* funeral. Do they even have funerals?

I knew him inside.

He sat back, swigging from his bottle of milkshake. Suppose I could ask the missus. Her kid brother's at uni. Only got exams to do. Might be glad of a day's work. He's not a grafter though. Fucking student. Fucking useless fucking student. Can't see the point. He's only going to get a job in Morrisons at the end of it.

Sorry, Steve.

Fuck it. I want you back on the job Thursday though. Right?

No problem.

And listen, cuntyballs, you see that fella right.

How do you mean?

You see him off proper. Just cos *he* was a Muslim, doesn't mean *you* can't get shitfaced. So get shitfaced – that's an order.

This was as close as Steve got to a sensitive side.

I dropped him back at the lock-up. Fancy a beer?

Not tonight, Steve. I've got a date.

Got a date. Fucking hell. Good for you. Give her one from me. Fill your boots, he said, Fill your boots, and we walked off in opposite directions.

I walked into town, getting there an hour early so there was plenty of time to find the bar, Milos, near the Corn Exchange, next to a tattoo parlour and a retro clothing shop. I went in and ordered a Heineken. I was on my second pint when Ramona arrived. She was wearing a white dress, a chunky black belt and clutching a black handbag. She looked pretty hot and I was immediately conscious of my own appearance – did I look too drab? Or even worse, did I look like a loser? I bought her a Magner's. Cider with ice – it was 2011, not 1989, and ice with cider was yet another sign of the times. We sat down.

So who's looking after your child?

My grandma. She only lives down the road.

Boy or girl?

She's an old woman.

No, I meant your kid.

I know. Joke. His name is Jake.

Is he at school then?

We chatted like that for some time, swapping bits of information about ourselves, building up a profile of each other. With me trying to avoid saying too much.

Have you eaten? she said. I told her I hadn't. We should maybe get something, before we get too drunk. I really need to eat something. Food is calling me. What do you like to eat? I like anything. I don't care what it is as long as it's edible. Although I'm not keen on seafood. Especially oysters. I find them too slimy. Do you like oysters?

I'd never eaten an oyster.

Er ... they're ok, I said.

Urgh! How could you? It's like eating snot.

We finished off our drinks and found a place that wasn't very busy. I had cauliflower and almond soup for starters as though this was a normal thing to eat and some potato and bacon dish with a French sounding name. Ramona had a beetroot blini and risotto for the main. I'd never heard of a blini. This was 2011 not 1989. I was heartened to see that England had upped its culinary game. We drank a bottle of rioja.

So what is it you do? she said.

It never takes people long.

I'm between jobs at the moment. Just doing a bit of casual work. Setting up my own business. I told her about the venture.

What about before. What were you doing then?

Oh, you know, this and that.

Such as?

I worked abroad. Did a lot of travelling.

Really? Where did you go?

It would be easier to list the places I didn't go.

I've always wanted to travel. Where was the best place you went then?

Tough one. Probably India.

You went to India? What's it like?

Well, at first, the total poverty of the place gets to you. I saw a dead baby floating down the Ganges.

No way! That's gross.

So many people, kids, begging. A lot of poverty and squalor but also it's so colourful. Everyone seems happy. You don't see that many miserable people. Even the beggars are cheerful. This man came up to me and said, with really good English, 'I'm a collector of coins and I'm collecting English coins, I don't suppose you have any do you.'

Bit of a dark horse. A man of mystery. And she gave me a look. Was she flirting? I wasn't an adept reader of the signs.

What about you? What do you do?

I seek to improve the wellbeing of an individual.

Maybe you can help me.

I don't know about that, she said. You look beyond help to me. Have you had your human rights violated recently?

I think I'm about to.

I can evaluate you.

I'm guessing you're a social worker.

That obvious?

We went to another bar. They had an offer on cocktails.

I love cocktails. Do you?

I nodded. My preference was for neat spirits.

I love the colours and the names.

I hated the colours. I hated the names.

We bought a jug of woo woo – whatever that was, a lurid red concoction with too much ice.

I love going to galleries. I love looking at art.

Er ... yes, I do too.

Really? You do?

In fact, I had never so much as been in an art gallery. But I had seen plenty of paintings and drawings in category A. A category A prison is like mid-nineteenth century Montmartre, full of writers and artists. And drug addicts.

I've been to see Manet, Pollock, Lowry, Louise Bourgeois, have you heard of her? She's great. Rothko, Turner. I saw Blake at the Tate ... she was beginning to slur her words.

I like Blake, I said. Pleased I could contribute something.

(I saw him once in Strangeways, George Blake – murdered his wife and two kids).

We ended up at her house. A short taxi ride. Her dog greeted us at the door. I said hello to grandma. Jake was in bed. Grandma lived round the corner. Ramona walked her back. Then we were on our own. I felt out of my depth, Ramona seemed relaxed, I couldn't sustain the easy conversation I'd had with her earlier. I was very aware of her body. She put some music on: Kings of Leon. A complete turn off, like being wrapped up in a cold wet blanket. We got comfy on the sofa and she started kissing me. It all felt very rushed, and I couldn't help the rising sense of panic in my brain. I stood up.

Are you ok? she said.

Excuse me, where's your toilet?

I found the room and locked myself in. I pressed my back against the cold tiled wall. I felt like a virgin. Ramona would be able to tell. She would sense my inexperience. She would laugh, or worse, she would think there was something wrong with me. There *was* something wrong with me: I was a freak.

I looked at myself in the mirror and took a deep breath. You're forty years old Nick, you've been waiting for this for twenty-two years. You've had sex with women before, and apart from that first time, which was a disaster, sex has been pretty good. Well, there was that other time when you were caught in the act, but don't dwell on that. It will be ok this time. Why won't it? She's not here to taunt you. She doesn't want to test you or judge you. She just wants some fun. Come on, you've got to see this through, get a grip of yourself. I took another deep breath and went back.

Everything all right? she said.

I nodded.

Come on, let's go through to the bedroom.

My heart started to bang with fear, counterbalanced by a whack of excitement. Biologically, my body was getting ready for action. Psychologically, my mind was trying to persuade my body to run for the door.

She took off her dress. Matching polka dot bra and knickers. I thought of Liv, that night, that dress. Then it was my jacket and long sleeved shirt. I had forgotten in the rush of passion, about my arms.

What happened? she said, looking at the scars along my forearms.

It's all right, I said, undressing, flesh, kissing.

You sure?

Long time ago.

She was all over me, I was all over her. She was kissing the scar tissue. I was fumbling, groping in the dark. She must have felt my clumsiness … she was taking me in her hand and guiding me in. I was inside her. I dug into her flesh. I bit on her nipple. She scratched my back and pulled at my hair. Her tongue was in my mouth. But I couldn't do it. I stopped what I was doing.

Are you ok? she said.

Then I was getting out of bed, getting dressed.

What are you doing? Where are you going?

I'm sorry. I can't. I've got to go.

I left her in bed. I needed air.

Outside, I filled my lungs. I ran along the street until I came to the main road. I stopped and rolled a cigarette. I was confused. What had happened in there? I lit my cigarette and walked along the pavement. The road was deserted. I thought about Keyop. I tried to hold back the tears.

You are in Wakefield prison – you've been here some time. You have category A status. You hang out with the most notorious prisoners. You have one hour of visiting. You have just been to the room. You sat at the table and dutifully waited. He has stood you up before, your dad, but for some reason you are convinced he is going to turn up. So you wait. He's five minutes late, then he's ten minutes late. He must have missed his bus, you think. That will put on fifteen minutes. So you wait another five minutes. So it's not a bus he's missed then. Maybe he's missed two buses. So you wait another fifteen minutes.

You look around and see all the others, with their wives and daughters, sons and brothers. And yes, some with their fathers. You recognise them: the sons and fathers. The traits they share, the same mannerisms. When they smile at each other, it's a distorting mirror. When they laugh, they do so in unison, the same pattern, the same tenor. Two men sitting opposite each other, one an older version of the other, his hair thinner and greyer, his ears and nose bigger, his skin more creased, his eyes more sunken into his skull. How many minutes do you wait? How many years can you wait? How many years have you already waited? Your life is now defined by waiting.

Eventually, you get it into your thick head that your dad is not coming. He's pissed in a pub somewhere, or passed out in a park or unconscious on the couch, the television on in the background. Your dad never comes. Who are you fooling?

Darren Lease, the prison officer, takes you back to your cell. He unlocks the door. He opens the door and he comes into the room with you. You both sit down. Him on the chair, you on the bed. He tells you a story about his own father standing him up on sports day. Darren was a fast runner. He was running the hundred metres. He won the race. But no one he cared about saw him do it. His dad had promised him he'd be there. His dad had broken his promise. He felt worse than if he'd lost the race. Dads eh, he says, and laughs. The laugh is there to comfort you and you manage to summon up enough human feeling from somewhere inside to laugh back. But it's a hollow laugh. A laugh that mocks the very act of itself.

When he has gone you find the broken shard of glass taped to the underside of your bed and you attack a fresh vein. You tell yourself this is the last time, like you did the last time. It feels good to start on a fresh vein. They only last so long before the pain dulls. Before the nerve endings die. But a fresh vein has a pain so pure. You crave this pain. Another few months of this and you'll be sectioned. It's very hard to commit suicide in prison. Most of the time you're stopped by staff. When you attempt suicide you are stopped by Sam Farnworth. He's just doing his job.

You are placed in Health Care with all the other physically and mentally ill prisoners. Karen Kenning is the nursing manager. She takes to you. Looks after you. Tells you not to be silly. Why should you let the system win? she says. Thought there was more to you than that. The only way you are going to beat the system is to survive it. And she hugs you. She is not allowed to hug you, it goes against her NMC code of conduct. She could be suspended for hugging you, or even sacked. But nevertheless, she hugs you. You go weak in her arms. You cry like a baby. You feel so sick and weak. Your misery has unmanned you. But you can't stop crying. It's ok, she says. And she hugs you harder. She builds you up from nothing, from less than nothing, to be almost human again.

It was one o'clock and I was waiting outside the chambers. It had just started spitting. Then I saw you in yet another pinstripe suit, glasses low on the bridge of your nose, striding out of the doors and down the pavement. You were coming towards me, although you hadn't seen me. I walked towards you, only a few feet away, but you didn't even give me a look.

Andrew?

You stopped, looking over your glasses in a puzzled fashion. Then I could see recognition form on your face, followed by shock. Perhaps even horror. Certainly disgust.

Nick!

Fucking hell, mate. Fancy seeing you. You look so different, I said, trying not to sound smug. I watched your hasty recovery, feigning excitement at seeing me.

Do I? You don't, really. You looked me up and down. I mean, you've not really changed a bit. You seemed almost hurt, that nature should treat our aging processes with such injustice.

What you up to now?

I'm a ...

You hesitated.

I'm a criminal barrister.

That's great.

You hesitated again, Well, in fact, I'm a QC.

You couldn't look me in the eye.

Hey, just like you said you would be all those years ago. Well done, mate. And I shook your hand.

You fiddled nervously with the buttons on your suit. How about you?

I'm not up to much, to be honest. I shrugged.

You stared at me for a moment then shook your head. I can't believe it.

I told you I was about to go for lunch and invited you along. You were hesitant at first, made a big show of looking at your watch, mumbling something about an important client, but I insisted.

Come on, Andrew, I've not seen you for twenty-two years, surely the client can wait?

Go on, why not. And you rang your clerk and rescheduled the meeting.

We went to a pizza restaurant round the corner from the chambers. It was clearly somewhere your barrister chums frequented. Pinstripe suits and Oxford brogues. We were allocated a table near the grand piano. We ordered a bottle of Merlot.

So, are you pleased to see me? The look of horror on your face hadn't completely gone away.

Course I am Nick, why wouldn't I be?

You attempted a smile but it was a rather formal one. You kept staring at me and shaking your head.

Anyway, you haven't told me why you're here, in Leeds.

I live here now.

You live in Leeds?

You looked aghast.

Yeah, what's so strange about that? I'm sharing a house with this old hippy just past Hyde Park.

Right. Great. And are you working?

Well, it's just temporary.

What you doing?

I'm working for a joiner. Sort of a dog's body really. I drive him about, do a bit of labouring. Fetch him his breakfast, fetch him his paper, fetch him his coffee.

I see. And is it all right?

It'll do for now. But I've got plans.

I waited for you to say something like, 'go on, do tell', but you were fiddling with your buttons again and messing with your tie. I told you about the club. You nodded. I could see you thought it was a cuckoo idea.

Sounds great.

And how's Liv? You two still together?

Yes, yeah. Got two kids, boy and a girl. We're living in Ilkley.

We talked about the kids for a bit. They were in boarding school. I raised an eyebrow.

The thing about this club, Andrew, I need an investor.

Right, you said and studied the pizza menu. You seemed to find it of particular interest, although I imagined you knew its contents off by heart.

The waiter who came over clearly knew you and you enjoyed his deference as we ordered.

Sort of a sleeping partner, Andrew. They wouldn't need to get involved in the day-to-day. And they'd get their money back plus profit. It's a win-win.

You nodded but your body was tense. You looked round the room. Spotting another colleague, you waved hello.

And if it fails?

I'll not lie to you, Andrew, if it goes tits up, it goes tits up. I shrugged. Then I said, But it won't. It won't fail.

The pizzas arrived. We managed to avoid *the* subject. You made a big deal about settling the bill at the end. We were walking out of the restaurant. Outside we swapped numbers.

I'll give you a call, you said, and put your phone away.

Will you?

Of course I will.

We shook hands.

Listen Andrew, you owe me this. And I looked you in the eye. Because you did owe me this and you *knew* you owed me this. You were a maggot on the end of a line, eyeing the fish with its mouth agape. But I was not going to let you wriggle out of it. It was time for payback.

<<<< IIII

White man, white bread, white van. Steve Taylor. The wasp in the jam, the snake in the barrel, the shark in the pool. Steve Taylor. My only friend in the world.

We went to the pub for lunch while we waited for the cement mixer to be delivered. Steve ordered two pints of lager and two steak and ale pies with chips.

You see him right then?

Eh?

Your mate. Your dead mate, you daft cunt. The Muslim fucker.

His question took me by surprise. It was nearly a week ago that I'd had the day off. But that was Steve, you would think he wasn't interested, days would go by, and then he would come out and ask it, as though he hadn't seen you in between.

Oh yeah, had a right session, I lied.

When my old man snuffed it, we drank the boozer dry. Only way to see out a man's life.

Is that in your will then?

I'll tell you what's in my will, I don't give a flying fuckeroo – that's what's in my will.

We drank San Miguel and waited for our food. There was no one else in except for an old man in a flat cap in the corner and a kid in a baseball cap at the bar.

Did you do her?

Eh?

That bird.

You mean Ramona?

Well, did you?

Come on, Steve, that's private.

So you didn't fuck her?

I'm not saying that.

So you did fuck her?

He patted me on the leg. Don't call you cuntyballs for nowt, he said. Good for you. Working, drinking and fucking. That's what life is.

Once again, I thought about a shark that had to keep moving and breathing at all times, but remained cheerful, a grin like an upturned banana. When you need to travel from the depths to the surface, you cling on to the shark's fin.

I hadn't heard a word from you, Andrew. It was now Tuesday – almost a week. I'd had several awkward phone calls from Ramona, but nothing from you. A week was long enough for you to get back to me. Why hadn't you rung? Perhaps you were too busy, or perhaps you were avoiding me. I decided that if you hadn't rung by the next day, I was going to ring you.

We did a day's graft and I drove Steve back to the lock-up. I had one in The Royal then went back to the house. There were no signs of Richard other than the usual stench. I had a shower, standing on plastic carrier bags, and brushed my teeth, taking my brush back to my room where it would be safe.

I went for a walk. Ray's leg was now healed, though he was still limping. I watched him run after another dog. I felt normal. I felt like a human being. It was a rare moment of balance. I got talking to the dog owner, a man in his thirties.

I love watching dogs play, he said. They're really caught up in the moment. It makes you realise, you know, that the most important thing is the here and now. Don't you think?

Did I think this? He was asking the wrong person. I was a man entirely consumed by the past. Perhaps I needed to change. I tried to picture you without feeling any emotion. Impossible.

I wondered if I concentrated on the exercise enough it would become easier with time or whether you would always have that hold over me. Because, despite what you think, Andrew, I didn't want to think of you and I didn't want you in my life. That hold made me feel weak, it made me feel beneath you. You were a snake coiled around my neck. I was holding the snake, but the harder I held it the more it squeezed. There was no shaking free. I had to grab the snake by its tail and let it bite me. Only then would it let me go.

The next day I picked up Steve and drove us over to Horsforth to start a new job. A couple in their sixties. Photos of their grandkids in fancy dress on their mantelpiece. The girl was a witch in green and black, the boy was a Buzz Lightyear. All these things people take for granted. It's amazing to me now, it was amazing to me then, that someone can walk under a rainbow and not see it. Did you know that rainbows are complete circles? There is no end. There is no crock of gold. All the colours of the universe are going round and round. It never stops.

I like to watch the sci-fi channel, she said, showing us around her house. He's only into documentaries. That's the idea of the conservatory. Get a TV in there, make it cosy. My sister thinks it's odd, but it works for us. Do you both want a cup of tea?

Another happy family. I left it till about two o'clock before I made the call, so I knew you'd be out of court and probably already leaving the chambers.

Andrew, it's Nick. How you doing?

Nick, I was going to call you … It's been mad. Big case on.

I could hear the panic in your voice.

That's all right. Not to worry. Have you had a think?

Well, yes. I have. I talked it over with Liv over the weekend.

And?

Liv suggested you come over for a meal. Give us a chance to discuss it properly.

Great. When's best for you?

We thought the weekend. Saturday. Five o'clock?

Look forward to it. See you then.

I put my phone back in my pocket. It was warm against my thigh. Liv had suggested it.

It seemed to take forever for Saturday to come round, but I was used to biding my time. The world divided into those who wait and those who act, those who say no and those who say what the hell. I was spending too much time in the pub with Steve, but I needed to sedate the snake around my neck.

Eventually, Saturday arrived, and I was on the bus. It dropped me off in the centre of Ilkley and I walked up the tree-lined avenue, the air thick with bird song. It was quarter to five. I stood close to your house. I badly needed a roll-up to settle my nerves but I didn't want to smell of cigarettes, so I waited until the time on my phone said exactly five o'clock, then I took a deep breath and walked past the gates, knocking once on your door. It was you, Andrew, who answered.

Hey, good to see you, Nick.

Was it good to see me? Somehow, I doubted that. We shook hands, your palms were clammy. The shake turned into an awkward hug. I could feel your corpulence. You were wearing a navy hooded sweater with white drawstrings. There was some meaningless insignia over your left breast. The top was loose fitting, and it made me smile. Was this your attempt to make me feel at ease or was this genuinely how you dressed in the comfort of your own home? Wearing pinstripe suits and robes all day, walking round in a seventeenth century wig, some of those straight lines must rub off.

Good to see you too, I said.

Liv's upstairs, come through.

We walked into the grand hallway and into the living room. It was quite a place you had, full of light and colour. The paintings and the sculptures were very tasteful and I wondered whether that was you or Liv. In fact, I didn't wonder at all.

Have a seat, you said, indicating the sofa.

I could see you'd been sitting in the leather armchair as the cushions were still showing the impression of your expanding backside. I must say, I derived much pleasure from observing your physical decline.

Drink?

You fetched us both a bottle of Sol and we chinked. I sat down in your armchair and you tried not to look distressed, resigning yourself to the sofa opposite. Above your head was a photograph of you and Liv. You were standing on top of a skyscraper. In the background was The Empire State Building. You had your arm around Liv and you were both smiling. Reaching up behind you was the antenna spire, soaring to the heavens. You had a bit more hair and less of a double chin. What an idyllic image, I thought.

Is that New York?

Top of the Rockefeller. Second trip. You been?

I let the silence answer your question.

Sorry, of course not. What I meant was, you should go. You'd like it.

I used silence again, let it fall like a lead hood over your head. There was a wooden chess set, but it didn't look as if it had ever been used. There was a thin layer of dust over the tops of the pieces. A black cat was trying to scratch the legs of the table, but you batted it away with your bottle.

Bloody cat.

The animal hissed at you. It stiffened its back legs and offered you the raw pink flesh of its anus, then stalked off.

So where are the kids? I said, at last.

They're at school. It's residential.

Boarding school?

Yes. I told you before.

You were scratching the ink off the side of your bottle.

A public school?

Megan was getting behind. She's not very academic. It didn't seem fair not to do the same for Ben.

Scratch, scratch, scratch. I enjoyed your discomfort.

Comprehensive worked for you, Andrew. How old's Megan?

Fifteen. You might get to see her later. She's popping over to pick up some books.

So, I said, There's money to be made from crime, and looked around the room.

It helps that we bought at the right time. Just luck I suppose.

Just luck. I knew about one form of luck, you knew of another.

I'm made up for you, Andrew. Really, I am.

I pointed through the window to the oak tree I'd hidden under. Nice tree, I said.

Have you been in the garden? you asked.

I got here early. I had a wander. Killed some time, I lied.

Neither of us said anything for a while. I watched you shift in your seat, trying to get comfortable.

About what happened ... you said, looking a little afraid, but I cut you off before you had time to continue.

It was twenty-two years ago, Andrew, we were just kids. Water under the bridge. Forget about it.

You sure?

Absolutely. I'm not one to bear a grudge. I've come to terms with the past. It's about the future now. And it's exciting.

Well, here's to the future, you said. I could see your body relax for the first time. You took a deep breath and we chinked again.

So tell me more about your plans.

Well, I've been looking around Leeds for properties. I want somewhere round the Corn Exchange. Somewhere a bit boho, studenty. I've been working it all out. I reckon I need somewhere with a capacity of about 150 people to make it work. Live entertainment. Paid performers at weekends, the rest will be open mic. Anyone can get on stage, sing a song, perform a poem, tell a joke, do a magic trick. I'll MC at first, but once it picks up, I'll pay someone. Good beers, good wines, a few choice spirits and cocktails. Snacks, suppers, tapas. Nothing fancy. It'll be a members club, so we won't need bouncers. We vet the clientele. If they become trouble, we cancel their membership.

Have you thought of a name?

Café Assassin.

You nodded your head. Why Café Assassin?

You know I was always a reader, Andrew, well I did a lot of reading inside. French nineteenth century Romantic writers: Charles Baudelaire, Théophile Gautier, Gérard de Nerval.

Baudelaire, you said, trying to sound cultured. I thought about my pet budgie with the same name. He showed a similar level of literary awareness as you.

They were part of this group in Paris, called themselves the Club des Hashischins. They met once a month at this hotel for drug-induced experiences – mostly with hashish. They didn't smoke it, they ate it as a sweetmeat. Like having a really strong hash cake.

It's not going to be a drug den is it?

Don't worry about that. We're just trading on the mystique, the sense of freedom and adventure. That's the thing. This is a free place for free spirits. I'm trying to create a scene. In an age of austerity, a bit of decadence.

It sounds ... interesting.

You were about to say something. There was probably going to be a 'but'. Something like, 'it sounds interesting, *but* a bit ambitious for a first time business venture', but you were interrupted by the door opening. You stopped and we both turned round. There was Liv in the doorway. Everything else in the room blurred.

I can't believe this, she said.

She was shaking her head, looking at me, taking it all in. I couldn't decide if she was pleased to see me or merely shocked. She shook her head again. I decided it was shock, perhaps even fear. Then she came over and gave me a tentative hug. She patted me on the back. Her body was rigid. Still, I felt a jolt shoot up my spine. You fetched her a beer and we sat down.

Nick was just telling me about his idea. Tell Liv.

So I went through it again, this time in more detail. All the time, Liv kept catching my eye and looking away. Was it fear I could see in her eyes, or merely caution? I smiled at her to reassure her, but I was thinking: twenty-two years and you didn't visit me once. You didn't write to me in all that time. Not one note. Not one word. *You fucking bitch.*

She had her legs crossed and her arms too, like she was bracing herself against an assault. She was wearing a sixties-style dress, big chunky ring and necklace. Your wife has great taste. Unlike you, Andrew. You never had any idea about how to dress yourself. I suspect that the robes and wig uniform was something you relished, as it took away the burden of choice. It took away the very real possibility of you looking like a dick.

Sounds too good to be true, she said, after I'd finished my pitch. What did she mean by that? I'd hoped to captivate her by my description, but she shared your scepticism. This was not the reaction I'd hoped for.

You're going to run it yourself? she said.

That's the idea.

But you don't have any experience.

Well, thanks for the confidence vote.

Have you got a business plan?

No.

A cash-flow forecast?

What's one of those?

Have you done an analysis of your competitors?

No.

Look, Nick, eighty percent of new businesses fold in the first twelve months. What makes your business any different?

I looked her in the eye, Because my life depends on it. I don't have a plan B. This has to work. Do you understand?

That doesn't mean it will. I'm sorry Nick, I'm just trying to be realistic.

Liv's speaking from bitter experience. She's had quite a few ups and downs with her catering business, haven't you, babe?

I watched Liv wince as you called her 'babe'. Things weren't as rosy in the garden as you were both trying to make out.

I'm sorry to hear that, I said, But be honest, it's not a matter of life and death for you is it?

She tensed at this. I wanted to say, 'so fuck off' but held my tongue. I saw her relax a little. She took a deep breath and she loosened her shoulders.

Ok, you've got a point, I suppose.

She looked over to you, Andrew. She shot you a look. It said to me, 'I could have done with more support from you'. I wondered to what extent your ambition had stifled hers.

Don't you think I can make a go of it then? I said.

I'm not saying you will fail, Nick. I mean there are quite a lot of bars a bit like that in town already, but to be honest they're mostly crap. Aren't they, Andrew?

You just shrugged.

We've been in them all. Shabby rather than decadent, with the exact same furniture and pat prints on the walls. Boring.

That's not quite true, Liv. There are some good ones.

What you're describing, Nick, if you can pull it off, and I'm sorry to put a dampener on it, but it *is* a big if, you're taking it one stage further.

Remember the Dry Bar? I said.

Course I do. She smiled for the first time, and you nodded.

I mean, a totally different place, but it had that thing about it. The thing I'm trying to create. You felt like you were part of something just being there, part of a club, a family. Remember that man who used to dress like Alex out of Clockwork Orange?

Oh, I do, yes. I'd forgotten about him. He used to sit with his mates wearing a white boiler suit. She laughed.

Black boots and a black bowler hat. He even had eyelash extensions on one eye.

What a cock!

I know, but at the time we all thought he was so cool.

No, you thought he was cool. I thought he was a cock.

And we both laughed. Me and Liv. Not you. You just sat there scratching your bottle, unable to join in. You hadn't noticed these people even though you'd been there with us. You had your mind on higher things such as punishment and justice. And shafting your best friend.

Then we were back there: 1989. Talking bars, talking nights, talking people. Pretentious people, desperate people, drunken people, extroverts, nutters. She was laughing awkwardly at first but as she drank she seemed to relax. Every now and then we would catch each other's eye and Liv would return my smile. Her guard was slipping, but whatever caution she was feeling hadn't entirely vanished. You hardly said anything at all.

We went into the dining room. Mushrooms, pasta, wine. More wine.

You like mushrooms right? she said.

Course I do. Edible ones.

Every mushroom is edible. At least once, she said, with the glint of mischief back in her eye.

I heard the front door open and a voice shout through.

It's only me!

We stopped talking. There was a pause, then the dining room door opened and in she walked, your daughter. She looked at you and Liv, then she looked at me.

This is Nick. An old friend. Nick, this is Megan.

She walked across and shook my hand. I was stunned by how like Liv she was, even more so in the flesh. Again, I thought back to that party.

I've heard about you. You were in prison.

It's not polite to say that, Megan, you said.

I don't mind. It's nice to meet you, I said.

I think it's interesting, Megan said.

The books are in the hall, on the stairs. I've put them in a bag for you, Liv said.

Don't I get a drink?

Liv poured her a half glass of wine. She took the glass and gave you a look. As if that glass was a small victory over you.

Megan thinks she's eighteen.

Don't start, she said. He's such a miserable–

Don't say it.

I had fun trying to guess the missing word. There are plenty in the English language that would do the job.

She sat down at the table. Are you really the same age as dad?

Give or take a month or two.

You look ten years younger. Doesn't he mum?

Don't think she's flattering you, Nick. It's just another way of insulting me, you said. You helped yourself to a top-up.

So what was dad like at school?

He was a good student. Worked hard. Always revised for his exams.

You mean he was a swot?

I thought boarding school was supposed to show you the benefits of a good education, you said.

You thought wrong. She laughed in your face.

Are you stopping for something to eat? Liv said.

I've had a KFC.

You looked relieved. We ate in silence. You stared at the end of your fork. Megan was looking over at me.

Well, I know where I'm not wanted, she said at last. She knocked back her drink and left the room.

Sorry about that, Liv said. She's at that age.

She sees me as the enemy, you said.

It looked like Megan and I had something in common.

We finished the pasta and moved on to the steak. The food was good, the meat was succulent, but you didn't seem to have much appetite. I noticed Liv watch you move your food around your plate without eating it.

Is there something wrong, Andrew? she asked you at last.

No.

I made it how you like it.

I noted the irritation in her voice.

I know.

Medium rare.

There was an awkward pause. You reached over again for the wine and filled your glass to the top. Liv's glass was nearly empty but you didn't fill her glass. She took the bottle off you and poured an inch into her own glass, as though demonstrating what restraint looked like. She moved the coaster from near your setting, where the wine had been, to the centre of the table, and put the bottle back. I thought about that chessboard in the other room, untouched. This is how you both play chess. I excused myself. You told me where the bathroom was and I went upstairs. Megan was sitting at the foot of the second set of steps.

You ok?

She shrugged, without looking up.

You sure?

I hate him. He's such a dick.

He's only doing what he thinks is best.

Bollocks. He's a twat.

Is that your bedroom up there?

Why do you want to know?

She stared at the floor. I watched a vein on her neck pulsate.

Do you like boarding school?

It's all right.

You look so much like your mum.

Is that a good thing?

She looked into my eyes.

Did you and mum...?

There was an awkward hiatus. Then I said, I best be getting back.

As long as I don't look like him.

I left her moping on the step, used the bathroom and went back downstairs. It was good to see how popular you were with your only daughter. I wondered if things with Ben were any better.

I didn't return to the dining room immediately. Instead, I wandered into your study. I wanted to look at that family photograph again. I could see now that Liv was holding a bag of bread. There were ducks everywhere and she was laughing. Ben was holding out a chunk of bread, but he looked nervous – a mallard about to snatch it off him. Megan was throwing a handful of bread in the air.

I was mesmerised by the photograph. There was a pond in the background and some trees. The trees were reflected on the surface of the water. To the side there was an old-fashioned lamp-post. I leaned against the wall and tried to draw in deep breaths. I felt a tightness around my chest, the snake constricting me.

After a minute or so the feeling wore off and I went back to my meal. We finished the steaks. You opened another bottle of wine. Liv went to get some cheese out of the kitchen.

So, have you had chance to discuss it? I said.

I'm sorry?

Come on, Andrew, no games.

Yes, we've talked about it.

And?

We've agreed on fifty thousand.

I need more than that.

That's what we agreed on.

Are you suffering from amnesia?

What do you mean?

Saturday the ninth of September 1989.

You gripped the stem of your glass. You rubbed the stem with your thumb, up and down, over and over.

I can probably get more.

I need a lot more.

The door opened. It was Liv with a wooden board of cheese. I didn't bring up the subject again. We talked about the cheese.

It was locally sourced. It was organic. The farmer used to be an actor. You seemed comfortable with this topic. We started talking about Liv's catering business. You drifted out of the conversation. Before long it was just me and Liv. You were in the shadows filling your face with locally sourced organic cheese.

The door opened again, this time it was Megan.

I'm going.

Have you got your books? Liv said.

I need some money.

What for?

I just need it.

Well, I've not got any, you said.

I need twenty quid.

I've told you, I've not got it.

You must have twenty quid, don't lie.

You cut a chunk of cheese and skewered it with the end of your knife.

Andrew, give her the money, Liv said.

Megan stood in the doorway, looking defiant. Looking like Liv. Eventually you stood up and took out your wallet. You counted out two tens and handed them over. She snatched them from you and slammed the door behind her. We had something else in common, me and Megan. We both wanted money off you.

Then it was ten o'clock.

You should stay over, Liv said, That's all right, Andrew, isn't it? She smiled at you, knowing very well it wasn't all right.

The guest bed is made up, why not? You smiled back. You weren't going to give in that easily.

I was the net you were both batting your ball across. I thought about how I could use that net. How I could tighten it.

I better not, I said. And I told you both about Ray. I told you both about Richard. My last bus is at midnight.

You made a big show about it being no trouble, now you were out of the danger zone. At some point you must have left the room. We were talking about the business. We both forgot you existed. About eleven o'clock we found you in the other room in your chair asleep.

He had a few single malts before you got here.

Nerves?

Partly that, and partly work.

How long's he been a QC?

Two years. It's a lot to take on. We hardly spend any time together these days.

I thought again about that net.

I better be going soon, I said. We've still not talked about the loan.

Let me make you coffee. You've got ages yet.

We went through to the kitchen. Liv took out a packet of fresh coffee and tried to open it.

Here, use my knife, I said, and I handed it over.

She took it in her hand and looked at the Celtic pattern on the handle. For the second time I saw her register shock. This isn't … is it?

Yep. I nodded.

The knife she 'bought' me for my eighteenth birthday, a few months before I got sent down, looked after by Her Majesty's custodians and returned to me in almost perfect condition. She turned it over in her hand.

You kept it all this time?

I think of you every time I bleed.

She laughed as she remembered the scene, with me holding the knife with the blade out. You just standing there staring at the blood pumping from my finger, your Robert Smith hairdo wet and limp with rain water. Then Liv running around finding a towel. Me just standing there watching the blood pour onto the cream bedroom carpet. Onto the cushion and even onto (and into) my coffee mug. The final drips landing in the milk jug. All of this lit by candlelight.

She looked at the knife again. She turned it over in her hands. I held out my hand, my finger with the scar along it. She took my hand, she ran her finger down the groove of the scar tissue. She gave me a hug. This time she hugged me with conviction. We stayed like that for some time.

I'm sorry about tonight, Nick.

What for?

You know.

She took the knife and pulled out the blade. She used it to cut through the coffee packet. She poured coffee beans into the pull-out drawer of the red and chrome machine.

We were both a bit ...

She made an apologetic hand gesture. She put the packet back, closed the drawer and fiddled with the settings. There was a dial on the front. I have no idea what it was for.

It's understandable, I said.

I can't believe ... you've hardly changed, Nick. You look–

She blushed.

So do you.

She laughed at this.

Well, the hair's out of a bottle these days, she said.

The coffee machine kicked into action. She took out two cups. She poured the coffee.

I don't want to be pushy, Liv, but Andrew made me an offer. The business of the loan.

If it was up to me, I'd just hand it all over to you. Like that.

And she clicked her fingers. I could see now that she was a bit drunk, a little unsteady on her feet, her words slurred. I was also inebriated, the alcohol giving me a nice buzz.

What you were saying before.

What about?

About me not having the relevant experience, I said.

Well–

You were right.

Well, I could help you find a property.

Really?

I almost laughed, I hadn't even needed to ask her.

I think it'd be a laugh. Milk?

Not for me. Not since that evening, I said.

She looked at me and then at the knife on the counter. She picked it up and turned it over, deep in thought. She handed it back to me.

I'd like to help you. I mean, you know, with the club – I like snooping around. It's not exactly riot city round here, more Camberwick Green.

That money, it's not going to be enough. I need at least five times that amount. He said you'd agreed on it.

That's bullshit. He told me how much he was giving you and said did I think it was fair.

And what did you say?

I didn't say anything. I didn't think he actually wanted my consent … Listen, I'll talk to Andrew. I'll see what I can do.

We finished our coffee and I went into the room where you were sleeping to get my coat. Liv followed me in, clearing away a few things. We both looked over to where you were slumped in your chair. There was a bit of drool coming out of your mouth and onto the cushion. A trail of slime. Liv made a face, one of mild revulsion, and I made one back.

Isn't that disgusting? she said.

'He' or 'that'? I said.

There was a pause, while she weighed it up. I could tell that a part of her was thinking 'he'. She didn't answer me.

We said goodnight at the door. We hugged for maybe a moment too long for it to be just a goodbye hug. I kissed her on the cheek. She gave me her mobile number like it had been a date. I was walking back into town, rolling a cigarette, Cramps songs in my head, looking at the stars. I sparked up and inhaled the smoke. It felt good. I was singing What's Behind The Mask? and How Far Can Too Far Go? I thought about that photograph of you and Liv on top of the Rockefeller. And I wanted everything that you had.

A few days afterwards, you'll remember, I received a text from you: I've spoken to my accountant. You'll need to make an appointment to see him.

There were various stages before it was possible to release the funds, but just over two weeks later, the money was transferred into my account. I printed out a statement. There it was: £250,000.

I looked at the numbers printed in blue on the white page. I couldn't quite believe it. I kept putting the statement down, then picking it up again. The numbers were still there. All of them. The most money I'd had in my life was £225. Now I had £250,000. This sum of money was nothing to you. It was merely the cost of guilt. There was no follow-up note, which didn't surprise me, the money was self-explanatory, but it did strike me as an indication of your emotional aloofness.

The first thing I bought was a laptop. I'd had access to computers inside, but they were never networked, never connected to the internet. I'd really just used them as word processors, to do my OU work. I was familiar with some of the software and the layout of the keyboard, but email and the internet were exciting spaces that I entered with the enthusiasm of a child. I won't say they were easy to navigate at first, but I was determined and persistent. I sent you a text to ask you for your email. The first email I sent was to you, saying thanks for the money. You didn't email me back. Instead, I received this from Liv.

To: Nick Smith

From: Liv Honour

CC: Andrew Honour

Hi Nick,

Andrew says, thanks for your email. Andrew (cc-ed) agrees that it would be a good idea if I get involved. It sounds like an interesting venture, and I do have quite a bit of experience of starting a business. Setting up a bank account, registering the business, sorting out a website, negotiating prices, stuff like that.

So where are you thinking of looking? Have you done any research into places similar to the one you have in mind? I'm asking because last year I did some catering for a bar in Manchester in The Northern Quarter called Casablancas. They were doing a similar thing, live music, cabaret, comedy.

We should go, Liv

I responded to say that I thought this was a good idea. Secretly I wondered why you were so keen for Liv to be involved. I sent you both some potential dates we could arrange. She emailed me back a few hours later.

To: Nick Smith

From: Liv Honour

CC: Andrew Honour

Hey Nick, (Hi Andrew)

I think you'll really like Casablancas. It's very cool and has a relaxed vibe.

How about the three of us check it out soon? I think they have a cabaret themed night on the last Thursday of the month.

Liv.

I replied to say that I'd love to come along. It would be good for the three of us to go, just like old times. Again, Liv replied fairly promptly. If only she had been this keen while I was inside. Twenty-two years. Not one letter.

To: Nick Smith

From: Liv Honour

CC: Andrew Honour

Hey Nick,

I'll drive and pick you up at 8 next Thursday. Can you send me your postcode as I'm crap at directions.

Thanks

Liv

The Thursday arrived and Liv picked me up outside The Royal Park. I was too embarrassed to have you pick me up from Richard's. I didn't want either of you to see me in such a lowly state. But particularly you, Andrew. However, when she pulled up, I was somewhat taken aback to find Liv was on her own.

No Andrew? I asked, as I got in the passenger side.

He didn't get back in from work in time, the case ran over. Again. Will I do? she said.

I tried not to look too pleased. We chatted in the car on the way there.

You don't mind me being involved do you, Nick? That was the only way Andrew would agree to the loan. Are you ok with that?

Perhaps she thought I had forgotten our drunken conversation where she had suggested she be involved. I wondered how long it had taken her to persuade you.

Of course I am, I said.

It's not that he doesn't trust you Nick, it's just that ... well, lots of things have changed. You'll stand a better chance with some help. A lot of the buzz we'll need to generate, we'll need to use social media. Have you seen anywhere yet?

I've not had chance to do much looking, but I've seen a few places.

I'd been walking around the Corn Exchange area of Leeds, not really knowing what I was looking for. It hadn't occurred to me to use my newly acquired computer. We drove into the northern quarter of Manchester in plenty of time and found somewhere to park. Casablancas was easy to find. The cabaret was entitled Cabaret Heaven, and so had a lot to live up to. The venue seated 250 people, which was larger than the place I had in mind. Liv had bought the tickets in advance, which was just as well. I was heartened to see, when we eventually got through the entrance and exchanged our tickets for a smiley face stamp on the back of our hands, that the place was packed.

Cabaret is dead, long live cabaret, Liv said.

I bought us both lagers and we found somewhere to sit at the back. The stage was a good size and decorated with spangly strips of silver, gold and red curtains. There was a mirrorball reflecting an array of coloured lights around the room. The audience were a mix of bohemian, arty types and regulars of the club.

The temperature was rising and I took off my coat and placed it on the back of my chair. Liv did the same. Then she took off the red cardigan she was wearing. My eyes were immediately drawn to the low cut neckline of her dress.

Tits of a twenty year old, she said. And I blushed.

Sorry, I said. I thought about Megan.

Don't be daft, she said, and grabbed my hand. I was only joking.

There was some delay, much talk about the interval buffet, and a great deal of emphasis on the raffle. We both bought a few strips.

You never know, we might be lucky. Liv said, First prize is a bag of pork.

I thought she was joking, but she pointed to the table at the front where the prizes were displayed.

Are these ironic prizes? I asked.

I was having trouble trying to work out what level of irony the night's entertainment was aiming for. It seemed to be a pastiche of a traditional cabaret, but to what extent it achieved this, and to what extent it merely presented a traditional cabaret was debatable.

The first act was 'Mr Mann and his Wizard Dog' and was billed as 'psychic canine magic'.

This should be fun, Liv said, and raised her eyebrows.

The act relied on four volunteers and a pack of giant playing cards. The dog was supposed to guess the card, through an elaborate system of biscuits and arithmetic. Mr Mann was adding up and taking away sums that were in some way connected to the treats. He must have been in his eighties and looked like he'd been doing the act all his adult life. Practice hadn't made perfect. The sums didn't add up. The dog wandered off the stage. The errors were funny, but not in that Tommy Cooper intentionally funny way.

I feel sorry for the dog, Liv said.

Mr Mann was shouting and pushing the dog, trying to get her to select a treat.

We all feel sorry for the dog, I said.

I looked around the room. There was indeed a general air of feeling sorry for the dog permeating the venue. Next was an ABBA tribute act which featured two women, one blonde and one brunette. They said they had lost the two men.

I hope it gets better than this, I said.

I wouldn't count on it, Liv said.

The next act was called Madame Légume, and was subtitled, 'for all your vegetable entertainment needs'.

I wasn't aware I had any vegetable entertainment needs, Liv said.

The act consisted of Madame Légume in a tent of a dress, a bowl of vegetables on her head, re-enacting the story of the film Jaws, with vegetables as replacements. The first victim of the shark was a leek. The lifeguard was a parsnip. Richard Dreyfuss's character was played by a potato.

She's not going to re-enact the whole film is she? Liv asked with a look of horror on her face.

About half-way through, Liv stood up. Come on, she said. I think we get the idea. Let's go somewhere quiet for a drink.

We found a bar round the corner with lots of space, where the music wasn't too loud.

I shouldn't have another lager, she said, looking at the pint glass I put down beside her. Then she took a sip, Fuck it ... well, we know what we don't want, she said. That wasn't even cabaret. I wouldn't call that cabaret, would you?

What would you call it?

Shit.

Well, yes.

It was more like variety. I think it has to be more coherent for it to be cabaret. You know what I mean? It has to hang together, and it needs to be more satirical and edgy.

Or just better, I said.

Liv's leg was pressed against mine. I looked around the room. There were only a few people standing by the bar.

Is Megan ok?

Why wouldn't she be?

She seemed upset, the other night.

Teenage girls.

She's very attractive. She looks like you.

I watched her blush.

We had one more drink, then she drove me back.

Well, the bad news is, that was shit. But the good news, even shit sells, she said.

She pulled up outside the pub and gave me a peck on the cheek as she dropped me off. When I got in, I poured myself a large whiskey and emailed Liv, to say thanks for a great night, and to say how much of a laugh I'd had. It was a shame Andrew hadn't made it, I lied. I can't remember if I CC'ed you or not. It was gone twelve, so I was really quite surprised when I got an email back just a few minutes later.

To: Nick Smith

From: Liv Honour

Hey there!

I had a great time too. The acts were a bit lame – I expected ping pong balls plopping into our drinks at any moment.

It's good to see how not to do it though, don't you think? I was thinking a little more classy really. Red velour seating and heavy drapes, that kinda thing.

There's a place in Leeds close to the courts we can try if you like.

Let me know.

Lx

I noticed, Andrew, that her email had omitted CC'ing you. I wondered about this. Had she merely replied to my email, which hadn't been CC'ed to you in the first place? It sounded like the obvious explanation, but when I went into my sent items box to check, I discovered that my email had in fact CC'ed you.

A hundred and ten press-ups, a hundred and ten sit-ups, eight minutes of shadowboxing. We were meeting at the station. I caught a bus from Richard's. I got to the station two minutes before Liv's train. There I was standing on the platform watching the tracks, parallel lines, converging on the horizon, when her train came in and she was stepping out of the carriage in a red frock coat. Black hair, grey eyes, a grey pencil skirt and those white ballet shoes again. She hugged me and kissed me on the cheek.

Let's grab a coffee first, she said.

We went to a deli and sat outside in the morning sun. Liv stirred her coffee and I watched her fingers play with the spoon. There were purple foxgloves growing from the gaps in the flags. A bee was flitting from flower to flower. The bee was just the right size so that the bell of the flower perfectly encapsulated it. Liv opened her bag and took out an iPad. We went through some of the properties she'd been looking into.

This one, she said, and we peered at a photograph of the outside.

It doesn't look like much, I said.

Wait a minute.

She touched the screen and an interior photograph appeared.

It's bigger than it looks.

We looked at a few other places.

Do you like what you see? she said.

She was staring at the interior of a club. It was very plush, but it wasn't big enough. I was staring right at her.

Yes, I do.

She looked up. She blushed.

Come on, she said, Let's have a scoot round.

The one we looked at first was by far the most promising, needing the least work. When we got there, the owner was taking out some pans from the kitchen, loading them into a van.

Can we see inside?

It's sold, he said.

He told us he'd just accepted an offer just below the asking price, but he let us look around anyway.

Are you both going into the business? he said. Husband and wife?

Neither of us corrected him. We finished looking round and left.

Shame, I said, afterwards, It would have been perfect.

Plenty of others to look at, fuck it, Liv said.

We spent two hours or so looking around properties. There was a place for rent, which had been a shop, that was a good size and was near the market. It was very suitable but I didn't want to rent, I wanted my own place, I wanted to own it. It was late afternoon when we'd finished.

Let's get something to eat, I know a place, she said, You'll like it.

It was a chop house near the railway arches. A waiter brought us two leather-bound menus. We ordered wine. I can't remember what we ordered to eat.

So what did you think of the other places?

We talked about what we'd seen. There were a few that needed work, but not much more than a lick of paint, new furniture, new decoration.

You want that first place, don't you? Liv said.

It was true, she'd read my mind. It was exactly what I wanted. She took out her phone.

What are you doing?

I've got the owner's number.

She rang him up but there was no answer.

What were you going to say to him?

I was going to ask him what it had gone for.

What's the point?

So we could offer him more, you bozo.

But he's already accepted the offer.

It's called gazumping, Nick. Everyone does it. We can try again later. If you want something, you have to take it.

I was going to take it, all right, Andrew.

We ate in silence. Eventually I said, Is Andrew still stressed at work, or have things calmed down a bit now?

I don't know, we've not discussed it.

But you agreed on the money?

Eventually.

Hope I've not caused any tension?

Don't worry about it.

She was going to say something else, but changed her mind. I wondered what it was. Something like, 'there was plenty of tension before, without you.'

We ate in silence again. Then she said, I wrote a thank you letter to myself this morning, from Andrew.

Really? What did it say?

Here, I'll show you.

She took a crumpled piece of paper out of her bag. She handed it to me. The note read:

> Dear Liv,
>
> Thank you so much for cooking my dinner, washing up the pots, drying them, putting them away, feeding the cat, watering the plants, picking up my underwear, putting it in the laundry basket, hoovering, cleaning, tidying, making my bed, ironing my shirts, washing my clothes, drying my clothes, putting my clothes away in the wardrobe, picking up damp towels from the floor, putting the milk back in the fridge, the lid back on the butter dish and my coat on the hook. Thank you for doing this every single day. I really do appreciate it, even though I appear not to notice any of it.
>
> Love,
>
> Andrew

I wanted to laugh, inside I was crying with laughter, but what did I do instead? I defended you, Andrew. *I* was *your* advocate.

Perhaps he thinks with the long hours he works, that he's contributing in an equal but different way.

Liv didn't say anything. She fiddled with her fork.

Do you know what I did my dissertation on at uni? she said eventually.

No, I said, What was it?

The Third Wave: a Post-Structuralist Interpretation of the Gendering of Domestic Space.

She held her glass and stared into the red liquid. She gulped it down then topped us both up.

We listened to I Wanna Go All The Way. Her leg was resting against my leg. I could feel the warmth of her flesh. Her bare skin against my jeans. I looked into her eyes and she was pouring into me.

I'm talking about your wife, Andrew.

You have been transferred to a maximum security prison as a Category A prisoner. Wakefield is so quiet in comparison to Strangeways. There is no clatter of metal against bars. There are no voices echoing down the white stone corridors. Not everyone in Wakefield is a murderer. Some are terrorists too. There are bombers, rapists, armed robbers. There are drug dealers. But mostly murderers. Murderers are a different type of prisoner to the others.

You are playing chess with a man called Ian. Ian interests you. Ian never gave any cheek at school. He always handed in his homework on time. He never taped off the radio or dropped any litter. He has never smoked a cigarette. His hair is parted at the side. He is clean shaven. Ian intrigues you. You have known him for three months and you can't understand why he is in prison.

Eventually you ask him. Eventually he tells you. He tells you that he left school at sixteen. He tells you that he worked in a warehouse. There he met a woman. She worked in the office upstairs. She made all the moves. She asked him for a drink. He was twenty-one and still a virgin. After some time, they slept together. They were married in a church in the village where she was born. They went to Lanzarote on their honeymoon. They had a daughter.

Ian worked extra shifts, to buy her all the things she wanted. Jewellery, dresses and shoes. Holidays abroad. A dream kitchen with a real marble top. A leather sofa. He put some of the money away in a trust fund for his daughter.

He came home early from work one day. He parked his car and went to the front door. Before he could put the key in the lock, he could hear a noise. It sounded like someone was hitting someone. He ran to the back window. And there she was. His wife. She was naked and she was on top of another man, rutting like some beast. He'd never seen her like this. He'd never seen her so animated.

Very slowly, he put the key in the lock and turned it. He walked down the thick wool carpeted hallway, into their dream kitchen. He took out a chef's knife of the highest precision from the solid wood knife block, which was placed on the pristine marble top. He went into the living room, where they were still rutting. He stabbed her eighteen times in the back. He stabbed the man three times in the chest and twice in the face.

Ian shows no sign of emotion as he tells this story. He studies the chess pieces. You are in the endgame. You think about your own story. You don't judge Ian. You look at Ian. He looks like the innocent flower. You and Ian have something in common. You are both the victims of betrayal. You wonder if you can be friends with Ian. You haven't had a true friend since Keyop. Is it possible to love someone again? You think it probably isn't.

Instead, you focus on the game. You are close to checkmating Ian. You are going to win the game and that is more important than love.

THE DIET OF WORMS

'Do not despair, one of the thieves was saved; do not presume, one of the thieves was damned.'

Falsely attributed to St Augustine by Samuel Beckett

‖‖ ‖‖

We didn't like French but we liked our French teacher. I say we, but I'm not talking about me and you, Andrew, not this time. You weren't in our French group. I would always sit with Mark Jones. When we got put into French groups I was automatically put in the bottom group because I was in the bottom group for English. The reason I was in the bottom group for English (and Maths) was because I'd been excluded for a year and had missed a great deal of work (unlike you who had been sitting outside the headmaster's office, working diligently at the coursework). Our French teacher was called Miss Mulrennan and, like Richard, she had the mannerisms of a dormouse, with the same quick nervy movements, pointy nose and big eyes. She was single (we all imagined) and drove a yellow Citroen 2CV. There was a rumour that she was still a virgin. She seemed old to us but was probably no more than thirty. Her dress sense was that of an older woman, long shapeless skirts, Arran jumpers and flat mannish shoes. I realise now that her dress sense was entirely appropriate for 'teaching' pubescent boys. It was the sartorial equivalent of a dose of bromide. She would always walk into a classroom that was in complete disarray.

Because we were the bottom group, nothing was ever expected of us, and as long as we were kept out of the way we could do as we liked. There was a wooden hut behind the school which was freezing in winter and scorching hot in summer. This is where we were kept, a comprehensive gulag.

Me and Mark would play hangman. Some kids carved their names on the desks. Some kids wrote 'fuck' on the blackboard and some drew a giant cock complete with curly pubes and spunk coming out of the hole in the helmet.

It was one such morning, with us sitting in our corner, looking out of the window, thinking of words for hangman, that Miss Mulrennan walked in with a large hessian bag. She knew from experience that there was no point in asking for order, instead she stood at the front and watched, ignored as usual. We were curious that morning to see, instead of fear on her face, a smile. We wondered why that was and we wondered what was in the large hessian bag. Then she opened it and we saw that it was full of bread and chocolate.

She walked to each desk and placed a baton-like loaf and a bar of chocolate on each one. When she had finished she stood at the front and she smiled again. The class was quietening down and the boys who had been playing basketball were sitting at their desks, and we were all now seated, looking to the front for the first time.

She explained that in France there was a tradition of children eating chocolate sandwiches. She explained that the small baton-like loaf was called a baguette and that chocolate in French was *chocolat*. And this was why she had brought the bread and the chocolate. She had gone to a special bakery first thing that morning to buy the bread. She had brought the chocolate back from France when she had visited a few weeks ago, especially for us. She wanted us to make chocolate sandwiches. She had bought the bread and chocolate out of her own purse because the school would not give her any money. An act of desperation or kindness? Either way, it got our attention.

She had been teaching us for two months and nothing had worked. It was now November and we hadn't learned a word of French or anything about French culture, even though we had started class in September. We felt touched by this gesture and we felt ashamed of the giant penis on the blackboard behind her which was positioned so that it appeared to be spurting spunk into her ginger hair.

We wished just this once that it wasn't there, that it was just a blackboard. She smiled again, realising at last that she was getting through to us. She had our attention and she seemed to grow and shine. We were actually sitting at our desks in silence and we were actually listening to what she was saying.

She was, for the first time in two months, doing her job – she was teaching us. We, for the first time in two months, were doing our job – we were learning. There was a sense of stillness that we didn't recall ever experiencing before. I wasn't really friends with Mark Jones, in fact never saw him outside of this class, but I sensed he was experiencing what I was experiencing.

And for one moment, we were behaving like human beings to one another and we were happy. We wanted that moment to stretch out across time. The air seemed to shimmer as though it were a hot afternoon in summer. Our ears were alive to every sound. The clicking of the clock on the wall, the gentle creak of the timber as it relaxed in the warmth of the room, the white-yellow glow of the fluorescent strip lights.

Then this moment was shattered like a sheet of glass. A baguette was hurtling through the air. We watched as it revolved, as it moved in an arc, a baton of bread, making the shape of an 'X' as it flew towards Miss Mulrennan. We watched it whirl and we watched as her smile turned into a look of terror, but it was too late to dodge and the end of the loaf hit her hard on her forehead and made a dull thud as it bounced off and hit the floor. She made a quiet gasp – not physically that hurt, although probably some sharp jolt of pain registered – and then the silence was replaced by shouting and laughing and swearing and baguette after baguette rained down on her head.

She was standing in front of us, with her hands over her face, not protecting herself from the onslaught, but covering her eyes, and we realised then that she was sobbing. She made little gasps and her tiny frame was shaking. We watched and we did nothing.

Then she was running. Out of the class, out of the hut and down the path. We watched her until she disappeared across the car park.

We never saw her again, nor did anyone ever mention her name again, no teacher and no pupil, but we knew that day that we would never forget what we had done and that we would always regret it. We had transgressed beyond our usual bad behaviour. We had driven a good-hearted woman over the edge. I felt ashamed to be part of this group. I longed to be in the other group, with you.

It must have been very different for you, Andrew, in your top class with the top kids and the top teacher (a strict teacher with a beard, you were all in awe of). Actually learning to speak French. Actually learning something about French culture. Actually going to France on holiday for two weeks, sometimes three weeks, every summer with your parents.

We never went on holiday. Not one I remember. Not after mum died, and I was too young to remember the holidays before. Dad wasn't a holiday person. To him a holiday was getting up when he liked, doing what he liked and drinking as much as he could. So in that sense, in the end, his life became a permanent holiday. He'd been abroad when he'd done his national service, so he had, in his own words, 'done all that shit'. Holidays were a thing of the past. Holidays were what proper people did. Holidays were for others. They were not for us.

Why am I telling you all this? Well, I suppose it's because it's something you don't know. Despite us spending nearly every day in each other's company from being aged three (although we didn't actually become best friends until we were six), this was one experience you were excluded from along with English and Maths. Because you were in the top group for all of these subjects and I was in the bottom. Not because you were smarter than me but because you sat outside the headmaster's office while I stayed at home watching television. Not because you were more competent than me but because your parents made you do an hour of homework four days a week, and because when you didn't make the grades they paid for a private tutor to come to your house twice a week.

I've never told you this, Andrew, but I loved you more than a brother loves his brother. It was the opening night of the club and I was thinking of the love I'd had for you once as I was getting ready to go on stage: how that pure love had changed into a twisted shape. How the resentment had built. How the feelings of inferiority had built. But now I felt equal.

I was thinking about my mum too. Did I actually remember her, or had I manufactured those memories from photographs and often-told anecdotes? The memory of her voice, with its soft lilt. The memory of her reaching into my cot one spring afternoon when a breeze was building, and covering me up with a soft blanket. The memory of her coming into my room at night to check I was asleep, kissing me tenderly on my forehead. You must admit, those memories are suspiciously chocolate box. A praline of implanted images.

I was thinking of Miss Mulrennan standing at the front of the class. I was thinking of you with your loving parents and your stable home. And I was thinking of my dad, stumbling up Peter Street, colliding with the lamp post, falling down, lying on the pavement. My mates around me laughing. You next to me, also laughing. Him passed out. Me laughing along, but inside wishing an assassin would come along and shoot a bullet through my skull.

From the stage, it was hard to see where she was sitting. The lights were bright and the club was dark. But then I saw her. I beckoned her onto the stage. She looked sheepish but wended her way through the crowd. Then I was offering her a hand and she was on stage beside me.

I just want to thank Liv for all the hard work and help she's given me over the past few months. First finding a place, then getting it ready. Help with the menu, help with the bar, booking the acts, promoting our opening night. She's been absolutely brilliant. So please, a big round of applause for Liv.

Your wife had been extremely useful, Andrew. I'd spent over four months in her company. I was completely inexperienced in the beginning. I'm not sure I could have done it without her. Particularly things like setting up a website, a Facebook account, Twitter. These things were entirely new to me. That's not to say some prisoners didn't have access to these things. There were smart phones in prison with internet access. Smart phones that had been smuggled in up someone's arsehole (it's amazing what you can push through the orifice of the human anus), or wrapped in foam and thrown over the wall. Or even sewn into dead rats. But I never used them. I had no one to contact and nothing to say to the world. But it wasn't just these things she'd helped with, she'd also helped me with the painting and decorating, and all the other work involved in turning an empty building into an inviting club.

I poured us both champagne from the ice cold Jeroboam. There was an audience of students, hippies and bohemian types. It was great to see the place so packed on the first night. It helped that there was no charge and we'd worked hard handing out flyers all week. Liv had designed them. I felt that your wife was my partner, Andrew.

I hadn't asked her to do any of this. She'd volunteered her services. A little push from me was all it took. I wanted to bring in as many as possible so tickets were free. In money terms I was going to have to write this one off. Three acts – three of the best for the money we were paying. It was possible that I might make it back on the bar but my business model was to have two nights a week where members paid £6 and non-members £12. Membership was £25 a year. This meant I could easily control who came in and who didn't. Anyone who became a pest would get the boot.

I had two Polish student helpers going round from table to table with forms, Pawel and Socha. They were wearing specially printed T-shirts: black, with the Café Assassin logo in silver – a mid-nineteenth century typeface with an ornate frame around it. Just like the sign above the door and the sign behind the stage. Liv had designed the sign, with a single contribution from me: a final flourish, concealed in the last curlicue. It was surrounded by concentric circles, and it was a human skull. A grinning totem. In my mind, it was looking at you, and seeing right through you.

It was the cellar bar Liv and I had seen that first day. I was surprised you never came to see it, but it seemed that your work consumed you. Liv helped me to gazump the other offer. It wasn't difficult. Your wife is good at Risk. I wanted somewhere dark and cavernous. Somewhere you had to descend the stairs to get to. Really, Andrew, I was thinking of how The Venue used to be. I always got a thrill leaving the pavements and plunging into a hidden world beneath. The bar was at one end and the stage at the other. I had decorated the walls with an 1840s-style damask flock wallpaper – pink with a crimson pattern. Liv had helped me choose it. The effect was to create an environment suggestive of nineteenth century Paris. Black tables, black bentwood chairs, candles, black chandeliers. Gilt framed photos of Baudelaire, Gautier and Gerard de Nerval.

I had quotations from their writing also in gilded frames. The photograph of Gerard de Nerval was staring out intently, looking a little mad. Theophile Gautier was dapper in a rather eccentric hat and cape. Charles Baudelaire looked a bit like a neo-romantic Anthony Burgess. The quote underneath: *the music I prefer is that of a cat hung up by its tail.*

I was very pleased with the overall effect. It was exactly as I'd envisaged. In fact, looking around the room, I was filled with immense satisfaction. I had dreamed about this place many times. It was a world I had disappeared into when the reality of prison life was too much. And now I was inside this world and what's more, it was a world entirely of my own making, helped along the way by your wife and, financially, by you. Now

I found myself in the space I had dreamed of, dreaming of the space I had escaped.

I had my own place and it was an anti-cage. Steve had knocked together a stage. It was quite small and only elevated by about twelve inches, but it represented freedom. It was a portal, a gateway. It was draped in crimson velvet curtains. There was a simple lighting rig (that Richard had set up) which bathed it in a warm glow. Steve had also built the desk that Richard was sitting behind. In the background was the Café Assassin logo. I nodded my approval to Liv.

I wish you hadn't done that, she said.

Done what?

Invite me onto the stage. I felt like a right tit.

Don't be daft, I shrugged, Credit where it's due.

Well, you do have a lot to thank me for, she said, and smiled.

It's a shame Andrew can't be here, I lied. Because, although I wanted you to see the club in all its glamour and finery, I wanted Liv all to myself. You were a man who could not think beyond the bars on your pinstripe suit.

I instructed Pawel to fetch four glasses for the others and I poured out the champagne. They joined us at our table. We all chinked glasses. True happiness induces a generosity of spirit, it wants to share itself with others – it doesn't sit on its own in its study. Pawel seemed thrilled to be drinking good champagne. He quaffed it with relish, spilling some of it down his scraggly beard.

I have always detested facial hair of any kind, particularly beards, but I liked this Pawel character. I don't think I have ever been more content before or since than I was then, sitting drinking champagne with *your* wife on the opening night of *my* club. Paid for with *your* money.

I knew I could do it, I said. I knew I could make a go of it.

Yeah, right, rent-a-crowd.

What do you mean?

111

It's only the first night, Nick, and we've enticed the audience with free entertainment. Wait until they have to pay for it.

You shouldn't be so cynical.

Look, I've put a lot of my own time into this. Andrew has invested a lot of dosh. You're not the only one with something at stake here.

Don't you think I've got what it takes? I said.

Probably not, but luckily you've got me. You'd be fucked otherwise.

Flipping cheek! If you're so smart, what happened to the catering business?

Long story, she said. Not now.

You were the real problem, Andrew. I knew you well enough. Your scepticism did not surprise me. Really, it was a form of cowardice. I had fully anticipated it. But despite what Liv said, I could tell she thought I could make a success of it. That is what I had been missing all my life. Someone to believe in who I was and what I was doing. It takes guts to believe in someone. You have to put yourself on the line. Anyone can doubt, anyone can deny, anyone can piss on someone else's fire.

I waited until the bulk of the crowd had been served then I mounted the stage to announce the last act. They were a comedy punk band – Liv's idea. The band played for half an hour before announcing their final song. I waited for them to finish then went into the back room behind the bar, where the safe was. Pawel was in there, fetching some more ice from the machine. I pulled the key from under my shirt, where it was suspended around my neck by a silver chain, and unlocked the safe. I had been to the bank that afternoon and had all the money for the three acts in cash.

What is this for? Pawel said.

He was holding an iron bar which I'd concealed behind the settee.

In case we get any trouble, I said. But I had no intention of ever using it. He examined it briefly.

In Poland I see a man have teeth out, he said.

He weighed it in his fist, then put it back. He picked up the now full bucket and left.

I counted out the money and folded the notes. They were nice and crisp. There was a mirror above the safe and I caught my reflection. I was wearing a suit and an open-necked shirt. The suit was off-the-peg, but I promised myself that as soon as the money came rolling in I would be travelling down to London to get myself a tailor-made Savile Row number.

I paid the acts then went over to Liv, who was chatting with a young couple sitting at the adjacent table.

I'm nipping upstairs for a smoke, I said.

Can I cadge one off you?

You don't smoke.

I know.

We went upstairs and stood in the doorway. Ray joined us. I rolled, first Liv's cigarette, and then my own. I torched them. My first memory of Liv was of her cadging a cigarette off someone at that party, before she even saw us. I wondered if she'd been clocking me then as she'd wandered round the room. I also wondered about what she said in The Venue that night, 'I chose the wrong one'. She was something else you had stolen from me.

I'm glad we got back in touch, I said.

Me too.

I hadn't realised how much I'd missed you.

Well, it's been a blast helping you out with this place.

It wasn't always easy to read her, but I think she meant it.

Did you ever give Andrew that note? I said.

What note?

The one you wrote from him to you. The one you showed me. Remember, that day we saw this place for the first time.

No, of course not.

So you sorted everything out then?

You know–

Go on.

Things are fine, really.

But I didn't think things were fine. Not with you and her, not with you and the kids.

And you'll stay on?

You'd be screwed without me.

You're not just here to keep an eye on Andrew's money, are you?

I couldn't give a fuck about Andrew's money.

She finished her cigarette and threw the butt in the gutter. She stamped it out.

Let's go back inside.

I took the last few puffs from my own cigarette and trod on it. As I did, I noticed a man in a doorway across the other side of the road. He was staring at me. Half his face was in shadow, but he was mouthing something at me. I tried to lip-read. I couldn't tell what it was supposed to be. Then he was holding up his hand and waving at me. He waved in an exaggerated way, a sort of sarcastic wave. Something unnerved me about this. I didn't recognise the man, but perhaps he recognised me. As he waved at me, I felt a chill trickle down my spine. I turned to Liv.

What's that bloke doing over there?

She looked across to where I was pointing, but a van had parked in between us and when it drove off there was no one there. I explained to Liv what I'd seen.

Don't worry about it, she said. Just a nutter, more than likely – the world is full of them.

You have been sentenced again. This time you are guilty of your crime. You are about to cut yourself. You reach for the jagged half razor blade that you have concealed with packing tape under your bed. You watch the light gleam along the metal. It looks so clean and pure. So beautiful. You have tourniqueted your arm with a ripped piece of bed sheet. You are twisting it tighter and tighter, so that it brings veins to the surface. You think about the makeshift noose that Keyop made from torn bedding. You see him in your mind, how you found him, bent over, as though he were praying, the noose like a leash, tied to the radiator behind him. Above him are the four sheets of wallpaper with the poems you both wrote on them, staring back at you: 'what might have been and what has been point to one end.'

You watch the blood in your veins coalesce and pump harder, the green-blue tubes swelling up, roots of a tree breaking through the earth. You take the blade and in one quick move, you slice through the most prominent vein on your wrist. Red is pumping everywhere. As the blood pours out you can feel the pain of losing Keyop leach from your body. As the vivid red blood gushes, you feel dizzy. You see the yellow spear and the torn bed sheet noose. It is Paddy you see now, gasping his last breath. A yellow spear in his chest. Standing over him watching him bleed. Images swim. Now it's all reds and whites and yellows.

You feel hot. You feel cold. You think about that night in Liv's bedroom. Blood like red paint dripping into the white paint of the milk jug. A towel around your finger. You feel the blood seep. Flowing from your muscles, flowing from your brain. You feel numb. You are finding it hard to breathe. You see the spear and the noose dance in front of you. You wish he was holding you. You wish you were in his arms. You feel like you are on the edge of sleep. You are falling to the floor. You are going down. You are hitting the cold stone. You hear your body hit the ground. You feel no pain. You are a minute from death.

||||| ||||| |

S teve was putting the 'pain' in Spain. He'd taken the family on holiday to Torremolinos. His absence gave me some club time. The club was slowly building up a clientele. I was able to open up Mondays and Wednesdays for an open-mic night and Fridays and Saturdays for paid-in entertainment. I wasn't making enough yet to pack in the labouring, but it was getting there, ticking over, word going round, and I had faith that I'd soon be able to give up the day job. It was hard keeping both jobs going. I'd started using speed as a pick-me-up, not to get off on it you understand, Andrew, but just so I could function with the long hours.

Mondays and Wednesdays were the toughest. Locking up at two o'clock. Getting home for half past. In bed and asleep for three. Three hours sleep. Nine hours of graft. It was a killer, but I kept telling myself it was still better than being inside. And it was. Even if I had done that every night, surviving for the rest of my life on three hours, keeping two demanding jobs going, it would still be better than being locked in a cell all day.

I spent over ten years in Wakefield. Probably the longest I did in one prison. Twenty-five hours of either education or work every week. Have a guess what the inmates chose to do? The vast majority chose work over education. How about that. I always chose education. I'd like to think I managed to educate myself to a reasonable level. Enough to hold my own with the likes of you, Andrew.

I had a burning urge to see you in action, and so on Wednesday, with King Steve still in Spain, I made my way to the Crown courts in Bradford where you were prosecuting. It was a retrial, Regina v Reaben Kareem and Jwanru Osman. Regina. How archaic it all sounded, quaint even. Kareem and Osman were two Iraqi Kurds who had conned their way into a student house and spent six hours robbing and torturing the three occupants, murdering one. There were three students involved. Two from Hong Kong and one from Poland. You had already seen this through once, last summer, but the judge suffered a heart attack on the final day and the whole thing had to go again in front of a new jury. You were going through the motions really, but I suppose it was easy money for you.

I'd left the knife at home this time, where it was safe with Ray. Ironically, the Bradford courts were more opulent than Leeds. Opulent not quite the right word, but you understand what I'm getting at – at least some attempt at decoration. Squares on the walls, squares on the carpet, squares on the ceiling. Squares within squares within squares. The lion and the unicorn dominating one wall, positioned high above human height so that it imposed itself over those passing. The royal coat of arms. An animal that has never lived in this country and an animal that has never existed. I smiled at this, as it seemed rather fitting as an emblem of our legal system.

I was sitting in the public seating area, but I had a very good view of Kareem. He looked scared. He was shaking. He was wearing a white shirt and a plain tie – the uniform of the ignoble. He was pleading guilty to causing harm to Sally Ho, one of the Hong Kong students – grievous bodily harm. He was pleading guilty to stabbing Gavin Stolarczyk, an eight centimetre stab wound that just missed his vital organs, but he was claiming this was an accident. He was not pleading guilty to murder. I could see that the jury were already measuring the rope, loading the gun, sharpening the axe.

Kareem's team was blaming Osman for the murder of Tony Ho, Sally's brother. There were no witnesses to this as Sally and Gavin were downstairs at the time. But there was a body with eighteen stab wounds, several of them fatal, including a slashed throat. You wanted to get both Kareem and Osman for murder.

There were six barristers in court, a judge, a jury of twelve, various legal people. Six barristers at three hundred pounds sterling an hour. £1,800. Plus a judge, plus a jury and all the rest. I worked it out to be in the region of at least £4,000 an hour to run this court. There was a court like this in every city. Then there were the solicitors, the security companies, the constabulary, the prison officers, the prisoners. The thousands a week it cost to keep each and every one of them locked up. Hundreds and hundreds of millions a year. Crime costs. Crime pays. Police and thieves. Barristers and murderers. Big business.

Liv told me that the cost of sending your kids to private school was thirty grand a year each. Sixty grand between them. You don't fork out that sort of dosh for nothing. What are you getting? A guarantee of power. A guarantee of being one of the elite. The rich feed off the poor. The poor get angry and steal from the rich. The rich lock them up and make more money. It's a good system. For the rich.

I watched you standing near the front, questioning Kareem, your stance one of authority. In your robes and your wig, you seemed to grow a foot in height. Everyone else seemed to be beneath you. You were clearly in charge and everything about you exuded power. The clerk and the other legal people looked up to you – you were the king of this court.

Why did you steal aftershave? you said.

It must have come into the case by accident, when I was putting the clothes in.

Four bottles? you said, raising an eyebrow and giving a look to the jury. Playful, I thought. I could see that the members of the jury were all impressed by your performance.

Yes.

Two from Gavin and two from Tony.

You didn't have to look at the jury. Your words did all the work. Job done.

I put it to you, you are a murderer.

I swear to God and my missus I'm telling the truth, Kareem said. He was crying now.

The jury had to leave the room while the barristers and the judge discussed the notion of *res gestae*. They flicked from page to page of their Archbolds, the big red book. The bible of the court room. Exception to the hearsay rule, if given spontaneously and out of emotion. It was important for Kareem's defence. His barrister wanted to include a conversation they had in the Group Four van. Kareem and Osman and two prison officers. Osman had whispered something to Kareem in Kurdish. Kareem had blanched. Kareem had shown fear.

Later, one of the prison officers asked what Osman had said to him that had made him so scared. Kareem had told the prison officer that Osman had threatened him, said if he stood trial he would get someone to slash the throat of Kareem's 'missus'. It was important for them to show Kareem as the weaker force so they could get him off with a lighter sentence. But you were having none of it. You stood your ground. You found it easy to persuade the others.

To say that you were good at your job, would be an understatement. You weren't just clear-headed and able to cut through the crap, you were a skilled orator too. I could see why you were a QC at such a young age. I supposed you must have worked hard at it, but you made it look effortless. In court all day, bundles of evidence to go through every night. Speeches to write. Words to persuade, words to condemn. No wonder you had neglected the kids, no wonder you had neglected Liv.

I understood why you had taken to the vintage wines and the single malts with such fervour. And I could see the chink in your relationship. Resentment building. A gap. A widening hole, like the one a moth makes in a silk robe. Liv and I had been working together a lot. Every week. Liv was doing the supper at weekends. She still wouldn't take a wage. It was your money in any case. Your money that had paid for my three-piece suit, my silk handkerchief, my new smart phone and my laptop. Your money, Andrew.

I went back to the flat and did a hundred and ten press-ups, a hundred and fifty sit-ups and ten minutes of shadowboxing. I had a shower in Richard's filth, and went over to the club to open up. But I couldn't get the image of you and Kareem out of my mind. For you it was a game – to condemn another man. I'm not saying Kareem didn't deserve to be condemned, he was certainly culpable, though not necessarily a murderer. In any case what he had done was very wrong. He had entered the sanctity of someone else's home, he had committed violence and intimidation. But what struck me then was the barely concealed glee on your face – you were relishing your power over this man and that made you less than him in my eyes. You were worse than a murderer.

When I got to the club I noticed, before I had even opened the door, that the window had been smashed. There was glass on the pavement. There was glass in the gutter. As I got to the door, I could see red spray paint. 'losT aNd fouNd', it said. I puzzled over the meaning of that phrase. It didn't make any sense. I sat on the kerb smoking a cigarette. As I rolled the paper round the tobacco, I noticed my hand was shaking. I rang up Liv and explained.

I'm coming over, she said.

It's ok, I said, I can handle it.

But Liv wouldn't listen to reason and within thirty minutes she was there by my side. She helped me tidy up. I'd already rung a window replacement firm who did an emergency service and I was painting the red off the door, painting it black again. Within no time at all there was no trace of the damage.

What do you think it means? Liv said.

I don't know.

Maybe it's the name of a band.

I've never heard of them.

That doesn't mean a great deal.

Thanks.

What about the window? Liv said. You don't smash windows to show band loyalty do you.

No, you don't. You smash windows because you want to break something.

She swept the broken shards down a grating in the gutter. A van pulled up and a man in overalls got out. I went over to him and explained the situation. He had a look round.

Listen, I can fix this for you, but I can't get the glass tonight. Best I can do is board it up, secure it, pop back in the morning.

That's fine, I said. The window isn't essential. It's a cellar club. The window just lights up the stairwell.

In which case I'd advise you to keep it boarded up or even get it bricked up. Is it rented?

No, it's mine, I said, with some pride.

Listen, I do a lot of these, if you get my drift. Think about it.

I got his drift. He boarded it up. I paid him and he drove off. I painted the chipboard panel black. I turned to Liv.

Come inside, I said. I'll make us a cuppa.

We sat down with our tea.

Who do you think's behind it? she said.

I don't know.

I was thinking about the man in the doorway, waving at me. Why had he unsettled me so much? I cast the image out of my head.

Andrew still away?

He's staying in a hotel. Two more weeks left of the trial. It's easier for him to be close to the court. The defence are throwing everything at him.

I wondered about this. Bradford is not that far from Ilkley. Two short train journeys. An hour and a half in a Jaguar car. Perhaps you were busy, perhaps you were taking the opportunity to have some time to yourself.

Kids at school?

Staying over at their grandparents.

Those two cunts.

Because that's what they were and still are: cunts.

Steady on! They're not that bad. Totally biased when it comes to Andrew, I know. It fucks me off sometimes.

I took her hand in mine. I'm sorry, I said.

Come on, tell me why you think that, Nick.

Forget it, I just wanted to say thanks, and I don't just mean about this. I mean thanks for everything. You know, for not judging.

Why would I judge you, Nick? I know what happened.

You do, I said, And you don't.

What do you mean, Nick?

Forget it, I said.

I rolled us both cigarettes. I lit them.

Nick, tell me what's up. Please.

That night, things got out of hand, as you know. But there's something I've not told you.

What? What is it?

I didn't want it to come between you and Andrew.

Perhaps if you'd showed any interest when I was inside, you could have found out, you bitch.

Nick, tell me what it is.

So I did. I didn't lie to her, Andrew, I told her about that night, everything she knew about the night, everything that came up in court, and then I told her what she didn't know.

Andrew was stood against the wall, watching. He'd taken a pretty bad pummelling as you know. The man was out cold. I'd stopped kicking him. I'd gone to look for a phone box. I was going to ring for an ambulance.

Go on.

When I came back, Andrew was over him and he was stamping on his head. Swearing at him. I had to pull him off. We both stood over the body. I knew he was dead. I leaned over him, listened for his heart. It was Andrew who ran off. I should have run as well but I couldn't move, it was like my feet had been riveted to the pavement, and the next thing there were people around me, grabbing hold of me. The police.

Are you saying Andrew killed him, Nick?

Yes.

The colour drained from her face.

But, why didn't you say that in court? Why would you keep that to yourself?

My defence. Andrew had an alibi. Both his parents said he was home for twelve o'clock. Andrew's parents – they lied. There were witnesses who saw me over the body. I had no alibi. There were two types of blood found on the dead man's shirt. 'O+' and 'B+'. The dead man was 'B+'. I'm 'O+'.

Same as Andrew, she said.

We have the same blood, Andrew, me and you.

My defence said it would be better to come clean. A drunken crime. I'd get a lesser sentence if I just pleaded guilty. No need for a jury. The judge would go soft on me. But I couldn't do it. I couldn't plead guilty.

Andrew killed him?

She stood up, but then she sat back down again.

I don't believe you. You're lying.

Don't you think Andrew's parents are capable of lying too? Don't you think Andrew is capable of lying?

And I'm meant to take your word for it? Where have you been for twenty-two years, Nick?

Twenty-two years you didn't come and see me. Twenty-two years with the wrong man.

Things happened inside.

What do you mean?

Things happened in there.

I don't know what you're talking about.

I'm a murderer, Liv. Inside, I murdered a man. It was premeditated.

There you go, Andrew, you didn't know that did you, but there you go. Both of us murderers, although I'm not the one judging others.

I ... I can't cope with this, she said. She got up again, unsteady on her feet, grabbing her coat and bag.

I've got to go, Nick.

And before I got chance to say anything, she was out the door.

You have made the handle of a plastic toilet brush into a yellow spear. You are walking down a corridor. You have concealed the spear down the back of your pants. You are entering Paddy's cell. He is on his own. He is sitting on his bed. He is holding up some silver foil. He is lighting the silver foil. He is inhaling the smoke coming off it. You smell the burning foil. You smell the sick-sweet smell of burning skag. Paddy sees you and he's smiling at you.

He asks you if you want some. He tells you it is good. You tell him that you would like some. He offers you the foil. He is saying sorry. He is sorry about Keyop. He is talking about Keyop. You want him to tell you what he said to Keyop. You already know but you want him to say it. He told Keyop that he fucked you. He said it to piss Keyop off. He didn't think that Keyop would believe him. But Keyop did. He is reaching down for more skag. You are taking out the yellow spear. You are thrusting it. You are looking at the yellow spear. It is half in and half out of Paddy's chest. Paddy is wheezing, blood is pouring. Paddy is falling, splayed on the floor. Blood. Red. Paddy's eyes, pleading. Gasping. Fists clenching. The foil by his side. He is staring at you. The pain in his eyes. His last breath. For a moment, you feel like laughing. How easy it is. How much power you have. Now you are an equal. Now at last, you are in the right place. Then your chest turns to lead. Your head thuds with a dull ache. You stare down at the body, at the lump of meat that was a man a moment ago.

You never fucked Paddy. Now you have fucked him proper.

||||| |||| ||

I was sitting at my table with only a bottle of Belgian beer for company. I was thinking it all over, making sure I'd covered every piece. Had Liv spoken to you? Had you denied it? You were bound to deny it. I figured that much. I was thinking about the best move. I was still shifting pawns. I needed to get my knights out or my rooks.

I looked around the room. The club was becoming a haven for alternative types. The membership system was working well. I had installed a magnetic sensor on the door and issued each member with a card. That way I could keep the door locked at all times. You might think there was an irony in wanting to keep the door locked, having spent twenty-two years wanting it open, but I needed people to feel safe. The outside world wouldn't penetrate this haven. I knew practically everyone who came in and they all knew me. It felt like home. But not quite a family. I still yearned for a real family.

Two weeks had gone by since the vandalism, but there had been no follow-up. I hadn't seen the man again and I felt sure it was an isolated incident. Two weeks had gone by since I had last seen Liv. I'd rung her, texted her, emailed her, Facebooked her, direct messaged her on Twitter. Nothing. I was trying to keep everything ticking over. Still working for Steve during the day and running the club four nights a week. I had upped my consumption of amphetamine. Pawel knew a good supplier, who dealt in pharmaceutical quality gear. I hadn't been to bed for three days. I had a couple of Valium in my pocket to knock me out later. Richard came over.

I'll get off, Nick.

Thanks, Richard. A good night.

And sorry for messing up that cue.

Don't worry about it, we got away with it. Again.

In fact, we hadn't got away with it. Richard's mis-cueing was gaining him notoriety.

Sure you don't want a lift?

Things to do still. See you Friday, Richard.

After everyone had gone home and I'd locked up, I sat downstairs on my own finishing my beer and going through my emails. I pressed send/receive and an email came through. It was from Liv. The subject said: 'I wasn't going to send this but ...' I immediately felt my stomach turn over with a sort of dark excitement. I let the cursor hover over it, I hesitated for a few seconds, before clicking and opening it. This is what I read:

I've spoken to Andrew. We need to talk.

I was thinking of lunch in Manchester.

Can you make it?

L x

After I'd read the document, I stared at it for a while. What had you told her? I wondered. What fresh calumny had you concocted? And why Manchester? I drained my bottle and switched off the laptop. I thought about that shark again and I clung on to its fin.

‖‖ ‖‖ |||

We met in a café just off St Ann's Square. I got there first and ordered a pot of tea. I found a secluded corner as far away from the counter as I could get. I read the paper and murdered the tea. She walked through the door. She was wearing a fitted fifties-style jacket, tight jeans and a red top. She had her hair tied back. She didn't see me at first, half-hidden in the shadows, but then her eyes adjusted. She smiled awkwardly at me and I smiled back. She walked across and sat down beside me.

Hi, she said, and shook her head. I gave her a few seconds to come round.

Well, you're here, I said.

Only just, she said.

I ordered another pot of tea. We made small talk until the waitress had been and gone and we were on our own once more.

So what is it you need to tell me? I was almost whispering.

I've been so fucking stupid.

What's happened?

I never thought he was capable of … twenty-two years, two kids. How could I be so thick?

She stared into the cup.

Take your time, Liv. Tell me what you need to say.

She took a gulp of her tea.

A few nights ago I confronted Andrew.

And?

He denied it. He said you were trying to poison me. It was all part of your plan. He said you were trying to destroy us, that you wouldn't be happy until you'd split us up.

I'd guessed right.

Is that what you think? I said.

I thought, that has to be right, that has to be your plan. I believed him, Nick. I said I was no longer involved with the business. He seemed apprehensive about that, asked after his money. How was he going to get it back, he said, if I wasn't keeping an eye on things?

So that's why he agreed to you being involved?

You were right, Nick. I said, fuck the money, we don't need it. He shrugged but I could tell he wasn't happy. Anyway, I went to bed. He said he had to stay up, work on some notes for tomorrow.

She finished the tea in the cup and I poured her some more. I gave her a few moments, then I said, Go on.

I must have been in bed for an hour. I couldn't sleep. Something about Andrew's response, when I told him what you said. I don't know, it rattled him. Surely if it was a lie it shouldn't have rattled him like that?

She looked at me. I shrugged.

I could hear him talking. So I crept downstairs. He was in his study. His voice was low ... had to almost stick my head in the doorway before I could make out what he was saying.

Who was he talking to?

He was on the phone. 'Nick's told her.' I guessed he was talking to his mum. There was a long pause. She must have been saying something, giving him one of her bloody lectures. Then he said, 'Don't worry. There's no evidence, even if they re-open the case.' That's when I walked in. 'I've got to go', he said, 'I'll call you back.' And he puts his phone away.

She stopped talking. She looked around the room. We were still on our own.

Take your time, I said, There's no rush.

I told him he was a liar. He didn't say a thing. It's funny, I've always had this feeling, this ... well ... that Andrew was covering something up. And his parents too. I've noticed it in the past, when your name's been mentioned. I don't know exactly, it's like something ... it's like a need to move on to another subject ... Believe it or not, I wanted to come and visit you.

Really?

Yes, really. But whenever I brought the subject up, I was rounded on by Andrew and his mum and dad. I was made to feel it was a bad idea. One time I wrote you a letter, but I tore it up and threw it in the bin.

Why?

I don't know.

I stared at Liv, measuring her, weighing her up. Perhaps she was telling the truth. People do that occasionally. Liv had gone quiet. She was hugging her teacup and staring at the table.

Are you ok? I said.

I feel completely betrayed. By Andrew, by his parents ... but mainly by Andrew. He came up afterwards and tried to explain. He said he had no choice. He said it was his parents' decision. I said it didn't matter whose decision it was, they had taken a part of your life away. He said to me, 'would you rather it was me that was locked up?'

I wanted to ask her, 'Well, would you?' but I remained silent. She put her cup in its saucer and leaned back in her chair. She tilted her head back and took a deep breath.

Do you want a cigarette? I said.

She nodded. I took out my pouch and papers and started to roll.

They never liked me, you know, she said.

Who?

Andrew's parents ... I used to think it was the way I dressed. They were a bit judgemental.

You know, I don't think they thought I was good enough. Not good enough for their high-achieving son.

I thought back to how kind they had been to me once and I felt the stab of pain afresh. How I had loved them, and wished that they were my parents. How, when my grandma had died, they had comforted me. They had saved me. How, when I had nowhere to stay, they had taken me in, clothed me, fed me, provided a bed for me on their sofa. But they had denied me. They had sold me to a house of torment, in order to save you. I was cast aside. I was no longer part of your world.

Andrew's been lying to me, Nick. He's been lying to me for twenty-two years. Twenty-two years. He's a murderer. I've been living with a murderer for twenty-two years.

I didn't need to say anything, Andrew. Everything was slotting into place, by itself.

This may sound self-centred, she said, But actually the lying hurts more than knowing he's a murderer. I can actually understand how things can get out of hand. I think we're all capable of it, given the right circumstances.

I nodded. I didn't need to state the obvious.

You know, I think part of me knew all along. Perhaps I didn't want to think about it. Perhaps I didn't want the truth.

Who does want the truth, Andrew, if it brings no consolation?

I knew she wanted me to say, it's ok, I forgive you. But I wasn't able to do that. It wasn't ok, I didn't forgive her. I thought about all that time she could have come to see me. I wondered how hard she had fought your parents, fought you, or whether she had given up easily. I pictured her tearing up the letter and throwing it away. I wondered what it had said. We sat in silence.

At last I said, So what do you want to do?

I don't know.

Why don't I pay the bill and we can go for a walk. Ok?

Outside we walked and smoked. We wandered down Deansgate, across Blackfriars Bridge, over the Irwell. We watched the river carry the filth of the city out to the sea. We walked up Chapel Street, towards the cathedral. We wandered up Shudehill. I hardly recognised the place. All the little stalls selling second-hand books and records had gone. The pawn shops and the shops for nerds selling parts for radios, rare stamps and collectable coins, had been replaced by wine bars, bistros and a tram station. We found ourselves on Oldham Street outside Affleck's Palace. We'd been walking for over an hour.

Fucking hell, she said. Look at this.

We stopped outside the entrance. It looked exactly the same as it had in the eighties. You'll remember Affleck's Palace, Andrew, you weren't as much of a fixture as we were, but you certainly frequented it. Who would have thought an old mill complex off Oldham Street would be such a regular hang-out for teenagers? On Saturdays it was teeming with life. A maze of retro clothes shops, gothic jewellery stalls, cafés, second-hand records, posters, badges ... there was a 1950s jukebox that played, 'That's Alright', 'Latest Flame', 'Summertime Blues'. To be honest, I didn't like that fifties scene with its slavish imitation of a bygone style – the right jeans, the right suede jacket, the right pomade in your hair. I wondered again why Liv had suggested Manchester. Perhaps subconsciously, she wanted to return to a time of innocence. When the world was still unsullied.

There was a barber's shop that we used to sit outside and watch all the painfully shy young men enter, wearing their turned-up jeans and cardigans, to ask the barber in a painfully shy voice if he would do them a quiff like Morrissey's, and there was a ladies hairdressers upstairs where the punk girls would get the side of their heads shaved, and get their hair dyed red, blue or green. Then when The Stone Roses, The Happy Mondays and The Inspiral Carpets got to be the new thing, it was all sixties-style mop-tops. Always, in one way or another, looking back to the past. And I didn't want to look back, I wanted to look to the future.

Shall we have a wander round, for old time's sake?

Ok, she said, and we went inside.

It was funny being back. It was exactly the same. It was completely different. They still had retro clothes shops, although eighties clothes were what was classed as retro now and there were several places that specialised in eighties 'vintage' sportswear: Sergio Tacchini tracksuits, Fila sports shirts, Ellesse jumpers, Farah slacks, Kicker boots. But there was still the same punk and goth shops, and a sixties retro shop that seemed to have the exact same polka-dot dresses and mod suits as I'd remembered.

The woman running the shop could well have been the same woman as twenty-two years ago – preserved in retro aspic. The barber's shop looked the same and there was a café in the same place as the old café, although it had been refurbished 'ironically' to look like a greasy spoon, complete with red plastic sauce bottles in the shape of tomatoes. There was a lot of tat – I don't remember the old Affleck's being that full of tat. Lots of cheap fancy dress. Liv tried on a faux-leather German officer's cap, I tried on a fake felt Victorian top hat. There was a hat which looked like it had been made from cat fur with cat ears and a scarf attached which had stitched-in gloves to look like cat paws. Liv put it on and did her cat impersonation. We spent a couple of hours just walking around, reminiscing, picking stuff up, laughing. Through an act of alchemy, we'd returned to the time before. Only this time, one thing was different: I knew I could have your wife.

We walked past Casablancas, then further up Oldham Street, where we found a restaurant next to the old fish market. Remember how run down that area used to be? It was all pet shops, sex shops and knocking shops. Tib Street used to smell of piss-soaked sawdust and lubricating jelly. Now it smells of rosemary and lemongrass. The area has been re-branded the Northern Quarter and is rather trendy now in a bohemian way. Anyway, the restaurant looked stylish. It was by the crumbling facade of the old market. The brick and wrought iron had been left in this state of disarray for effect. We peered inside the restaurant. It was modern but cosy. Lots of black leather, glass, oak, ivy. We chose a bottle of wine that the waiter was keen to recommend. He had been on a wine-tasting course and spoke passionately about the list. He told us both about the blind tasting that was required to pass the course.

So, Liv said, looking at me with those molten silver eyes, Why didn't you tell me?

Why didn't you visit me, Liv? I said. Why didn't you believe me?

There was an awkward pause.

I filled her glass. The waiter was right – the wine was very good. (Though to be honest, I was no expert back then, but I've been on one of those courses now too – and I'm a bit of a wine buff. I'd beat you in a blind taste any day of the week).

I've told you, Nick, that I wanted to visit you.

And I told you about Andrew.

You waited twenty-two years to tell me about Andrew.

Look, I said, It wasn't my place to tell you. It was Andrew's secret. You should be asking Andrew, not me.

I can't forgive him. Not the lying, or what he did to that man, but what he's done to you, she said.

And another piece moves into its place.

You don't need to forgive him. It's not for you to forgive him. Only I can do that. And I have, I said.

But how can you?

It was an act of cowardice, not one of malice. Who's to say, boot on the other foot, I wouldn't have done the same thing.

Liv stared out of the window, at the crumbling facade.

How are you feeling? In yourself, I mean, I said.

Not good.

Have you spoken some more to Andrew?

What's the point?

So what are you going to do about it?

The waiter returned and we ordered.

Liv looked out of the window again, deep in thought. At last she said, It's an impossible situation.

I raised my eyebrows. I could think of a solution. You could leave him, I wanted to say, choose the right one this time.

Instead I said, Perhaps you can patch things up. His parents were only doing what any parent would do in that situation. Don't be so hard on him.

We went to a bar afterwards, The Night and Day Café – of course you'll remember this old haunt? I hadn't drawn on it consciously, but in some ways I think it must have been one of the inspirations for Café Assassin.

We used to go there a lot, to see bands, to watch stand-up, to see (in theory) good performance poetry. It's an interesting side issue this one. We did see some good performance poetry there but the vast bulk of it was mediocre doggerel delivered by talentless fops doing a rat-a-tat copy of John Cooper Clarke. Everything else seemed to come first: the clothes, the make-up, the hair, even the predictable left-leaning opinions. It was almost like they had forgotten about the words. As though the only reason for a word to exist was to rhyme with another word. You may or may not be interested to note that twenty-two years later the scene hasn't really changed. Bad dress, naive political opinions, no life experience, just a rhyming dictionary.

Anyway, what I liked the most about the Night and Day café was that it was always busy and convivial. But as we stood at the bar and gave our order, I looked around and there was hardly anyone in. The atmosphere was grim. It was the middle of the day, I supposed. I imagined it would be quite different during the evening. Or perhaps not. The brightest stars, at the end of their lifetimes, contain little more than degenerate matter. In my mind I made a note: as one star dies, another star expands to become a red giant. We sat on two bar stools and drank Peroni.

I've got something to confess too, Liv said.

What's that? I said.

When you were in prison.

What about it?

I missed you.

Bang. Her words shot into my brain. They were burning hot. They were luminous. I made sure not to allow any expression on my face.

She looked me in the eye and I returned her gaze.

These few weeks have been really hard, she said. I've come to really like my routine with the club. I enjoy the atmosphere, got to know quite a few of the regulars. I've made friends with the staff.

They like you.

It's pretty sleepy in Ilkley. We rarely go out, if at all. All I seem to do is worry about what the kids are up to at boarding school. I hate them being there. Or when they're back home, drive them around. Since when did my life get shoved to one side?

I wondered why she hadn't fought you over the boarding school. Perhaps she had. I'd seen you in action and I knew you were a master of persuasion.

I didn't tell you how I came to murder someone.

I can imagine, inside, things got pretty dark.

Do you want to know?

She thought about this. At last, No, not just now. I've lost my taste for it.

Lost your taste for what, Liv?

The truth.

We sat in silence and finished off another beer. I walked Liv back to the train station.

Can I hold your hand, she said as we walked along, a little unsteady. (Not quite cuckolded, Andrew, not quite). I tried my best to stay calm.

You'd best get the first train. I'll get the one after, I said.

She nodded. She knew how it would look if we both got off the train together. So we headed to the platform hand in hand. I kissed her on the cheek. A rather chaste kiss I thought. She kissed me full on the lips. We held on to each other. Then her train arrived on platform four and she was getting on it. She was getting on it, she was getting on it. Then she was gone. I went to the station bar and ordered a double shot of vodka. I waited for the next train. I could still taste Liv on my lips. Time for a little celebration.

卌 卌 IIII

I t was a matter of life or death. I had to make a success of the club – I had to show you I could be as successful as you. But I couldn't keep on going as I was. There were staff to pay and bills. Food, tobacco, drugs, booze. I needed to open every night of the week just to break even. But would I make enough on those nights? Would the cost of amphetamine required to work two jobs full-time outweigh the profit? This was the gamble. I was making good money labouring and managing to save some of it. But not enough to cover any big loss. I needed to be solvent for at least another six months before I could give up the labouring job. It was back-breaking work.

Steve came out, clutching his diary and scratching his balls.

Fucking quids in, he said, and went over to the van. We got inside and I started the engine. Took longer than I thought though, he said. If we want to get a decent run at the job in Adel we'll need to make it a late one. Five o'clock. You ok with that?

I can't, Steve, not tonight.

Why the fuck not?

I've got to open up the club.

Thought you only did Mondays and Wednesdays during the week?

It's a new night.

What sort of night?

Storytelling.

What the fuck's that all about?

People on stage, telling stories.

He laughed and shook his head. What's wrong with sitting at the bar telling stories?

They're not those kind of stories.

What other kind is there?

Traditional tales, fables, folk stories, ancient myths.

He gave me a look. He was not impressed.

What's on tomorrow? Making jam? Knitting jumpers?

Burlesque.

We were driving along the ring road, slowing down every minute or so for a roundabout.

Strippers? he said, getting interested.

They don't call themselves strippers.

Do they get their kit off?

Well, yes.

So they're strippers then.

It's more about the tease. It's a form of theatre. They use peacock fans and feather boas.

Do they get their tits out?

Sometimes.

Then they're strippers.

It's not what you think, Steve, trust me.

Do they get their minges out?

Not very often.

I might come along anyway. Wife's out with her mates. Mother-in-law's babysitting. What time does it kick off?

It's a members only club, Steve.

You saying I can't come?

It's not that.

I helped build it, don't forget.

I just don't think you'll like it, that's all.

I'll be the judge of that.

So that was settled.

I did a hundred and twenty press-ups, a hundred and thirty sit-ups and eighteen minutes of shadowboxing. I took Ray on a three mile run, building up his strength. Only a slight limp now. As we ran down the old railway track, Ray spotted a rabbit and gave chase. It felt good to watch him run after that rabbit. No other thought in his head. His muscles taut. His ears pinned back. His forelegs stretching out, towards the quarry that was running for its life. I was running too. You were my quarry, and I was running faster than you, Andrew.

Ray was running with a limp beside me, panting. I was running all the filth out of my body, the way you bleed a radiator until all excess air has escaped and the rotten water has spurted out. I ran until I couldn't run anymore. We came out of the woods and climbed over a stile, into a farmer's field. The footpath skirted the borders. The path went through an area of five houses. I had my headphones on. I was listening to The Destroyers. The path cut through the gardens of the houses. Whoever owned them had cordoned them off with fences, walls and hedges. Ray was walking a few feet in front of me. I became aware of something moving in my peripheral vision. I stopped. There was a big fat man with a red leathery face, standing outside his house, waving his arms at me. He was shouting. I took off my headphones.

Get that fucking dog on a fucking lead! He was screaming.

I stopped in my tracks. I don't have a lead.

What?! You thick bastard! I could shoot that fucking dog. Do you know that?

I walked over to him.

Did you see that film last night? It was on telly.

What?! What the fuck are you talking about?!

There was this film about a farmer. He stopped this bloke and told him to put his dog on a lead. Do you know how the film ended?

The fat red-faced man didn't answer.

It ended with the man going back to the farmer's house when he was asleep. He poured petrol through the letterbox. The farmer was burned to death along with his wife and kids.

Are you threatening me? The man had stopped shouting now.

No. I'm telling you about a film, I said, and carried on walking through his garden.

I'd lost count of how many size sixteen French knickers I'd seen hurtling through the air in the club, but for Pawel it was all new. As I chatted to him, it struck me just what an odd character he was. How little I really knew him. Is a man with strange friends, a strange man? I noticed that Liv was in the corner with a friend. I gave her a wink and she grinned back. I left Pawel at the bar and went over to Liv.

I'm just nipping out for a cig, want to join me? I said.

She didn't respond at first but then turned to her friend.

Excuse me a minute.

Outside we lit up. The streets were quiet. Somewhere I could hear a fox screaming.

It's good to see you. I wasn't sure I would, I said.

Been doing a lot of thinking.

Are you coming back, to work I mean?

No, that's what I've come to tell you. I've decided that it's not a good idea.

So you just came to snoop around, check on Andrew's cash?

Fuck off.

You here for the size sixteen French knickers then?

Fuck off.

What then?

I wanted to see you.

What for?

Look, it's not easy. There's a lot at stake. We've been together a long time.

I get it Liv. You don't have to explain. He lied to you, but you've got a nice house. A nice magazine life.

Fuck off. That's not fair, Nick.

The truth hurts, eh?

Perhaps I shouldn't have come. I'm cold. I'm going back inside.

I watched her go through the door and descend the stairs. *Yeah, fuck off then. I'll get you when I'm good and ready and not before.* I finished my cigarette and lit up another. I filled my lungs with smoke and watched the blue-white vapour snake around the orange streetlight. Inside, the next burlesque performance was about to begin. I went and sat back next to Pawel at the end of the bar.

Just trying to persuade the chef to come back, I said.

Good looking, he said, nodding to where Liv was sitting. I was shocked at how strongly I felt for her. It wasn't supposed to happen like this, it wasn't the plan. I thought about a shard of jagged glass – pressing it hard into wounded flesh.

Then I saw Steve coming down the stairs, stumbling, looking a little worse for wear, still in his work clothes, stained white with silicone sealant. He had threatened a visit and now here he was.

Here's trouble, I said. I'd already pre-warned Pawel.

Can I get you a drink, Steve?

Have I missed the tit show? he said.

Lager?

There were over a hundred people in the club. Lots of drinkers. I had three bar staff on and they were struggling to get the drinks out in time. Socha looked flustered. I watched her bend down and reach for some cold lager from the fridge. Young skin has a luminous quality, have you noticed that? As if there is a light inside, shining through. Like your daughter's skin, Andrew. The queue at the bar was four deep. I went round and gave her a hand.

Richard was doing sound and light. He'd not fucked up any of the cues, which was a first. It was crucial that the cues came in on time for burlesque (reveal, tableau, black-out). He must be getting the hang of it finally, I thought. It was the start of the second half and he was dimming the house lights and fading the backing track. The audience quietened down, the bar thinned and people made their way back to their seats. Too low a seats-to-punters ratio. Some were standing at the back. I was thinking about introducing a standing policy for people who drank soda water, or students, or anyone with a beard or a moustache.

The finale took the burlesque idea into different territory: it was a black mass. All the performers came together. At the centre towards the back of the stage, there was a throne. There sat a woman dressed as a high priestess in a black cloak. Around her, positioned in a pentagram, were five women, their breasts bared and their faces hidden by black crow masks. They lit candles and started to chant, behind a repetitive tribal drum and a demonic bassline. The effect was sinister.

You may find this amusing, Andrew, but in my desperation inside (or should I say one particular period of particular desperation) I sought solace in witchcraft. My thoughts were so deranged at the time. I would kick the opiates. I'd go cold turkey, crawling up the walls, uncontrollable spasms, sweating, shivering, shitting, vomiting. Then a sort of normality, but a cycle of struggling, craving, struggling. Then just needing something – an open door.

I read Crowley and Anton LaVey. In my cell I would conduct a black mass and I would cast out all that was good and invoke all that was evil, to avenge me of my enemies: of my one abiding enemy. I even carved an effigy out of a bar of soap, it wasn't a very good likeness but it was supposed to look like you, Andrew.

For a moment I was back there. I was under the spell of the black arts. I started to sweat. A lizard chill crept down my spine. I felt shards of ice form around my heart. I was trapped by the ever-present reality of the past. By all that I had done and by all that had been done unto me.

Then the music switched. It was a song from the 1920s Broadway show Running Wild. The high priestess pulled off her gown in one flourish and revealed a Josephine Baker style outfit. Fast kicking steps, the frenetic kicking of feet, and the rest of the girls were doing the jay-bird. The effect was comic, the audience loved it. I laughed out of relief. Steve stood at the back and looked bemused. I looked over to Liv, she seemed to be enjoying it.

The music stopped abruptly and the lights went black. Silence. Darkness. A few seconds, nothing, and then they came back on again, but the moment was lost. I looked over to Richard, he shrugged and gave me an apologetic face. Once again he'd fucked it up at the crucial moment. The dancers realised there was no way of clawing this back and started to tidy up their discarded clothes: dress gloves, stockings, size sixteen French knickers.

Steve looked outraged. He walked over to me.

Where are the fucking minges? I paid twelve quid to get in.

Look, I told you Steve, it's more about the tease.

What's the point of that? he said. What's the fucking point? He looked genuinely horrified.

One of the dancers' partners was up on stage having an angry word with Richard. I was trying to do two things at once: explain the basics of burlesque to the great ape Steve, and keep an eye on the fracas that was building between Richard and this dancer's dick of a boyfriend. The dick of a boyfriend was shouting now but I couldn't make out what he was saying. Then he reached over and started to mess with the PA. Richard was not an aggressive man, but someone else touching his PA was guaranteed to rile him. More words were spoken. The man pushed Richard, Richard pushed him back. The man squared up to Richard, then he landed him a punch. It caught him on the side of his head and Richard went down, falling onto his desk. Steve saw what was happening and, quick as lighting, was on the stage punching the life out of the man. He had him on the floor in no time. He was standing over him. The man stayed down. I went over to them.

Nice one Steve, I said, genuinely pleased for the first time to have Steve in my world.

The cunt was going to damage the desk. Took me ages to build that.

We got the man up on his feet and escorted him to the doors at the top of the stairs. Steve flung him into the night. We went back to the bar and I got Steve a fresh bottle. Apes eat ants. The cat catches the weasel. The man with blood on his hands and the man with blood on his face.

I went to freshen up. When I leaned over the sink to wash my hands I saw it, sprayed in red paint on the mirrors: I fouNd U Nik, it said. I stood back. The letters were about six inches in height. It was evidently the same hand as the graffiti on the door outside. The same use of capital 'N'. I could feel a vein in my neck pulsing. I leaned back against the wall. I closed my eyes. I'd been working long hours, I needed more sleep. But when I opened them, the words were still staring right at me. I went over to the letters and I touched one. The paint was wet.

Could the culprit still be on the premises? I rushed back into the main room and scanned the crowd. I went over to Pawel.

You seen the graffiti in the toilet?

He hadn't. I ushered him into the gents.

It's just been done, I said, It's still wet. Have you seen anyone behaving strangely?

It is burlesque, Nick. Everyone is strange.

I looked down at my hand. It was stained red.

ꟷꟷꟷ ꟷꟷꟷ ꟷꟷꟷ

The next week I made a trip to the court again. The case was almost through. There was just your speech (which I'd come to listen to. Believe it or not, I like your voice), then the defence's, then the judge would give the jury directions. It wasn't just your voice I was here for though, I wanted to see my opponent at his best.

It brought it all back. I remembered waiting in a holding cell. I'd been confined there for hours while I waited for the jury to come to a decision, with nothing but a Styrofoam cup of cold coffee to keep me company. Pacing the concrete floor or standing staring at the wall, reading the same graffiti over again. A large part of me clung to the hope that I would be found innocent. My barrister had done a reasonable job of presenting my case, I thought. At some point a prison officer brought me another cup of coffee, but I couldn't drink it and I put it on the floor where it went cold and congealed next to its companion. Then I heard the rattling of keys and I knew the call had come for me to be returned to the courtroom.

I looked over at the jury. I wondered if they understood the full weight of their responsibility. It would all be over for them soon. They would go back to the routine of their lives, to the jobs they had been temporarily seconded from. Perhaps they had even enjoyed this brief spell away from their ordinary existence. Builders, hairdressers, plumbers, waiters, teachers, office workers: normal jobs for normal people. It would all be boxed up for you soon as well and then you could go on to your next job.

There you stood in the middle of the courtroom, like a king. You were addressing the jury. You made the case against Kareem very straightforward. Kareem had already admitted he wanted to punish and rob the victims and he had already accepted the possibility this could include harm. Kareem was in real financial difficulties and there was a pressing need. Kareem had pleaded guilty on count four – conspiring to commit a robbery. And he had already pleaded guilty to manslaughter.

None of this mattered, you pointed out. The position of the prosecution was that they did not need to rely on Kareem's plea. Osman was clearly lying when he said he had gone into the house for a cup of tea. The men had a common cultural heritage, had known each other since childhood, and saw each other as brothers. In Iraq they'd gone to the same school, had sat next to each other in class. They'd played games together, gone camping together. Not for the first time, I thought about me and you, Andrew. I wondered if you were thinking of me?

Kareem and Osman were sitting in a glass-fronted box to the side of the courtroom. They were accompanied by prison officers. They betrayed no emotion but I knew, perhaps better than anyone else in the room, what they were feeling behind the facade.

In life the simple answers are often the correct answers – is that not so? And is that not the case here? It is simply not possible to know what happened with Tony Ho in his bedroom – only two men alive know.

You looked over to the defendants for effect. Again, a touch of theatre. The members of the jury were hanging on your every word. You had them where you wanted them.

Kareem and Osman, and we cannot rely on anything they say on that matter. We do not need to know in order to prosecute. The fact is Kareem was in charge but Osman was still responsible and *is* a murderer.

You were enjoying saying the word 'murderer', fully aware of its dramatic effect. I wondered if you were thinking of yourself as a murderer, or whether you'd been able to put that to one side.

Duress, as you know, cannot be used as a defence to murder. The taking of an innocent life can never be justified, so no amount of fear or intimidation can justify murder. Osman bears responsibility for Tony Ho's murder. He is therefore guilty, along with Kareem, of count three. When he said to Sally, 'I'm going to get your brother now', he meant that he was going to confront him, going to use violence against him. And when he said later at the police station, 'I am not ashamed', he meant that he was not ashamed of murder.

Of course, you may have been right, Andrew, Osman may have meant those things. Or when he said, 'I'm going to get your brother now' perhaps he meant precisely that, he was going to bring him into the room. And when he said, 'I am not ashamed', maybe he meant he was not ashamed because he wasn't a murderer. There you were putting thoughts into the jury's head. You looked over again to the glass-fronted box, and stared this time at Osman.

That was when I noticed him: Darren Lease. One of the prison officers at Wakefield who had told me stories about his shit dad to make me feel better about my shit dad. One of the prison officers who showed me kindness. The only prison officer who listened to my story and believed it without question. I'd known Darren for a long time. And what Darren had told me inside was to prove very useful.

I caught up with Darren outside during a break. He was having a cigarette.

Fucking hell, Nick. Good to see you on the outside. You look well. What you up to? Keeping out of trouble?

I told him about the club. He seemed impressed, perhaps even envious. We chatted for a bit. Caught up on a few characters. Sam Farnworth, who had stopped me topping myself, had left his job and opened up a bar in Spain. Karen Kenning had transferred to Broadmoor, which wasn't as perverse as it sounded. There were lots of advantages to working in Broadmoor. It was more of a hospital, less of a prison.

Listen, Darren, I'm glad I bumped into you. I wanted to check something with you.

Go ahead. What?

When we were talking that time, the QC who's prosecuting, you remember me telling you about him?

Andrew Honour. Course I remember. He was the bloke put you inside. How am I gonna forget that?

Well, I know you've seen him at work a few times.

Sure. He's good at what he does, one of the best, but he gives me a creepy feeling.

That's right, Andrew, you gave him the creeps. Darren Lease was a man of compassion and what he saw in you that made you such a good QC was a complete lack of pity. In fact, that's one of the reasons Darren believed my story. Because he'd seen you cross-examine a police officer. A police officer who happened to be a very close friend of Darren's and someone that you accused of being a liar under oath. And that police officer was angry. Perhaps his ire was excessive but nevertheless, he'd been incensed and full of rage at the time. Of course, you remember that police officer now, don't you, Andrew? You are unlikely to forget him. Perhaps you think him unbalanced, because accusing someone of being a liar is just part of your job.

That police officer. What was his name again?

He's called Paul Leadbeater. Officer Leadbeater to you. He laughed. What do you want to know for?

I just remembered it, it came back to me. I've been watching Andrew in action.

Right. You get off on a man in a wig do you?

Beggars can't be choosers ... Where's he based, this Leadbeater?

I think he's at Huddersfield. I'll warn you though, he's changed. He smiled and winced at the same time.

I shook Darren's hand and said goodbye. I walked to the nearest pub and ordered a drink. Thanks, Darren. Thanks for that. I owe you one. And I drank on my own to Darren Lease. Things were moving forward – falling into place. Outside I made a phone call.

Is that Huddersfield police station? Could I speak to Officer Leadbeater please?

I wondered what Darren had meant by Officer Leadbeater changing.

|||| |||| |||| |

I think it was the week after your fourteenth birthday. You had a new tent and we decided to camp by the chicken coop down the road. There was me, you and Steps in your tent; Rogan, Summers and Bob in Bob's tent. It was a Saturday afternoon and the sun was scorching the grass along the banks of the old railway track. We were erecting the tents and collecting fire wood when Bowie came across the adjoining field with an excited look on his face.

Hey, guess who I've just seen?

We had no idea. Madman Marz. That's who.

Bowie was not a close friend, not in our gang, but someone who was on the periphery of the scene. You didn't like him, Andrew. He was too feral for your tastes. But I always admired his capacity for hedonism. He was mates with Summers, had been in borstal with him. He was wayward, frequently in trouble with the police. He was a glue head and a thief.

What was he doing? Rogan asked.

Walking the slacks, with his hood up.

We were scared of Madman Marz, even though we had no reason to be scared of him. We would always see him on his own, walking the old railway track or walking the slacks. The slacks were the name we gave to the levelled out areas of slag. Slagheaps from the mines that had gradually flattened and were being reclaimed by nature. Madman Marz always wore an oversized green parka with the snorkel hood zipped up to the top so his face was hidden, even in the heat of a summer's afternoon. We'd never seen his face. He always wore jeans tucked into football socks. He sometimes carried a plastic bag.

We'd been told once that he carried a human head in the bag. We didn't believe this.

He was going, 'keek, brrrmf'.

He always made this noise as he walked. In rhythm with his walking. The 'keek' like something snapping, the 'brrrmf' like something stopping. We didn't know anything about him, where he was from, or what his real name was, or how old he was. We didn't even know what he looked like. We didn't understand him and that made us afraid of him. Somewhere in our darkest thoughts, we imagined him without a face, without a body, forever traipsing across a giant ball of dust.

We concocted a plan. Summers had some rope and Rogan knew how to tie a noose. He'd been in the scouts and collected a badge for knot work, at least that's what he claimed. I always thought he could tie a noose because he had taught himself to tie a noose in the eventuality that he would want to hang himself or someone else. Rogan set about making the noose, while we dug a ditch under the branch of the hanging tree, a grave sized ditch only not as deep. If Madman Marz should creep up on us in the night, we would hang him from the gibbet of the branch and bury him under a thin layer of top soil, rubble and slag.

We needed provisions for the evening: sleeping bags, knives, food, drink, warm clothes, torches, lighters or matches. We went back home and gathered the things we needed. Summers was sixteen and the oldest and could easily pass for eighteen. We collected all our money together and poured it into his cupped hands. He went to the off-licence to buy bottles of cider and tins of lager. You were always uneasy around any illicit activity but had the sense to keep quiet. I was the only one in the gang who sensed it but I never gave the game away. We were mates going back to the age of six. We were loyal.

We gathered back at the site and organised all our goods. Summers had a net bag and he submerged the cider and the lager into the stream to keep them cool. We built up the fire supply. We had Bobs dads axe and we took it in turns to chop wood. We went on missions to find more dead branches. Before long we had a sizeable pile. When it was dark, we wandered around the streets. Bowie said he was going to steal a motorbike and we could take turns riding it on the slacks. Something Bowie frequently did and one of the reasons we liked having him around. Again, it was something you never took part in. No one said anything about you not joining in – probably just pleased that they could have more turns themselves.

We went back to camp and lit the fire. The wood crackled and Summers went to get the bag of booze. We drank from the bottle, passing it around. Summers and Bob drank the lager, that little bit older, their taste buds that little bit more 'sophisticated'. We drank and joked and laughed until the fire wood had gone and the booze had been drunk. It was late. Still no Bowie, but again this was not unusual. It would sometimes take him all night to get the right motorcycle and he would appear at dawn going full throttle over the slacks, waking us up.

We were asleep. There was a noise and I woke up. I listened but I couldn't hear anything. The fire was still burning, no flames just the wooden sticks glowing red in the distance. Then I heard something smash. A bottle of Woodpecker. I could make out the silhouette of the axe, positioned between our tent and the dying fire. I listened again but I heard nothing. I was going to go back to sleep when I heard it: 'keek, brrrmf'. It was some way in the distance but it was the unmistakable noise of Madman Marz. I shook you awake.

What is it? You wanted to know. I signalled to you to shush and we listened together. At first nothing, then the familiar 'keek, brrrmf'. This time louder, closer. I could see the fear on your face. We shook Steps awake and whispered an explanation. We huddled together and listened. Nothing. Then we saw the silhouette of a man in a parka with the snorkel hood zipped up. He was in front of the fire and he was reaching for the axe.

We didn't say anything, we were too frightened, but we huddled even closer together in the middle of the small tent. We wanted to scream out to Summers and Rogan and Bob in the other tent but were too scared. We saw the silhouette approach. He began to circle the tent, making his repulsive noise. Then nothing. We heard nothing, we saw nothing. We were beginning to think he had gone away, when out of nowhere the axe came through the middle of the tent, ripping a hole in the thin canvas, just missing our heads. We screamed out. We huddled even closer. He had gone, but we didn't dare move.

We stayed like that for some time until Rogan shouted out asking us what was wrong. We shouted back. 'Come in our tent', he said, but we were too frightened to move. After some time, still afraid, we started to relax. Perhaps he had really gone, perhaps we were safe. But then we saw his silhouette at the entrance of the tent. He was unzipping the fly sheet. He was coming inside. We shuffled to the back. There he was, poking his hooded head through the gap in the sheets. 'Keek, brrrmf', 'keek, brrrmf', 'keek brrrmf'. We wanted to laugh. It was funny. In one hand he held the axe. His free hand reached for your leg.

You were shaking. We're not bad, you said. As if this would dissuade him in some way. Again I had to fight the impulse not to burst out laughing. Then you did something that shocked me. You grabbed hold of Steps and you pushed him in front of you. Steps was the smallest, the youngest, the quietest in the gang, and you had decided to sacrifice him to save your own bacon, although after you would claim that you were saving both of us. Madman Marz was grabbing Steps's leg and dragging him out of the tent towards the hangman's noose. Summers and Rogan and Bob were screaming. Steps was kicking and kicking. He managed to boot Madman Marz in the face, or at least the hole where his face must have been. And now he was running away, we could see the red and white stripes of his socks flash as he disappeared and we were safe. We looked at each other. I stared into your eyes. You had chosen what side you were on. You looked back in shame. I didn't need to say anything. I noticed a wet patch between your legs.

In the morning we went on a breakfast recce, stealing milk, bread and eggs from the door steps of red brick terraced houses. This time you even joined in, finding a lesser sin to cover up your bigger one. Then Bowie turned up on a 250cc Yamaha, or a Kawasaki – or whatever it was – and you were the first one to jump on the back. No fear this time, no disapproval. You just wanted to fit in, cover up what you had done, and I stood there and said nothing.

Steve had walked back to the suppliers. One of the frames was faulty. The job was nearly done. It was warm in the conservatory. I'd been given the mentally challenging job of cleaning the glass, filling the gaps with silicone and tidying up the site in general. There was about an hour's work. Steve wouldn't be back for some time so I lay down on a bench and closed my eyes.

I was woken from my sleep by Steve shaking me and shouting in my ear, What the fuck are you doing?!

It was not the first time I'd fallen asleep on the job and Steve, with more jobs lined up, was feeling the pressure. The job was a week overdue and Steve couldn't stand to not deliver on time. Even a day over brought him out in a sweat and a fit of Tourettes. I jumped up, barely aware of where I was. All right, all right, ALL RIGHT! This was the closest I'd ever been to striking him. My fists were clenched and I was screaming in his face.

I leave you for two hours to do a one hour job and you haven't done a scrap of work, and I find you asleep on the client's garden furniture. You've got a fucking cheek, you cunt!

Listen, I've had enough of this, Steve. I've had enough of you and I've had enough of your job.

I walked off.

You're fired! He shouted after me.

I didn't turn around.

I get my licence back in a few weeks, so I don't even need you. You hear me? You're fired, yer cunt!

It was only when I returned to Richard's place and was making a cup of tea, that it occurred to me that I had acted in haste. I'd walked out of a job that I needed in order to pay my keep. The club was picking up but it was still a long way from generating sufficient income to keep me.

I'm sure things will work out, said Richard, You'll see.

Richard was not someone I would immediately ask for financial advice, but I didn't want to hurt his feelings, so I gave him a nod. You think so do you?

Oh yes. Have faith, Nick.

Have faith in what? The mystical forces of the cosmos, the spiritus mundi, black magic, God? Perhaps I could simply barter for everything I wanted from now on, as Richard had previously suggested.

If it's the rent you're worried about paying, I don't mind if you miss a week, he said.

An act of kindness. I had great trouble then, and I have great trouble now, dealing with acts of kindness. I took Ray out for a walk. Ray had made a full recovery, and I watched him as he ran after rabbits.

Like Ray, I was almost there. I'd almost reached one object: that of financial independence. Another few months of the club building up and I would be there. But could I survive those few months? I was developing an amphetamine dependency. I was developing a dependency to alcohol and dope and Valium. Who was I kidding? I was a full on phet-head ... I was taking phet now just to get going in the morning. I couldn't even answer the telephone without drugs.

Financial independence was comforting but not the be all and end all. I still had some way to go before I had the rabbit in my teeth. There had been some developments. I hadn't managed to speak to Officer Leadbeater, but I had decided to go to his place of work. Perhaps if I met with him I could get closer to my goal.

I walked down a disused railway track. Just like in Manchester, the track had been developed into a cycle path. I spotted a comma butterfly on a fence post. I was remembering a hot summer. Before the Madman Marz episode. We must have been ten or eleven. It was almost the end of the summer holidays. For six weeks the sun had baked the earth. The verges of gorse were turned into straw. It was you who had the box of matches, Andrew. A full box. We started with a little fire of twigs but it soon took. Then there was a gust of wind and whoosh! The whole thing was up in glorious flames. The grass crackled and whistled. We laughed out of shock. We had to run as fast as we could to beat the fire roaring towards us. We just made it to the road in time. We stood leaning on the fence, panting and laughing. All we could see beneath was the light and heat and dance of the flames.

I was trying to pinpoint it in my mind: when you stopped being an ally. Internally you must have been changing long before there were any outward signs. Like the journey a comma butterfly takes, only in reverse. Instead of beginning life as one of the crawling things, hiding in a shell where the change was concealed, to begin again as a shimmering check of gold, you had begun your life as something that glimmered with the sun, and now you were encapsulated in your pupa. It was left to me to try and see through the shell, to see the grotesque transmogrification within. Not then. I did not see it then.

It was your initiative. The matches half-inched from your own kitchen. Your mum's matches. Your mum who said we could have been brothers. Your mum who dressed me in one of your old coats when I came to your door shivering one winter morning. Your mum who took me in when my grandma died. Your mum who fucked me over.

Your plan. But by fourteen you were on the side of the hangman. Still, I made excuses for you. Best mates. Loyal as a kicked dog. It's dogs that guard the gates, oblivious to what's going on behind them. The last to know. Past the white pillars, the golden hinges, the snake draws its winding length.

We watched as the fire spread, a momentary panic before we could see it diminish. We laughed again, this time out of relief. We walked up the embankment and across the recreational field. Past the Methodist chapel. I remembered that poster outside, something quite common now, but then it was a novelty to us: God is Love, it said. God is many things but he's not love, I said. You joined in the game: God is non-existent. God is absent. God is angry. God is jealous. God is insane.

As I walked along the railway track, not unlike the railway track we had walked then, I played the game again: God is a murderer. God is a sound wave, God is Charlton Heston. God is the sword of justice, God is a mote of dust, God is someone else. God is us. Playing the game on my own that we had once played together. And in this way, I vomited God out of existence, but I could not vomit you out of existence. You were bigger than God.

I thought again about that fire, about the fire we'd started and of the game we'd played. How we'd delighted in each other, how we'd been enough for each other, had needed no one else, had needed nothing else. Complete. But beneath your carapace something slimy was shifting down to a sunless sea.

I thought about that photograph in your front room, you and Liv on top of the Rockefeller. I dropped to the ground and curled up in a ball of hate.

You are training with Keyop. You are doing reps. You are taking it in turns, using the bench-press. You are doing squats. You are doing press-ups. You are doing curls. You are doing chin-ups. He says nothing. He doesn't even grunt. He is not himself. You sense this. He doesn't let on and you do your workout. You ask him if he wants more weight, but he doesn't hear. You ask him if he's ok, but he doesn't answer. You've seen him like this before. When he won't talk, when he won't answer.

Eventually he says, 'That story you told me.'

'What story?'

'The one about you camping when you were a kid.'

'What about it?'

'You said you'd never told anyone else.'

'That's right.'

'You lied to me.'

'Of course not. Why would I lie? Why are you even asking me?'

'Look me in the eye and tell me you didn't lie to me.'

'Don't be stupid, Keyop. Fuck off!'

'I'm done' he says.

He walks off. You don't say goodbye.

You are in the library. You are reading Dante. It is hard going but you keep at it. You have read Purgatory and now you are reading Hell. You read a few lines, then you stare at the wall. Something is bothering you. You read some more, but it won't go away. It is this: you have lied to Keyop. It is the one thing you both promised you would never do. But you have just done it. You didn't think it was such a big deal, but now it is something playing on your mind. It is picking away at it. You read some more, for an hour at least, but the feeling just builds. You think back to a few weeks before. Keyop said that Paddy had told him something when they were playing poker. You want to know what. Paddy had said 'I fucked your bird'. You told Keyop it wasn't true. You and Paddy have not fucked. But now he knows you are a liar, he does not believe you.

You are walking back to the cell, fear unsettles you. You want to run, but you stop yourself. Somehow you know. When you go into the room, the shock you feel is that you are not shocked by what you see. There is no sound. He is kneeling on the floor. His hands are by his sides. His head is tilted towards the ground. He is tethered to a radiator by a bed sheet. Like a goat tethered to a post. Somehow he has managed to strangle himself. You never said goodbye.

⦀ ⦀ ⦀⦀

The train pulled up at the station. I got off and picked up a paper from the vendor, went to a café, ordered and sat down in the corner. Then I noticed the headline: GUILTY OF SAVAGE MURDER. It was the same headline I'd read twenty-two years ago, but instead of a photograph of me there was one of Kareem and one of Osman. The sub-heading: pair face life behind bars for the brutal killing of student and rugby star Tony Ho.

There was the full story inside. Two full pages. Each had been sentenced to life imprisonment. Kareem would serve at least thirty years before he could apply for parole and Osman twenty-five years. There was no mention of you or the sterling job you'd done in bringing about justice. Andrew Honour QC: the invisible arm of the law.

I thought about both men. One guilty of murder, certainly. The other in all likelihood not guilty. Not innocent. But not a murderer. I thought about my own day of judgement. No *thing* that had happened in my life up to that point had prepared me for that day, for that reckoning. No *one* I had met had prepared me for it either. No one had prepared me for the moment when the clerk of the court approached the foreman of the jury and said, 'have you reached a verdict upon which you all agree?' No one had prepared me for the moment when the foreman said, 'yes'. Or for when the clerk said, 'Do you find the defendant guilty or not guilty?' And no one on earth could have ever prepared me for the moment when the foreman answered, 'Guilty.'

For those who are guilty, prison is tough. For those who are innocent, prison is worse. I was innocent when I began my sentence. I was guilty by the end. To be guilty of my crime, to be punished for what I had done rather than what I had *not* done – that was a huge relief. Reaben Kareem and Jwanru Osman: it was Osman I knew would find life inside the harder of the two, because Osman was not a murderer.

My full English arrived and a pot of tea. I read the rest of the paper but it didn't register. I turned back to their photographs. They looked like murderers. Just as my photograph did when it made the papers twenty-two years ago. They always do, we always do, because the person who looks on the image has decided that you are a murderer.

It was raining when I paid my bill and opened the door. I made my way over to the police station, past the statue of Harold Wilson: the man who abolished capital punishment. I stopped by the statue and said, 'Thank you'. I owed him my life. I arrived at the police station but didn't go in. What I had to say was better said on neutral ground. I decided to wait for Officer Leadbeater to leave the station – as I'd waited for you to leave your chambers. I took out my phone.

Hi, Andrew, it's me – Nick. Hey, listen, I've just seen the headlines.

Eh?

The guilty verdicts. Kareem and Osman. Congratulations.

Thanks, Nick.

It's a real achievement, Andrew. I was thinking, we should celebrate. Have a night out. What do you think?

I'm in Sheffield at the moment.

When are you in Leeds?

Not for a while.

Don't you get any time off over summer?

I'm not sure.

Come on, Andrew, for old time's sake.

I'm just so busy at the moment.

One night won't harm. You owe it to yourself. You need to unwind. Loosen a few screws.

There was silence from you. I could hear you breathing down the phone. Look, Andrew, Liv told me she had it out with you. I had to tell her the truth. Let me explain, face to face. We need to talk.

Well, I suppose ...

Now the worm waits for the apple.

It was band night at the club. It was a rockabilly band called Wanda and the White Trash. The music wasn't a million miles away from The Cramps. The same mix of early rock and roll, with surf and punk thrown in. The singer reminded me of a young Liv, a mix of punk, goth and rockabilly. Her hair was dark brown with a white-blonde streak at the front. She was wearing a tight fitted black pencil dress with metal hooks at the front and studs around the hem. The men wore zoot suits, bright coloured shirts, and crepe sole shoes, their hair quiffed with Dax.

They could drink, this rockabilly crowd, although a lot of it seemed to have ended up on the floor. Their drinking tastes were not particularly sophisticated, pints of lager or bourbon and coke. A few were drinking Sailor Jerry's. The audience had left some space at the front so that people could jive, jitterbug and lindy hop. I caught the eye of a man standing on his own in the far corner from the bar next to the picture of Baudelaire. He was wearing a military-style hat with ear flaps. He didn't seem part of this crowd – he seemed completely at odds with it. He was staring at me.

I tried to shrug it off, a feeling of unease. After two or three minutes I looked back and he was still standing there staring a hole right through me. The fucking cheek. I wanted to go over there and smash the back of his skull into the wall. I took a deep breath. I had to get a grip. I tried to push him out of my mind.

Ray had caught a rabbit a few days ago. He'd carried it over to me in his mouth, still kicking. I went to take it from his jaws, ready to wring its neck, but as I did it was like someone or something had switched it off. A moment ago it was jerking and writhing. Now it was limp. Its head loose and floppy, blood dripping from its open mouth. How easily they give up.

I held it by its front legs and took out my knife. I made a good cut between the legs and dragged the blade of the knife down, like it was a zip, reaching the genitals. The giblets slopped out, dangling by a thread. I cut this and freed the mess onto the grass, where they lay steaming. Ray gobbled them up. I fished out the lungs and fed them to him. I plucked the kidneys, still attached to the carcass, and gave them to him one by one, off the blade of the knife. Last I skewered the heart. He took it off the point and swallowed it whole. There is no such thing as a murderer in the animal kingdom. There is no such thing as a barrister either.

I looked over to the far corner by the bar again. There he was, staring right through me. Could I, if push came to shove, wring his neck? I made an excuse to Pawel and wended my way through the crowd.

Great night, mate. It was a punter in a blue teddy boy jacket.

Yes, it's a good one.

I think it's great you're putting on rockabilly nights. Are you going to make it a regular thing?

I might do, yes, excuse me.

And I carried on through the crowd until I came to the staring man in the military-style hat.

What's your problem? I asked him.

It's the trains.

What?

He smiled at me. It's the trains, they're never on time.

Do I know you?

He just stared at me.

Look, I said, I don't know what your game is, but you better lay off, have you got that?

He didn't say anything, just carried on staring.

Whoever smashed the window. Whoever threatened me. Whoever sprayed graffiti on the door and on the mirrors. That you, is it?

He shrugged.

What do you want?

I'll see you on Friday, he said, making his way through the crowd and up the stairs.

There are two reasons why I went back to The Royal: Steve Taylor and Vinnie Howell. I bought Steve a beer. He was easily bought. He'd found someone to replace me.

A cock of a student. Doesn't know his arse from his elbow. He's even worse at mixing cement than you are. And he drives like a fucking girl.

Thought you were getting your licence back?

Yeah, next week. Thank fuck.

I might have some work for you.

You! Have work for me?!

I'm right in thinking you're not too fussy where you drink?

Well, up to a point. What's the crack, cuntyballs?

I want you to drink at my place on Friday and Saturday nights. I'll pay the bar tab. In other words you get to drink for free. As much as you like.

So what's the catch?

You're my insurance, in case things kick off.

You mean I get to punch students and blokes with beards. Fuck me, I'd pay *you* to do that.

And it was that easy to get Steve on the payroll. I had to wait till later on to 'bump into' Howler.

I'll have to make a phone call, he said, when I popped the question. It's dead tricky to get hold of at the moment, proper MDMA. Bit of a drought.

But I knew that was the maggot, the wriggling slimy thing on the end of the line that would cause my eel to bite.

Why's it so hard to get hold of? I asked him.

Sassafras oil, he said. The main source comes from China. It takes hundreds of years to grow a sassafras tree. Then there's the process of synthesising it – it's dead complicated. A lot of the precursor ingredients are tricky to get hold of. I can get you tablets no problem, three for a tenner. But there'll be fuck-all MDMA in them.

It's got to be MDMA, I said. Old school.

It had to be the genuine article. I was going to take you back to 1989. He made a phone call.

It's dealt with. Happy days!

We took a trip in a taxi to a place a few miles away. A back-to-back terrace. A dishevelled man in his thirties answered. Unkempt hair. Bad teeth. He had a dog the size of a lion in a cage by the kitchen door.

Don't worry, he said, He can't get out.

He had some scales and he weighed out a couple of grams of the grey-brown crystalline powder. He had some coke too.

It's not that speedy coke is it? I don't want anything like that.

Howler grabbed my arm. Listen Nick, this int no speedy shit. This man sells coke to barristers. It's the real deal.

When he said the word 'barristers' it was as though he were saying 'people better than us'. Barristers, as though that were the true test. There were humans and then there were super-humans and these people were barristers and they had to have the best of everything. The dealer held it up.

Look, see the shimmer on it? That's how you can tell. Avoid floury stuff. Here, have a sniff.

I did.

It smells of kerosene, right? I nodded. It's the proper stuff.

I bought a couple of grams.

Back at the pub, I got us a round in. What you said that time Howler, about helping me out?

How do you mean?

If I got into trouble.

Sure, no problem. Why, do you need someone sorting?

No. As it turns out. I think it's sorted.

I'd done my research. The Top Cat club no longer existed, nor did The Venue. But I'd found another club run by a member of one of the Madchester bands from the late 80s. It played all the same tracks as The Top Cat and The Venue used to play. There was a train going from Manchester to Leeds that ran all night long so we could get back any time we liked. I found the sort of pub we used to hang out in: run down, studenty. I got the first round and we found a cosy place to sit.

You're only as good as your last job in this game. I've got work for the next six months then there's nothing in my diary, you said.

You were looking a bit puffy in the face, eyes rimmed with red, as though you'd been hitting the single malts a little too much. Must be hard to sleep, I thought, so much responsibility on your shoulders, but perhaps this concern was entirely unearned. You could, for all I knew, have slept like the dead.

But you'll get work later, right?

Who's to say.

Come off it, Andrew. With your reputation. You're one of the best players in the game.

Well, yeah, I should be ok. But it's a worry, that's all I'm saying.

How do you get the work?

Firms of solicitors. You have to be in with them all. They control the work-flow really.

You talked to me about how it operated, the social functions, the long hours, the poles that needed greasing, and the grease you needed to grease those poles. I listened and nodded, as though I were actually interested. Then you started talking about all the extra-marital affairs. It went with the job apparently.

Adrenalin plus ego plus testosterone equals infidelity.

Ever been tempted?

Nah.

Come on, Andrew, no one's going to blame you. Your secret's safe with me.

It's not my style, you said. You were not going to take this bait, but there were other worms in my pocket.

How's the club? Liv's not mentioned it for a while.

Well, she's not working there at the moment, Andrew.

Right.

This made me smile. You didn't even know. You didn't even know the first thing about your wife.

It's going well. You'll have to come down one night.

I will, Nick. I promise. It's just finding the time. My work takes me all over the country.

Do you like all those long hours, Andrew?

You thought about this for a while. Well, it's probably like you and the club. It doesn't feel like work. I love it, Nick. It gives me a buzz.

I laughed. Talking of 'buzz' – you're going to love what I've got.

It's all right though, Nick, right? I've not touched it in years.

It's the proper stuff, just like what we used to get. Loved up, old school.

You looked a bit nervous, but you had always had a soft spot for MDMA, indeed you enjoyed it more than me. Every occasion I took it, it was on your insistence. I imagined you'd continued your habit during your time in higher education.

I shouldn't really, you know.

But I could see beneath the nerves, there was excitement.

Come on, Andrew. You need to let your hair down. I pointed to your thinning pate. We laughed. You've got to be able to let off steam once in a while, Andrew. You're not telling me the rest of the chambers are drug-free?

Well, there is quite a bit of coke about.

There you go, see.

A lot of the big guys, they sort of see themselves outside of the system. Immune from its code.

Well, there you are. I mean, in a sense, you are the system. You're the golden hinges, the white pillars.

You shrugged. Somewhere not that deep down you believed you were. For those who write the code for others to follow, there is no code.

How's Liv?

Fine.

And the kids?

Ok.

Good to have them back, eh?

How do you mean?

Nothing, just that they've been at boarding school. Thought you'd be pleased to have them back.

Oh yeah, you said.

You probably hadn't even noticed they were home.

Listen, Nick, I understand about you telling Liv. She confronted me. I couldn't lie. She'd suspected for a long time.

How?

Something to do with my parents, being clammed up about it. I'm glad you told her. It was a relief to get it out in the open. Really. Look, Nick, I want you to know, for what I did to you–

You don't need to say it. We were young. I would have done the same.

I do need to say it, Nick. I absolutely need to say it.

Then say it.

I'm sorry.

Good. You've said it.

Really, I am. I'm sorry, Nick. All these years, every single day. I've thought about you. About what I did to you. I ... I ...

Your eyes were welling up.

Got to move on, Andrew. Don't beat yourself up about it.

It was unforgiveable.

It's over. It's the past. Done and dusted. I've got a life now. I've moved on. You've helped me with the club.

The money, it's nothing. If you want more, I can get you more.

I don't need any more. Forget it.

She's still angry. Liv.

She's bound to be.

She won't talk to me.

You need to ride it out.

I lied to her. For twenty-two years.

She'll come round. She'll see why you did it.

You nodded. I really think you believed she would. You went to the bar and ordered another round. The place was starting to fill up with students and members of various youth cults. Mostly all identifiable from our teens. Nothing much had changed: the same ways to indicate outsider status, the same ways to draw attention to yourself, the same ways to attract others. The music was sixties psychedelia. We talked about the old times, skilfully ignoring the elephant.

I went back to Affleck's Palace the other day.

Really, it's still there then?

I went back there with your wife, I wanted to say, on a secret date while you were hard at work.

Exactly how it was, only retro is now 1980s tracky tops.

That's funny. I was having this conversation with a colleague recently. All the young men we get in the dock in hooded tops. It's fashion as camouflage. Punks, hippies, skinheads, all the youth movements that have gone before were there to shock, to stand out from the crowd. Now it's the opposite. The point is *not* to be identified.

I know what you mean, Andrew, but it was only like us, back in the day.

How do you mean?

Well, you know, the whole Perry Boy thing.

Oh yeah! Skinny jeans. Dunlop Greenflash.

And the haircut – short back and sides with long fringes, the fringe flicked over one eye. I'd been growing my fringe all winter, remember, Andrew, so that it practically reached my chin, I could put the ends of it in my mouth.

I know, I'd been growing mine too don't forget.

You had a good head of hair in those days.

Cheeky fucker!

And we were laughing, Andrew, just like the old days.

We were both silent for a moment, replaying the old film stock in our heads.

Turner's night club. Remember that dive, Andrew?

Course I do.

Friday night up till 9pm was under-eighteens.

Salt and vinegar puffs, 6p a packet. And those pink shrimps.

Two for a penny.

Seems such a long time ago now.

Not to me it doesn't, I said. Because it didn't. The routine of prison does funny things to time. Every second seems to take an hour, but after ten years, nothing has happened, nothing has changed, and time shrinks. Pulling and pulling on an elastic band, then letting it snap back to exactly where it was.

Going to Wimpy for burgers and milkshakes. I used to love that place.

The world was our playground, eh, you said.

We were a club of two.

We needed no one else. It was the same Andrew sitting next to me now. It was a different Andrew. You had the same laugh, same smile, same gesticulations. But there was something cold and dead about you now. Cold in the same way a knife is cold and dead in the same way a knife is dead. The knife of authority. The knife that cuts the head from the heart.

We moved on to another bar. The beer was kicking in. Laughing, joking, reminiscing. Five beers into the evening. I have to say, I was really enjoying myself. Some of the old you was resurfacing. We were having a great time. But the alcohol was starting to take its toll. We went to the toilets and locked ourselves into a cubicle.

Christ, not done this in years, you said.

Again, I observed the mixture of nerves and excitement playing out on your bloated face. You actually giggled. I chopped up two lines of coke on the cistern lid.

Sshhh, I said. There was no one in but I thought it was best to play it safe. At any point we could have been disturbed by another toilet customer. Me neither, I whispered.

Not when you were inside? You whispered back.

Nah. Coke and MDMA – the worst things you can do. It's dope and opiates. Booze too if you can get it. But you can't get it. The last thing on the planet you want to be on in a prison cell is Ecstasy.

Why's that?

Because the last thing you want to be inside is horny.

We laughed. What is funny is truth and pain. Every time. I snorted the first line and moved out of the way to let you near the cistern. I had to be very careful as I took my phone out of my pocket and set it to video mode. I had to hold it up without seeing if the angle was right. It was pot luck really. I recorded for just a few seconds, making sure the camera was back in my pocket before you'd finished hoovering up the line.

You stood back, gathering your senses about you.

That hit the spot, you said.

You passed me my rolled up tenner. Your nerves had been settled by the drug.

Next, we went to a cocktail bar and worked our way through the menu. It was busy, less studenty, more aspirational city types. Young, fit, wearing expensive clothes, bodies taut with gym classes. The music was contemporary R and B.

When did you know, Andrew?

Know what?

That you wanted to be a barrister?

Don't know, probably about the age of fourteen.

Just as I thought. The day that you became the guy who handed the other guy to the hangman. Steps was a sweet kid. I suppose these days he'd be classed as having learning difficulties, but back then you were just thick. He was in all the bottom groups, but within these groups there was a range of abilities. Steps was at the bottom. He was picked on, beaten up, blamed, set up, ridiculed, the butt of everyone's joke. He was the one walking around with 'kick me' pinned to his blazer. His was the name and address you gave to the security guard of the mill if you were caught on the roof, or the shopkeeper if he copped you nicking sweets.

Every group needs a Steps. It helps the group cohere. It strengthens the bonds within the group. If Steps had left, we would have had to go to second from the bottom to replace him. Did you feel that was you? Were you worried about your place in the pecking order? That's why the higher up you are the safer your position, except for the top. The person at the top is the most vulnerable.

At about eleven o'clock we disappeared into the toilets again. This time I fished for the wrap of MDMA. I took out two smallish rocks. No wider than a grain of rice. We each swallowed one. About half an hour later we started to come up. Big smiles and a warm glow. You know it's the drug because your throat's gone dry and you no longer fancy lager, you fancy lemonade. I looked into your eyes and your pupils had dilated. Not that anyone else would notice. They weren't dinner plates, but to the close observer the signs were there.

We made our way to the club. It was called, I suppose ironically, South. There was no queue to get in. We walked past the door staff no problem and made our way down the stairs. As we descended, it felt like we were going back in time. The place was full. The dance floor was heaving. We bought bottles of water from the bar and joined the revellers in the middle of the floor. The unmistakable sound of a Farfisa organ. Dragging me Down, Inspiral Carpets. Kennedy, The Wedding Present. Loaded, Primal Scream. I looked over at you and you were grinning from ear to ear.

I was pleased to see that you still danced like a dizzy vicar. No sign now of the dead and the cold. You were alive – transported back to your youthful self. And I liked that you, Andrew. I wished you back into my life. I hoped we could be together as we had once been. For a moment, there was the possibility that we could be best friends again.

There was a smoking area out back and we made our way there. I smoked a rollie.

So what do you think? I asked you.

It's fucking ace, Nick. Why have we waited so long?

I had a good excuse, I said. We both laughed.

So what's your clerk like? She looked pretty hot in court.

Sarah? She's a good mate. We get on really well.

Nice body. Pretty face. How old?

Thirty five.

She seems to like you.

Like I say, we get on.

Well?

Well what?

Would you?

You laughed at this but also blushed. I get it, I said, and nodded.

You won't tell Liv will you?

Course not, I said.

It was only a bit of fun. We got tipsy one night after a big murder case. She helped me carry some files back to my hotel room. And, well …

Your secret's safe.

I finished my roll-up and we went back in. You were smiling and I was smiling. You were smiling because you had connected to a version of yourself that knew how to unwind and have fun. I was smiling because, although I had planned the evening meticulously, I had not anticipated it going as smoothly as it was.

On the train on the way back, you fell asleep. Your face was squashed against the glass of the window. It looked lumpy and misshapen. I took out my phone and played the video. It was no Oscar winner but it was adequate: the face was clearly identifiable, you hunched over the cistern lid, hoovering up a line. At this stage, I had no idea what would stick. Part of me even thought, leave it Nick, leave the past where it belongs.

S he's kissing me. And I'm kissing her. Hands all over. Ripping at clothes. I pull off her knickers and I'm licking her clit and she's writhing. I have to grip her hard to keep her in one place as I feel her spasm as she comes. And then we fuck over one of the tables in the club under a picture of Gerard de Nerval. And it's exactly how it should be and it's absolutely right. Afterwards, she gets dressed. We have just fucked, Liv and me, me and Liv. The fuck of a life time. Then I wake up.

Gerard de Nerval went insane before hanging himself. He left a note to his aunt: 'do not wait up for me this evening, for the night will be black and white.' It was Friday and tonight it was the cabaret night. The theme was black and white. Nerval had a pet lobster which he walked in the gardens of Paris on the end of a blue silk ribbon. He didn't care for dogs. I got up and went for a seven mile run with Ray.

We used to give each other dares. You would be the first to back out. I'd always go further. To me it wasn't just a dare, it was a test of character. There was a geography teacher called Mr Seddon, a depressive. These days, the doctor would have him on a course of Fluoxetine the minute she saw him. The first ten minutes of every class was him complaining about his kids, about his wife, about his job, about his life. He had a nasal whine. He had a speech impediment which made him pronounce, 'the ru-urban fringe' as 'the wuu-urban fwinge' which amused our small minds, but should have elicited our sympathy. We both hated him but it was your idea.

We used to have to stand outside the class until he'd turn up with his box of books balanced on his hump of belly, key in one hand, glasses falling off the end of his nose. It was your turn to dare me and you dared me to get Mr Seddon with the fire extinguisher. You had pointed to where it was positioned on the wall. It was exciting to take it off its bracket. It was exciting to smack the top until the foam shot out. He was striding towards me. 'Give it here Smith, stop messing about.' I gave it him. Right in his eye. He put his hands up to defend himself. He fell back over his box. You were laughing. The entire class was falling about laughing. For a moment, I felt popular.

Mr Seddon ran for the headmaster, like a small boy running for his dad. When the headmaster arrived, he got it too. I was on a roll. I waited after school for my dad to arrive, outside the headmaster's office. 'He's half an hour late Smith, we can't wait here all day.' Here's the thing, he let me go without punishment. He felt sorry for me. He knew my dad wasn't going to make it, that he was in a pub somewhere, half cut, the phone call completely forgotten about. I didn't count.

And I remember another time, in infant school. I was in the dining room. There were eight of us on our table. You were sitting next to me, and you dared me to take my spoon and flick mushy peas onto one of the dinner ladies. I selected the right one, Mrs Crossley – whose back was as wide as a barn door. Couldn't miss her from a mile away. I aimed the spoonful of mushy peas and splat, right across the back of her navy blue tabard. She turned around and eagle-eyed me. She paced across and grabbed me by the ear. I can still remember the sharp stab of pain – like being knifed. She marched me to the headmistress's office. She told the headmistress what happened. The headmistress was called Miss Pilkington. Miss Pilkington had looked angry. She had turned to Mrs Crossley and thanked her for bringing me to her. Mrs Crossley had marched back to the dining room, secure in the knowledge that I would be chastised, probably even caned.

Then Miss Pilkington had turned to me and smiled. For being so naughty, she said, I'm going to make you sit there all afternoon watching those fish. She pointed to a chair in the corner of her office, then she smiled again. That's where I sat, Andrew, staring into the tropical tank, at the small thin darting fish, brightly coloured. The slower swimmers, the strange grey-brown sucking fish at the bottom of the tank. And it became clear, that she had felt sorry for me too. That's what I was, an object of pity.

So I stood outside the headmaster's office, listening to him drone on about how it wasn't acceptable and it wouldn't do, and that it was the wrong attitude. All the while, I knew what he was thinking, that I'd go unpunished, because he felt sorry for me in the same way Miss Pilkington had felt sorry for me. Because the damned need no punishment. For being damned is its own punishment. And I thought about your face, as I'd been led out of the dining room. You had given me a sympathetic look, but then I saw you turn to Mark Longworth and you gave him a snide smile. You'd set me up.

I stopped for a breather, my heart beating hard in my chest, sweat dripping down my back. Ray was in the undergrowth, hunting out the young, the old, the weak and the sick. I thought back again to that afternoon, to Miss Pilkington, to the darting fish and the undulating fish and the fish at the bottom of the tank, eating the shit left by the other fish. Your face now was out of my mind. I was calmed by the water and the soft motion of the fish. By the flash of colour and the gentle bubbles from the filter. And I realised, that afternoon, watching the fish, was one of the happiest times of my life.

Remember that time we went camping in Bangor, me, you and Bob? We got barred from the Youth Hostel for smoking weed. First time we'd had any, aged fifteen (I've never managed to get so high on it since). When we got back from Bangor we went our separate ways, me to my gaff, Bob to his mum's and you to yours. Only when I got home I couldn't get in. I was locked out. I went to the pubs in walking distance looking for my dad. I asked Manny's dad. I asked Summers's brother. I asked anyone if they'd seen him. He was on a bender. He could be anywhere. There was a pub where you could ring a bell at the back and they'd let you in – any time of day or night. Had I tried there? I walked around for hours with my rucksack on my back.

Eventually, unable to walk much further with the rucksack digging into my shoulders, I went to your house. Your mum invited me in. You were having your tea, or as you called it, dinner. I was invited to join you. We had spaghetti. The first time I'd had it out of anything other than a tin. A revelation. It tasted completely different. We had meatballs your mother had made, actually made them from fresh ingredients, real minced beef and real diced onion. There was a tub of dried grated cheese with a perforated top so that you could shake it, that I later found out was called Parmesan.

Afterwards, we had pudding with fresh cream. Not condensed milk or Carnation. I went back to my house, which was now in darkness. Still no dad. I waited until midnight. I went back to your house. You were in bed, your mum was in her nightie. She let me in. Your dad was watching an episode of Kojak. I sat down on the sofa while he finished watching the episode. It was about this man who had been released from prison. A woman, who had driven with him to New York, was found murdered in his abandoned car.

Only Kojak knew the truth, that the prisoner was not the murderer, and in the last few minutes of the show, he proved it to the others. It felt so good sitting there with your dad watching Kojak. Your mum brought me a mug of Horlicks with two sugars and your dad a coffee, and we sat there in silence staring at the television screen watching Theo Kojak suck on his lollipop while he figured out what had really happened. He was in the sunken plaza of a huge building that dwarfed every other skyscraper surrounding it. I didn't know it then, but it was the Rockefeller. I looked at your dad, his face set in the same concentration as Telly Savalas, and I pretended that your dad was my dad.

After the show was over, your dad switched off the TV. Your mum brought me a blanket and they let me sleep on the sofa. I lay there in the warm glow of the dying embers of the fire and drifted off into a dreamless sleep. And that's where I slept for a week. When I eventually found my dad, he blamed me, said I'd told him I was going away for two weeks, not one.

You are watching Keyop play poker with Paddy and two other men. You are trying to follow the game. You do not play yourself, and have only a beginner's knowledge of the rules. They are playing for roll-ups. Paddy is dealing. Keyop is sitting to the left, and so he puts out the small blind. The player to the left of him puts out the big blind. You don't know why they do this, but you think it is to do with the chips.

Paddy deals the cards. As you watch the game, you kid yourself you're not in prison, you kid yourself you are in your club. The club that you and Keyop own. The club you have dreamed up to keep sane. A place you can go to be free. You replace the white walls with flock wallpaper. You replace the plastic furniture with oak chairs and tables. You replace the fluorescent strip lights with chandeliers. You replace the barred windows with velvet curtains. In the background a band is playing. You are drinking beer with Keyop and laughing.

You watch the game as it enters the showdown. Keyop shows his hand. Paddy's hand wins. Keyop is accusing Paddy of cheating. They argue without raising their voices. Both men are used to discord. Paddy is whispering something in Keyop's ear. You see something on Keyop's face you have never seen before: shock.

It was Friday night. The man with the hat had promised to return. I was sitting on my own again, clutching a bottle. I was scanning the room. So far, nothing. I made my way back to the bar. I wanted to know if Pawel had seen anything suspicious.

You should open up a club in Manchester.

Why Manchester? I asked.

I have sister there. Manchester, very good place.

I asked him if he'd seen the man.

The man with hat?

He hadn't seen him.

You're a good worker, Pawel. And Socha too. Is she your girlfriend?

Just friend.

Do you like running this bar?

Yes, I do.

Good. Keep on the lookout. He's barred from now on. Whatever you do, don't let him in. If for some reason he gets in, you come and get me.

When I got back to my seat, I grabbed my beer and my jacket. I wanted to sort the money, ready for the acts. I went through to my office and opened the safe. I put my jacket on and went to the mirror to straighten out my shirt. That's when I noticed it, a splat of red paint on my breast pocket. I touched it. It was still wet. I wiped the paint off my fingers with a towel. Inside my breast pocket was a folded up piece of paper. I could see the end poking out. I took it out and unfolded it. It was a ten pound note and written on it in red marker: 'U will pay'.

I put it back in my pocket and took the jacket off. I checked all the pockets: nothing. I hung the jacket up. I sat down with my beer. What was going on? Was he still out there? I stood up and went back into the main room. I scrutinised the audience one by one but I couldn't see anything. I wended my way through the crowd, hoping to spot something. But there was nothing. He'd been here tonight though. My jacket had been over my chair for about three hours. Plenty of opportunity. I told Pawel what had happened but he said he hadn't noticed anything. I opened another bottle and sat back down, determined not to miss anything this time. If he was here, I was going to see him.

It was the end of the night. Richard was helping the acts pack away their equipment. The bar was still busy but Pawel and the two other staff were coping with the traffic. I took Ray upstairs for some fresh air. The street was quiet. Everyone was inside a bar or a club. Ray had a sniff around. He found some chips and a half-finished burger. I stood and watched him eat greedily as I rolled a cigarette. So the man had been and left his mark again. But what did it mean? He didn't appear to want money, so why 'U will pay'? I tried to reason it out. He hadn't been violent. As creepy as it all was, it was relatively harmless.

I was halfway into my cigarette, when I noticed a black car approach. It moved slowly and the lights had been switched off. The windows were shaded. Something wasn't right. I called Ray over. He came to my heel. The car was level now. It slowed down to a near stop. The back window wound down. There was an eerie stillness. Then there was a 'phtt' sound and a clatter of something. The car pulled away. I looked round. We'd been shot at with a crossbow bolt. Miraculously the bolt had missed both me and Ray, flying through the one inch gap between us. I hailed a cab. Jumped in the back with Ray by my side. A black cab tailing a black Astra into the white and black night.

We followed the car for some time, but then we lost it at a set of lights.

What do you want to do? asked the taxi driver.

He drove me back to the club. I was surprised by how shaken up I was. I got Pawel to pour me a very large whiskey. I told him what had happened.

Not good, he said.

An understatement.

Why is he shooting you?

I had no idea. If it was a protection racket, it was a funny way of going about it.

You don't let him in. Under any circumstances. You got that?

Long after the club had closed, I was still sitting in the bar, with a bottle of whiskey. I was still thinking about the crossbow bolt, how close it had come. Was it aimed at me or Ray? Surely a protection racket would not want to kill the person they were trying to get money off, just scare them? But the man with the military-style hat did not seem interested in money. All he seemed interested in was putting the heebie-jeebies up me. It was working. But now this. This wasn't just intimidation, this was an attempt on my life. I didn't want to think about death, not mine or anyone else's.

I was on my own with just the past to keep me company. I thought back to that party we crashed. We were with Pete Wardle, remember? He could always sniff a party out. We'd been in the Red Lion all night. It was about half eleven. The landlord was calling time. It was a Friday or a Saturday.

There's a party down Bellfield Close, Pete said.

It was a student party. We bought some bottles over the bar and followed Pete. He got us in no problem. We both got chatting to some girls. We left Pete to his own devices. He would frequently end up naked on the floor with lots of students around him. We would hear the girls screaming followed by his manic laugh. His party trick.

I was getting on really well with mine. I looked over to you. You seemed to be getting on well with yours. Yours was better looking than mine. A stunner in fact: jet black hair, smoke-grey eyes, heavily kohled. She was wearing fishnet tights that were torn in strategic places, smoking a roll-up. A red plastic mac, a low cut top. It was a punky goth look that set her apart, made her look different, and I wanted her. But it was too late.

I was chatting away to mine and she was laughing at my jokes, it was all going so well. I kept having a sly glance over to you and thinking, wish I had yours. Mine was blonde and blondes were never my type. She had a nice body though. She was wearing a top which revealed an inch of cleavage.

I can't remember how it happened but the next thing I knew I was on a double bed with this blonde girl. She was naked and I was naked. We were about to fuck, the only light that of the moon through the window. Then the door burst open. The bloke whose party it was and about twenty of his friends surrounded us. This bloke hit the switch and the room flooded with light. There I was in all my 'glory'. In a state of arousal. Twenty-odd people staring at me. The bloke whose party it was – it was his girlfriend. They'd had an argument. I was a revenge shag. I'd been set up again.

I'd thrown my clothes across the room. I stumbled around. I managed to find a sock, then another sock, but I couldn't find my T-shirt, or my trousers, or my underpants. He was coming at me. Red angry face. Fists bunched. I ran down the stairs and out the patio doors at the back. It was December. Freezing cold. I stood in a bush shivering in just my socks.

You came looking for me. You let me in at the patio doors to reclaim my clothes. You helped me find my jeans, my shoes, my coat. We were laughing, giggling, drunk. Then he appeared, searching. I hid under the dining table. You said you'd seen me leave through the patio doors. He didn't believe you but then there were screams from the next room. Pete Wardle had taken his clothes off and was sitting in the middle of the room playing someone else's guitar.

Pete saved my bacon. We both piled out, laughing into the night. I knew my dad would still be out so we went back to mine for a nightcap. A good party, we both agreed. That girl you got off with, was Liv, of course. You always did have all the luck didn't you? You'd managed to get her number before we fled, so sharp of you, and you went on your first date the next week. I think you took her to see Blind Date, or was it Fatal Attraction? I stayed in and watched Cheers. Ted Danson's character, Sam Malone, was trying to get off with Diane Chambers, played by

Shelley Long, who would leave shortly after to be replaced by Kirstie Alley, playing Rebecca Howe. And he would spend the next few years trying to get off with her instead.

I just remember watching it on my own – I watched a lot of television in those days, on my own. I was imagining you in the cinema with Liv. You'd buy her popcorn and coke, or maybe hotdogs. You'd sit at the back. You'd make a big show of yawning, stretching your arm round the back of the chair. Or you'd let your hand touch her thigh. A test. If she let it stay there you'd gradually move it closer, edging to the hem of her skirt, to the area of bare flesh. I could picture Liv's face in my mind, but not the blonde girl I'd been so caught out with. I couldn't even remember her name. I imagined that I was in the cinema with Liv and you were sitting on your own at home watching Cheers. I imagined it was my hand that stroked the soft flesh of her thigh, that it was my hand that cupped her breast, feeling the nipple stiffen, that it was my lips that kissed her. And I masturbated.

I never went past that house again, the place where I had made such a fool of myself and where you had got off with Liv. I had to avoid Bellfield Close altogether. Turned out the host of the party was a headcase. One of the toughest guys on the estate, and a knifer. There was a rumour that he was coming for me. You were at college at the time doing your A levels. I was in the first year of my apprenticeship. Even up to the day of my conviction, I always had to keep my wits about me in case he was creeping up behind me with a baseball bat in his hand, or a knife in his pocket.

I should have confronted my fear, instead of running scared. The city I lived in was not the same as the city you lived in. My city was full of people I had to avoid. It was a place of dark ginnels, doorways in a perpetual shroud of menace, black shadows and black nights. Your city was shrouded in light, with white beams and golden rays. Yours was a city of sunshine. Your city was white. It was a laughing beautiful girl. My city was a knife-wielding psychopath.

I thought again about the man with the military-style hat. I went into the back room and sent Liv an email. It just said: I need you. I finished the whiskey and lay down on the sofa. I didn't want to leave the safety of the club. Outside there were dangers. It was dark and cold. I was drunk. I was thinking about you, in your magazine home, safe behind the golden gates and the white pillars. You would be in bed with Liv, your arms wrapped round her soft body.

Perhaps you had given her one of your persuasive speeches. Perhaps you had made it up with her and she had forgiven you. Perhaps you were having make up sex right now, while I lay on a hard sofa with a maniac waiting for me outside. Images of you fucking Liv came into my mind. I tried to block them out, but they kept coming, over and over. Your leering face, your contorted face, your pallid flesh, your cock entering and entering her. Your disgusting cock. I had no one, only Ray for company. You were fucking Liv. What fucking right did you have to your fucking life?

I fumbled for the phone ringing in my pocket. It was Pawel. I pressed 'ignore'. I was in the back room of the club. There was an empty whiskey bottle on the floor and an overflowing ashtray. Grey light was pouring into the room from the high cellar window. It was morning. My head was pounding and my tongue was coated in thick silt. Ray was still sleeping. I went into the bathroom and brushed my teeth. I drank some water and necked some speed. I rang Pawel back. He was down the cash and carry. They had run out of Peroni. What should he get instead. Use your initiative, Pawel.

I have just been to Lidl, he said. They have deals on. Very good.

Ok, well, get whatever you think.

Two for one.

I told him to get whatever he wanted. I put my phone away. I walked to a greasy spoon and ordered some toast and some coffee. I picked up a paper and pretended to read it, but really I was thinking about you.

I don't remember when I first became aware of you because memories of when I was three are rather vague. We both started at Saint Paul's at the same time. My grandma Smith dropped me off, my dad's mum. She was a stern woman but she had a big heart. Shame she died so young, perhaps she would have been able to keep my dad on the right track. He seemed to respect her more than anyone else. I'd anticipated school. Some kids a year older than me had told me you had to do sums, but I didn't know what sums were. In my head they were some sort of punishment. I suppose they are.

I do remember my first day. We were split into groups, six groups, one for each table, five or six kids round each table: Blue, Red, Green, Orange, Yellow and Purple. You were in Blue, I was in Red. I was sandwiched between Mark Longworth and Carl Lindley. The first task we were given to do was to draw a picture of our family: the house, the garden, our brothers and sisters, mum, dad, any pets. The teacher was called Mrs Fox. Someone must have told her my mother had died, because she corrected her list, 'or if you've not got brothers and sisters, or a mum and dad, just draw the family you've got.' Then she smiled at me.

I didn't see your picture. I can imagine what you drew though: white fluffy clouds, a perfect house, with curtains neatly tied either side of the window. A perfect door, coloured in with yellow or red crayon. A chimney with a plume of grey-white smoke. Green and brown trees with juicy red apples hanging from the boughs. Daffodils in neat little pots. Your cat and your dog lying down harmoniously together. The sun beaming down on you. Your perfect sister and your perfect father and your perfect mother.

I looked at both Mark and Carl's efforts with despair. They had drawn their family. A circle for the body, a circle for the head, lines for arms and lines for legs. I looked to Wendy and Lisa and Jane – they had all done the same. I drew my dad and my mum even though my mum had been dead a year. I still had a memory of her then. I don't now. It looked like a normal family. It was a normal family, just without a mum. Not for much longer though. I wish I'd kept that picture.

Although we'd known each other since we were three (sharing the same nursery memory of dipping malted 'cow' biscuits into orange squash) we didn't become close friends until much later. Perhaps three year olds are incapable of being close friends.

It was break time but it was raining so we were staying in. We could do what we liked. Some kids played snakes and ladders, some kids played Frustration, some played draughts. There was a game of snap somewhere and two kids were playing noughts and crosses. You were on your own, reading a book with such concentration, it drew me to you. I asked you what it was. You lifted it up so I could see the cover, a book of fascinating facts.

There's a man here who's eaten a plane.

You're kidding me?

You showed me the page. He was called Mr Eat-All and he was French. He had eaten eighteen bicycles, fifteen shopping trolleys, seven televisions, and a plane. The plane had taken him two years to eat. There was a photograph of him in front of a plane. In his hands he held an engine part and he was biting through it.

That's amazing, I said.

It's fascinating, you said. A fascinating fact. And you pointed to the book title on the cover.

How witty you seemed to me then. How clever. How different to the simpletons with their happy game of snap. I liked you instantly, I admired you. I sat down beside you and you showed me other fascinating facts. There was a plant that had eaten a bird. There was a photograph of a brightly coloured flower the size and shape of a bucket with the back end of a bird sticking out. Buckingham Palace had over six hundred rooms. It was impossible to sneeze with your eyes open. We were friends from that day.

Your mum would always pick you up at the school gates. At first my grandma used to pick me up but within two years she was dead. For a few months my dad would be waiting for me, parked up by the gates, with his name on his van. But then he lost his licence. Without his van, he couldn't work. Without his work there was no income. He became a full-time drinker. In those days, if you declared yourself an alcoholic, you got signed off. You didn't have to go to the dole office every fortnight to sign on, you were given some form of disability benefit and also an allowance for alcohol. The state actually paid you to drink.

Some days he'd forget to pick me up. I'd be standing at the gates with all the others. We'd be chatting and laughing, but gradually, all the other mums and dads, older brothers and sisters, grandparents, would come to collect them. We'd thin out until I was the last one there. It wasn't just the sense of being abandoned, it was the humiliation of everyone else seeing me being abandoned. Eventually, the head teacher would come out to her car. Miss Pilkington. She had a red sports car which was at odds with her frumpy image. She drove me home a few times, made sure my dad was in.

One day while I was waiting by the gates, I saw your mum approach Miss Pilkington. They were chatting and looking over at me, so I knew they were talking about me. After that I used to go home with you and your mum. You'd hold her right hand and I'd hold her left hand. I'd pretend that your mum was my mum. She'd make us a beaker of Vimto or sometimes pour us a glass of milk. Do you remember that milkshake we made by mixing Vimto with milk? I shudder at the thought now, but we believed we'd discovered penicillin or pasteurisation at the time. We even asked your dad about how you patented something. He humoured us, explaining about the patent office and the process that was necessary. Your mum would bring us a plate of biscuits. We'd eat the pink wafers first, then the custard creams. We would always leave the Garibaldis. You had a cupboard full of brightly coloured Matchbox cars. We'd drive them round the carpet. The lines of the carpet were the roads. We were not just close friends, we were brothers.

Your mum couldn't have been kinder to me. And your dad was always warm and friendly when we saw him, although he was normally at work. Even your sister, who was a good three years older than you, always made time for me to ask how I was.

It was a proper family, like the ones you see on TV. You sat down for breakfast together in the morning. You sat down for a hot meal in the evening and talked to each other about what you'd done that day. You went on shopping trips. You went to the seaside. You went for walks in the park. You fed the ducks. They read you bedtime stories. How I envied you. At night, in my bedroom, I would kneel at the foot of my bed and pray.

Please God, make Andrew's parents adopt me. If you do this, I won't ask for anything else and I will do anything you say.

We broke up for the summer holidays. You were excited because summer holidays meant a holiday in France. It was a family ritual. For weeks you would leave me. You'd send me postcards, brief notes, to let me know how you were getting on. You would always put some minor detail in to amuse me or make me feel less alone – 'I'm in a French café full of French people. The woman next to me smells of onions', 'they eat frogs legs here, yuk!' You'd come back tanned and full of stories. You'd always bring me back a present. One year it was a boules set. There were eight steel balls and one white plastic jack, and they came in their own box with a carrying handle.

It was the best present I'd ever had. There were two weeks of the holidays left and we'd take the set to the park and play boules there. The other kids would want to play too and we'd have tournaments. We started back at school but we carried on with those tournaments after school and at weekends. We were popular and the tournaments were a great success. We started to have leagues and tables – ranking players. We even had a little betting syndicate running.

Until one day I came home from school and the boules set had gone. At first I thought I'd misplaced it. It wasn't under my bed where I kept it but perhaps I'd put it in the wardrobe. It wasn't there either. I searched the house, every room, but it had gone. When I saw my dad I asked him if he'd seen it. He said he hadn't.

Then one afternoon, I was walking home from school. I went past the The Black Bull, and I saw two men playing boules. I watched them. The set looked just like mine. I recognised the men. They were men I'd seen drinking with my dad. Then

I realised what he'd done. That was the end of the boules tournament.

I was careful walking back to Richard's, checking out each person that I passed, especially anyone in a hat, checking out each car that passed me, especially if it was black. I took Ray for a walk through the woods. There was a mist that hadn't lifted. I tried to shed the grogginess of the night before – a combination of too much whiskey and a night on the sofa – by focussing on positive thoughts. The club was doing well. It was really taking off. I could quit the speed now, I didn't need it. I'd finish off this batch, then call it a day, I decided. I was making progress with you too, Andrew: a very interesting meeting with Officer Leadbeater.

As I walked down the path, as the light dimmed, and the leaves thickened, I saw the outline of a man in the distance. He was leaning against a tree. I couldn't make him out, just the shape. He appeared to be wearing a hat. I could feel anxiety claw in the pit of my stomach. It felt like a rat. Don't be a dick, I said to myself, keep your cool. Just walk past him. But as I got closer, all I wanted to do was run.

I stopped in my tracks. I pretended to answer a call on my phone. I took it out and faked a one-way conversation. My hand was shaking so much, I nearly dropped my phone. The man was still leaning against the tree. I put the phone in my pocket and said to Ray, Come on, that was Pawel, he needs a hand, we can go for a walk later.

I walked back with the rat in my gut scratching at my insides. I wanted to see if the man was following me. But I didn't want him to know I was concerned. I couldn't stand not knowing. I stopped and turned round. There was no one there. I looked to see if he'd walked further up the path. Nothing. I strained my eyes to see through the mist. Then he appeared from behind a tree. He was closer now and I realised he wasn't wearing a hat as I'd thought. It was a coat with a large hood – a parka with a snorkel.

I tried not to panic. I was almost running, getting faster and faster, my heart thumping. The rat frantic. Then I *was* running, I didn't care anymore about keeping cool. I ran until I was clear of the woods and halfway across the park. I stopped to check where he was, but he hadn't followed me. I took deep breaths, trying to stifle the panic in my gullet. I made my way to the club.

卌 卌 卌 卌

Black Art was playing through the PA and I was clearing up from the night before – sweeping the stage of glitter and feathers, tidying the bar area, re-stocking the fridge – when there was a banging on the door. It made the hairs on my arms stand on end. I went to answer it, my breath rapid and shallow. I stood behind the door for a moment, collecting my nerves. I wished there was a peephole, and I made a mental note to buy one. I unlocked the door and opened it a fraction. But there was no wolf. Standing there, in her school uniform, was your daughter.

Megan, what are you doing here?

I've been excluded.

I paused for a moment to gather my thoughts.

Come in, I said.

I locked the door behind her. I made us both a coffee and we went into the back room.

Sit down, I said, Tell me what happened.

She sat on the arm of the sofa. I sat in the armchair opposite.

I got caught, she said.

Doing what?

Smoking skunk.

Have you talked to your mum?

Not yet.

Does she know you're here?

I want to work for you.

You've got to be eighteen to work behind a bar.

No you don't, they've changed the law. Sarah said. Her dad's got a chain of pubs.

It's complicated.

I rolled a cigarette, lit it.

Can I have one of those?

I don't think that's a good idea.

But I handed her the packet. I watched her roll the paper round the tobacco inexpertly. She lit it but it soon went out. She'd rolled it too tight. I took another paper and re-rolled it for her.

Thanks. It's against the law to smoke one of these too, she said.

I think you should let your mum know you're here.

I could collect glasses.

Could you.

She blew out a plume of smoke. The cloud lingered between us.

My dad thinks I'm stupid.

He's just got high expectations, Megan. He wants you to do well at school. He wants you to be successful.

You don't have to do well at school to be successful. You didn't.

I passed her the ashtray. I don't think you want to go down the path I've gone down.

But you've made it now. This place is getting a name for itself.

Really, Megan. I'd avoid my way of doing things at all costs.

I'll work for free the first night. See it as a trial. If you don't like my work, you don't have to hire me.

I've got to open up soon, Megan. You need to talk to your mum.

She shifted down the arm of the sofa, her skirt riding up over her thighs. Her legs were so smooth. She caught me copping a look. She held my gaze.

You were excluded weren't you, Nick? My mum told me.

When did she tell you that?

Ages ago.

I wondered how many times Liv had spoken about me. I wanted to ask Megan, but it wouldn't do to seem interested.

This has gone out again, she said, You're as bad as me.

She leaned over and with her cigarette still in her mouth, lit it off mine. She was very close to me. I watched the end glow red.

Pawel will be here in a minute.

Who's he?

He runs the bar. And Richard, he does the PA. He'll be here too.

She leant against the back of the sofa. She took a few drags of her cigarette.

I need your light again, she said.

I thought about ringing Liv after Megan had gone. But then I thought better of it.

You have been sharing a cell with Keyop for six years. Keyop is from Chapeltown. He is inside for shooting a drug dealer in the face. He earned his money by taxing drug dealers. He would wait until they were in bed asleep, then he would break in. He would go into their bedrooms and point a gun in their face. He could get thousands each time he did this. It was almost foolproof as dealers tend not to grass and dealers do not use banks. But his main source of income was guns. A connection he got from his first trip inside. The university of HMP. Ukraine was left with massive stockpiles of military weapons after the disintegration of the Soviet Union. Keyop tells you how he set up supply chains.

Gang members, drug dealers, street people and other assorted criminals, all want guns. From a shotgun at £150 up to a sub-machine gun at £30,000, Keyop caters for all tastes and budgets. Bullets, silencers, infra-red sights. Death, that's my business, he says. Now he is inside, he has switched from selling guns to selling Subutex. From death to paralysis. Keyop is a reader. He reads Ed McBain and James Ellroy, Joyce and Shakespeare, Dante and Tolstoy. You spend all day talking about books. Keyop's favourite writer is TS Elliot. He likes the Four Quartets best.

'I'm going to see if I can get some old wallpaper,' he says.

'What for?'

'I want to take each poem and write it on the back of the sheets. I want to hang the sheets up so I can see how the poems look.'

You don't know why Keyop wants to do this but the idea of it excites you.

'I'll give you a hand,' you say.

This is why you love Keyop. And you realise something for the first time, that Keyop has replaced Andrew, that you have found someone else on this planet you can truly connect with. You are no longer 'I'. You are 'we'. But Keyop will never replace Andrew.

Socha was serving absinthe. I watched her pour the dose up to the first indentation in the glass, then take a cube of sugar and sit it on the slotted spoon over the emerald green liquid. She took an iced pitcher and slowly poured water over the sugar. I watched as the water louched the absinthe, turning the clear green spirit into a thick mist.

I'd been chatting to a gallery owner called David a few nights before. He'd approached me with a business idea. If he could exhibit some of his artwork in the club, he could guarantee so many extra punters through the door. I'd agreed to go and see him. It might be profitable. There was an exhibition opening. I'd immediately connected with David, and part of me wondered if we could become close.

Steve was chatting up two students. Pawel and Richard were on stage. I watched them play. I was given a guitar in prison as a privilege. Keeping hold of the guitar was a challenge because of all the drugs we were taking. We did all sorts of things to fool the regular drugs tests. We would drink lots of water before so the sample would be too dilute, or we'd tax a clean. Taxing a clean is risky. It involves the extraction of urine from a prisoner who doesn't take drugs, concealing it in a bag and then puncturing the bag in the sample container. The risk is this: prisoners lie about how clean they are. A third option was Keyop's favourite, he would cut his finger with a razor and trickle some blood in his sample. They couldn't force you to urinate if you had a medical condition which prevented you from doing so. Bingo.

I watched Pawel and Richard. I thought about that day when I used Keyop's favourite method, only I got caught with the razor and consequently failed the test. The punishment was to lose the guitar.

What do you think? Pawel said, when he came off stage.

It's getting there, I lied. Listen Pawel, I've got to nip out in a bit.

How long for?

Just a few hours. Are you ok to be left in charge?

He seemed a bit taken aback but pleased. Was this the most responsibility he'd ever been given?

Yes, of course. I will do job good, Nick.

I looked around the room. People laughing, chatting. Lovers holding hands, potential lovers flirting. I was overcome with a feeling of loneliness. You were probably at home now, in the same room as Liv, breathing the same air as Liv. No friendship I'd ever had in my life had come close to the bond we once had. I drank some whiskey in the hope of staving off the feeling. I thought about Gerard de Nerval. I wondered what he meant when he said that tonight would be black and white. I had this urge to ask Keyop, but of course I couldn't ask Keyop. I couldn't ring Keyop, I couldn't even write to him, because Keyop was a memory. Keyop was dead. Keyop topped himself.

I went over to Steve. He was sitting on his own now. I sat down beside him.

Fancy a whiskey? I said and produced another glass.

Go on then.

How's it going?

Alright. There's quite a bit of skirt in. Thought I was in with them two, he said, indiscreetly pointing. I'd love to cum in her hair.

You see that picture there, Steve? I pointed to the print of Gerard de Nerval.

What about it?

That's a French poet called Gerard de Nerval.

So?

He topped himself.

Daft cunt. What's the point of that, you're going to be dead in no time anyway.

Before he died he left a note. In the note he said that the night he killed himself would be black and white.

What you telling me for?

Just idle banter, Steve. What do you think he meant by that?

How the fuck should I know? Oi, cuntyballs! Steve shouted over to Pawel. Another beer.

Steve had stopped calling me cuntyballs and started calling Pawel cuntyballs. I'd been promoted. It sounds silly, but I actually felt a degree of pride about that.

I don't know whether I should be upset or not, I said.

What do you mean?

You used to call me cuntyballs, Steve, don't you love me anymore? I passed him the whiskey.

You're doing a good job of this, he said, looking round the busy room. I admire anyone who grafts and makes a go of it. Plus, there's lots of fanny about.

And that's why I'm no longer cuntyballs?

Like I say, you're doing a good job.

Pawel brought over a beer. Steve swigged from it. The posher they are, the more I seem to score.

Eh?

Student fanny.

I felt tired: physically and mentally drained. I looked around the room, a lot of familiar faces. Then I noticed him, the man with the military-style hat. He was sitting in the opposite corner and he was staring at me. How had he got in? I'd made it clear to Pawel that he was banned. But he didn't have a drink so perhaps he hadn't been to the bar. I excused myself and made my way over.

Thought I'd made it clear? I said.

I've told you before.

Told me what?

It's the trains.

Who you working for? How much do you want?

You've got it wrong pal, he said. I'm not working for no one. I don't want your money.

What do you want then? I said.

Oh, you know, a little cottage in the countryside, fresh bread, fresh milk, somewhere to keep chickens.

Come on, stop messing about.

He gave me a wink. Who was he, Andrew? Was the man in the parka in the woods the same man or did I have two men after me? Was this the man who had fired a bolt at me? I couldn't work out which was the more paranoid thought: that I had two men after me, or that they were both the same man.

I forced myself to appear calm. I went into the back room. I sat down. I didn't know what to do. I could get Steve to throw him out. I could get Steve to do him over. I turned on my laptop and opened up the spreadsheet with all the membership details. There were over three hundred members. I scanned through them, I read down the list. I don't know what I was looking for. It wasn't as though I knew his name. An act of desperation, I suppose. I scanned down the columns. I sifted through the cells and across the rows – nothing rang any bells. A lot of the names were familiar, but quite a few were new to me. People who had joined on the first night and never come back, I supposed. I stopped at the name 'Harry Maggs'. It didn't sound like a real name. It sounded like a made-up gangster name. I took out my phone and rang the number. A man with a Cockney accent answered. I apologised and killed the call. I sifted through the files again.

After half an hour I clicked on the 'x' in the right-hand corner. I emailed Liv again: please get in touch, I need to talk to you. I wondered what was going on between you and her. I felt jangled. I took out a bag of phet. With my knife, I scooped a half inch dose and necked it. I put the bag back in my pocket and went over to the bar.

Pawel, he's here. I thought I'd made it clear he wasn't to come in? I've got to go out. I want you to get Steve to kick him out. Make it clear he's not welcome back.

Who?

The man with the military-style hat.

Where?

It was only then I looked across to where he was sitting. Only his seat was empty and there was no sign of him.

I was in a taxi with David, the gallery owner whose exhibition I'd just been to. He was with his girlfriend, Lucy. We were meeting the artist for a drink. I'd bumped into Ramona at the opening and only narrowly avoided a heated altercation, but she seemed more upset than angry. She wanted an answer. Why had I run off?

Where are we going? I asked.

We're going to the Falcon Bar. David said. It's the other side of town, in the studenty bit.

The exhibition was by an avant-garde artist called Michael Gray. It consisted of two landscape projections. One was a snowscape and the other was a woodland scene. There were red neon lights superimposed over the canvas. Very few people had turned up to see the exhibition. I wondered where the artist's friends were. I wondered where his family were. I wondered where the artist was. David had invited us to have a drink with him.

I'd already decided that David's idea was a waste of time but I accepted the offer of a drink. I wanted to expand my social circle. Perhaps I could make a new friend, one with more than just 'fanny' on his mind. Yes, perhaps David was the answer.

Why wasn't the artist there? I said.

He never comes to his own openings, David said. As though this made him more virtuous, more of an artist. I had become anxious about what I was going to say about the exhibition. I was racking my brains: think of something clever to say.

What did you think? he asked me.

I don't know, I said. I like content. I felt a bit daft, saying this.

I like content too, he said. But I also like work without content.

We arrived at the Falcon Bar. The windows were steamy.

It looks hot in there, I said.

This is where the cool people hang, Lucy said, and laughed.

David paid the taxi man and we went in. The security was comprised of one grinning bald man from Belfast. You'll like Belfast, he said, You're English. The place was teeming with young men in check shirts and beards and young sparkly women with shiny hair and retro dresses. It wasn't a million miles from the Café Assassin audience. Still predominantly students, only students with richer parents. And therefore students who were trying harder to look like they had poorer parents.

Have a pint of Black Rat, David said.

It tasted of fruit juice and had a sinister red glow. We sat down. We were joined by two glamorous women, they were curators. They were sparkly with shiny hair and retro dresses. I could feel a jolt of super-alertness, as another dose of speed kicked in. Then a man in a check shirt and a beard approached. I was wearing a suit and an open necked shirt. I felt over-dressed.

This is Michael Gray, the artist, David said. We shook hands. We drank Black Rat.

Michael, this is Nick, the man I was telling you about. Nick owns the bar over the other side of town, Café Assassin.

Oh, yes, I remember.

Have you been? I said.

No. It's a live music venue isn't it?

Live music, comedy, cabaret, burlesque, magic. It's a bit Cabaret Voltaire.

What's that then?

I was surprised. I thought he'd get the reference that I'd made especially to accommodate him. You know, where Dada started.

Of course I know, Michael said. Which made me think even more that he didn't. David tells me you're interested in exhibiting work there.

It's David's idea, I said. It's a good idea, I lied.

Nick has just been to your exhibition, David said.

What did you think? Michael said.

I don't know, I said. I like content. I mean, I like things that are free of content too. But, you know, my preference is for content.

But that's the point, he said.

I see, I said. I get it. I didn't get it. I felt over-dressed. I took my suit jacket off and rolled up the sleeves of my shirt. I asked him why his friends hadn't turned up. I asked him why his family hadn't turned up. I asked him why he hadn't turned up.

I don't need an audience to validate my work, he said.

I see, I said. I was grinding my teeth.

What do you think of the Black Rat? Lucy said.

I like it, I said. It was the black rats that carried the bubonic plague.

I was imagining Michael Gray with swollen lymph nodes.

That's dark, she said.

We drank more Black Rat. The room was swimming. It was strong stuff, cutting through the pharmaceutical-grade speed I'd downed.

I need to go outside, I said, For some fresh air. David joined me. We both rolled cigarettes.

Are you from round here? David said.

No, I'm from Manchester. How about you?

Bristol, he said.

He didn't have a Bristol accent.

How long did you live there?

Twenty-one years, he said.

We stood in silence, smoking. Although I was buzzing from the speed, I couldn't think of anything to say to him. He was stubbing out his cigarette and putting his lighter in his pocket.

I'll just finish this, I said. And held up my cigarette. He nodded and went back inside.

I felt deflated. It was clear that there was no special bond between us. I felt like a fool. What was I thinking? The truth was that I was closer to Steve than I was to David and his crowd who didn't need 'an audience to validate their work'.

There was a golden nimbus of light emanating from the street lamp opposite, but everywhere else was quite dark. As I watched the halo it seemed to grow. It pulsated. I wondered if it was the speed or the Black Rat.

Then I noticed *him* standing in a doorway of a boarded up building, the man with the military-style hat. He was staring at me and beckoning me over. I felt my muscles contract and a cold steel wire wrap itself around my neck. I looked around. The street was empty. I looked back over to the doorway. He was in shadow now, the peak of his cap concealing his eyes. He was smiling. Then he waved.

I chucked my cigarette in the gutter and went back inside. I went over to David's table.

I need to go, I said.

Are you all right?

I need to go.

Can I take it as a 'yes' then?

What?

To the exhibition space.

He held out his hand for me to shake. I backed away from him.

Outside, I stood waiting for a taxi. He was still there, in the doorway. I flagged a taxi down and got in. I was shaking. I wished that I was driving, driving over the artist, and the gallery owner, over the curators and over the man with the military-style hat. I pictured a giant black rat, eating the man's face off.

Since the beatings stopped, life inside is bearable. You are no longer afraid of the world outside your cell. You are no longer afraid of other people. You play chess with Keyop and talk about life outside. You have known him for three years. He has a daughter and she has agreed to visit him for the first time. She is coming this afternoon. You have never seen Keyop this nervous. He is wearing a white shirt and a green tie. His hair is neatly parted. His shoes are polished. There are creases in his trousers.

'The last time I saw her on the outside, she was still a girl. Now she's a woman. I took her to a park. I pushed her in the swing. I bought her a milkshake from a van. We picked some blossom together. We stood against the railings by the side of the canal and reached up to the bough where it hung down.'

His daughter's name is Zoe. Keyop remembers watching her throwing the blossom into the water. He remembers how it travelled through the air, so soft and so slowly. They bought some bread and fed the ducks. His eyes are welling up. He asks you if you have ever wanted a daughter. You tell him that you haven't. But you have and you do. You want your own family: a wife and daughter and son. You want to take them to the park to feed the ducks, on a sunny day when the trees are full of lilac blossom. You do not talk about Andrew. What Andrew has stolen from you.

You finish your game of chess. It is time for Keyop to see her. 'Do I look alright?' he asks. He looks like a boy in a school uniform. 'You look great,' you say and straighten his tie. You wish him luck. You watch him stand up and walk into another room. You think about the family you might have had, had things turned out differently. You close your eyes and picture the park with the sun beaming through the trees. You feel its warmth on your face. In the background is a pond. By your side, your children. Your wife is holding your hand. You squeeze her hand tightly. She smiles at you. It is Liv smiling at you. It is Andrew's children by your side. You have nothing and Andrew has everything. You do not even have a sense of who you are. Andrew has even robbed you of this.

When I got back to the club, I checked my emails. There was one from Liv.

> sorry I've not been in touch or responded to any
> of your messages. I don't think it's a good idea to
> meet up. I don't think it's a good idea that I work
> at the club. I've been thinking about it a lot. I hope
> this doesn't upset you too much, Liv.

So that was it. Not even a kiss. Nothing. I closed the laptop and sat in the dark. I'd lost my queen. All the work I had put into having your wife had been thrown back in my face. I couldn't stand that. I couldn't stand to think of her in your arms. I couldn't stand to think of her with your cock inside her. Oh well, I would just have to play some of my smaller pieces.

|||| |||| |||| |||| |

K night time. I drank some coffee and sat back in my bed. I thought about how I could turn the game to my full advantage. I didn't need Liv. I could get her later. For now I could play Officer Leadbeater. I rolled a cigarette and lit it. I liked to smoke in bed. The meeting had gone well and I was convinced it would lead to full control of the central files on the board. As I drank and smoked and schemed, there was a knock on the door. Ray shot up and started barking. Richard was out, so I would have to answer it. I climbed out of bed and wrapped a towel around my waist. It was a postwoman.

Nick Smith?

Yes?

I need a signature.

I took the plastic stylus off her and used it to sign the box on the screen. I took the parcel inside. I hadn't ordered anything. I carried the parcel upstairs and took out my knife. Inside the brown packaging was another parcel, this one wrapped in Christmas paper – red with green holly motifs – and tied with black ribbon. I cut through the ribbon and tore the paper off. I opened the box. Inside was a large white cake of soap. I picked it up and turned it over. Scratched into its surface was 'yoRe tuRn'.

He had found out where I lived. Whoever *he* was. My first reaction was to grab for my bag of speed. I was about to neck a knife-ful, but I stopped myself. Instead, I took the bag and flushed it down the toilet. The drug was making my thoughts muddled. I needed to think straight. I went back to bed. Ray lay next to me. But I was no longer safe. Not at the club. Not at Richard's. Was he watching me now? I lay for some time turning it all over in my head. The man outside the club on that first night, waving in the shadows. The smashed glass and the graffiti. The message on the mirrors. The crossbow bolt fired from the black car window. The red paint on my suit pocket and the ten pound note.

He must have followed me the night of the exhibition opening, from the club to the gallery and from there to the bar. Perhaps he had followed me home that night. And now this. A Christmas present. It wasn't Christmas. I held the soap bar in my hand. I squeezed it. It was solid. I tapped the corner of it against the wall and it made a thud. It was real. Someone was after me, that was for certain, and it wasn't just drug-induced paranoia. I felt like a sitting duck.

I got up and got dressed. I put on my coat and went out with Ray. I walked the streets, aware of everyone I passed, convinced someone was following me, but each time I turned there was no one there. Eventually, I went into a pub and bought a drink for myself and a packet of pork scratchings for Ray. I sat down and sipped my lemonade. I didn't want anything alcoholic. I had to stay sober. I was craving phet. If I could just have a small dose, I'd feel better. Just half a knife. I wasn't sure to what extent my anxiety was down to the parcel or the phet withdrawal. I had to clear out my system.

There were only a few people in the bar, but I felt uncomfortable in their presence, like they were a jury and they were judging me. They hated me. Don't look at me. Don't talk to me. Don't say a word. I tried not to make eye contact with anyone. I stared at a picture on the wall. An old advert with a cartoon toucan. Lovely day for a Guinness. Pawel rang but I ignored the call.

I went back to Richard's. I closed my room door behind me and put a chair under the handle. I shoved it as hard as I could so that it jammed in. I crawled into my bed fully clothed. Pawel rang again. I texted him: 'sick as a dog. You'll have to manage without me.' I received a response shortly after: 'OK boss'. At first I couldn't sleep, my muscles ached and I felt completely drained. Outside I could hear gulls screaming. Eventually, I drifted off.

I dreamed that the man with the hat was fucking Keyop. As he fucked him his hood came off. He had no nose, just a big black hole in the middle of his face. I woke up sweating. I drifted off again, another nightmare.

When I woke up the next morning, I was lying in bed with Ray. I lay for some time staring up at the ceiling. I tried to cast the nightmare images out of my mind. I thought about the package wrapped up like a Christmas present, and I thought about you, Andrew.

I remembered that tape recorder you got for Christmas. We were six years old and we'd only just become close friends a few months after meeting over a Fascinating Facts book. It was a gift from your mum and dad. It was a big square parcel with wrapping paper on and a bow. We wondered what it could be. When we opened it, there was a tape already in the machine, a C-60 (or was it a C-30?). We huddled round the machine. You were excited because you already knew what was on the tape. It was Father Christmas, and he was talking to you, calling you by your name and wishing you a 'Happy Christmas, Andrew, ho ho ho'. There was an elf too, a female voice, telling you that you'd been such a good boy, that they didn't normally address the children in person but that you'd been so good this year, they felt it was only right to do so. You were so excited to share this with me. And I was excited too. I was excited for you, Andrew.

We found out later that Father Christmas was your dad and the elf was your mum. But at the time, listening to the tape, completely unaware of this, I remember thinking that you were one of the chosen ones, one of the elect. Not thinking with those words obviously, but with a six-year-old boy's equivalent language.

Then, one day, both of us huddled round the machine, you pressed 'play'. There was nothing. No sound: no 'ho ho ho' of Father Christmas, no giggling elf, no one telling you how special you were, and for a moment I thought that we might have imagined it. We listened intently, there was just the 'ffsshh' of the speaker amplifying a blank tape. You went to your mum, crying. She said that it only lasted the Christmas period and then it vanished. That was Santa's magic recording. And that made it even more special. It was years later that your parents confessed that in fact they'd wiped the tape by accident. I think that was probably the most traumatic thing that ever happened to you.

I lay there for hours re-living childhood memories. Eventually I noticed a feeling I hadn't had for a while. I was ravenous. I climbed out of bed and went to a cafe. I ordered a full English, with extra bacon, extra sausages and extra black pudding. I stuffed my face. I saved a piece of bacon for Ray.

My phone rang. It was Pawel.

What's the problem?

It happened last night.

Go on.

The man with hat.

He was in the club?

No, he was outside. He had a crossbow.

A crossbow?

Standing over the road.

What did you do?

I ring you.

Oh, I see, sorry about that.

I ring police.

And?

They ask me what he is doing.

Go on.

I tell them that he is doing nothing, just standing there.

And what did the police say?

They want to know what trouble.

You're taking the piss.

This is what they say.

Useless fuckers ... and what did he do?

He is standing there.

And that's it?

He was up to some game, Nick. Socha and Tim, they were working. They were scared. Police come, too late. What are we doing if he comes in again?

Listen, Pawel. I'll be back soon. If he turns up again, you ring the police but this time you say he's shooting people with his crossbow. Have you got that?

But what if not shooting?

What do you mean, what if not shooting? Say anything, but get the police to get their arses down there. Right?

Ok.

I want you to phone me if anything happens.

I will.

As I finished off my breakfast, I couldn't get the man with the hat out of my head. He was coming for me. He was creeping closer. I should have been afraid, but instead I was overcome with a feeling of intense loneliness. I'd had some shitty luck, then I'd had a few lucky breaks. Was this it? The end of the line? We walked back to Richard's. I was tired again. I went to bed again. I spent the rest of the day in and out of a fitful sleep. Each time I woke up I felt even more fatigued than the time before, as though sleep itself were the cause of my exhaustion. I got up to make some tea, but went back to bed. I knew if I could get some more speed, the feeling would go away. I lay on my own in the dark.

The Segregation Unit governor is Richard Vince. He's been here since the riots. It was his idea to put you with Keyop. Does he know what Keyop did for you? You wonder if it is an act of compassion, or just coincidence. You were both on the list. Perhaps this is the reason. Being caught with drugs means loss of privileges. No playstation, no TV. There are drugs and there is the gym. But for you and Keyop there are also books.

It's easy to feign madness. It's hard to prove sanity. For a long time you think Keyop is pulling the wool over their eyes. Experience teaches you otherwise. You are talking with Keyop. You are laughing with Keyop. Keyop is telling you about one Christmas Day. His uncle Nikolos had said, 'That's it, Christmas is cancelled.' Everyone had cracked up. What was so funny? You wanted to know. Uncle Nikolos had merely punctured the curled paper tongue of a party horn. That was what was so funny. Bathos. Normally a word you would keep to yourself. But in front of Keyop, you say it out loud. 'Bathos.' He doesn't even look at you. Something you share. He repeats your word, 'bathos.' And there it is, that connection between you. An echo in the darkness. And you are lonely. And you crave affection. His body is very close to your body. You know this man intimately. You think about it. You don't do anything. You feel weak, you feel small. Your loneliness has unmanned you. And you reach out.

The next day, I felt much better. I took Ray to the park and watched him run after a squirrel. I rang Pawel.

How's it going?

It is not going.

What do you mean?

I have closed club, Nick.

Pawel, you can't do that. We've built up a business. You can't just abandon it.

I wanted to reach through the phone and grab him by the throat.

Socha. The man with hat. He was following her.

Attacked?

Not exactly attacking, no.

What then?

He is following her as she is coming out of club, then he is grabbing her.

Did he hit her?

No, not hitting.

Well, what then?

He just say, 'aye up'.

Why didn't you ring me?

I did. Eight times. Five texts.

I put the phone down. I felt numb. I was throbbing all over. I closed my eyes. Falling backwards through a black tunnel. Faster. Nothing to hold onto. Bracing myself for the crash.

I opened them again. I was sitting in the park. Men in suits, women in heels. A girl selling Coca-Cola. A beam of sunlight filtered through the leaves, lighting up a wasp eating an aphid. There was a boy clutching a yellow spear, lunging it into an imaginary dragon. I watched him thrust and jab. I felt that lizard chill again. A flash of white, cold, the stench of piss, bleach, burning foil. The sweet-sick stench of opium smoke.

Paddy O'Brien's prison cell. He was hunched over the foil, sucking up the fumes. I was asking him what he'd said, knowing full well, but needing to hear it out of *his* mouth. He was looking up, puzzled. 'I just asked you if you'd ever played poker with Keyop, that's all. He was a good player.' He was smiling at me, an opiate smile. 'I meant to Keyop. What did you say to Keyop?' Paddy O'Brien was smiling again. 'I told him I fucked you. It was just a joke.' I was brandishing a yellow spear and Paddy wasn't smiling any more. Paddy was on the floor, a spear sticking out of his chest. A spreading red stain.

I walked over to Pawel's flat but I couldn't convince him to come back to work. Pawel must have got to Socha too, because when I spoke to her she refused to come back, saying 'not safe'. I tried to reassure them, said that we could issue new cards for the door, so that there was no way he could get in again, but he had got to them and I couldn't convince them. I opened the club myself. I wasn't going to let this man, whose name I still didn't know, ruin what I had built up from nothing. From less than nothing. I was the club. The club was me.

I cleaned up, washed the tables, hoovered the floor. I filled the soap in both toilets. I served behind the bar. I was front of house. I sorted out the PA. I introduced the acts. By the end of the evening, I was aching with exhaustion. It was a good hour or so after everyone had gone before I managed to get the place straight and I was ready for home. I craved speed but I was not going to give in to my cravings. I put the takings in the safe and turned the dial. I was about to lock the office and leave the club when Ray started to bark.

It's ok, Ray. There's no one there, I said.

But he wouldn't stop barking. In fact his barking became more frantic. I told him to 'shush' but it made no difference. I went to the outside door, where Ray was standing. I listened at the door. I thought I heard someone shuffling outside. Then the flap of the letterbox opened and a voice whispered, 'Nick ... Nick ... I know you're there.' Ray was going berserk, jumping up and down and barking. 'Nick ... let me in ... I've got something for you.'

I shouted for Ray to follow me and I locked us both in the office. I reached for the metal bar and I stood in the middle of the room, gripping the bar and listening. Ray stopped barking. Silence. I put the bar down and took a glass from a drawer in my desk. I uncorked a half-empty bottle on the top. I poured two inches and necked it.

'Bang! Bang! Bang!' on the door. I nearly dropped the glass I was holding. My heart punching its way out. Silence again. Then 'Bang! Bang! Bang!' Ray was going insane. I tried to calm him down but it was no use. The sound was not being made by a fist on wood. It was too loud. He must have a bar or a staff of some sort. Maybe a baseball bat or a hammer. The door was thick but given enough force, it would give.

I rang the police. It was gone three o'clock in the morning. They said they'd send someone out immediately. I stood in the middle of the room, necking whiskey and smoking, waiting for them to turn up. All about me was silence. There was a window in my office, quite high up. It was a frosted window and it didn't look out on anything as it was under the pavement. Its function was to allow some light into the room. It was illuminated by the street lights above, which shone down through a metal grate, projecting black bars across the pane. I noticed the pane darken, and I realised someone was standing on the grate. Very cautiously and very slowly, I went over to the window. I stood looking up, but I couldn't see anything. Then I heard a sound. A human voice making an animal sound. 'Keek, brrrmf', 'keek, brrrmf', 'Keek, brrrmf'.

This set Ray off again and paralysed me with fear. My head was banging. I felt ice cold talons trap me in their grip. I tried not to scream out. Eventually, the noise stopped. Ten minutes later, two policemen arrived. I told them everything. They showed me the outside door. The wood was bashed in and splintered. The first policeman said that whoever it was had almost broken through. They took the incident very seriously, writing everything down. The second one spoke into his radio.

They said that they were going to have some presence at the club for a while, until it was resolved.

The next day, I told Pawel and Socha about the police presence and they agreed to come back to work. There was a policeman there every night for the next two weeks. I had an idea about how I could turn this to my own advantage.

I rang up a journalist who had covered the launch of Café Assassin. I told her what had happened and how the police had reacted. I arranged to meet her at the club. She turned up with a photographer. We talked for over an hour, then the photographer took some pictures. I may have exaggerated a little. I may have given the impression that the man with the hat had been sent by a rival business or protection racket.

The feature was published a few weeks later. It was a double spread with lots of photographs. More papers and some magazines showed an interest. The police continued to monitor the situation, but there was no sign of the man with the hat. Nothing. Eventually, they said that they were satisfied that he had given up his campaign of intimidation and moved on to someone else. The police stopped coming.

Three or four months after re-opening, I was raking it in. One magazine did a feature on how I was at the centre of the redevelopment of the south-east side of the city. They ran it as a plucky-club-owner-puts-up-a-fight story. I framed one of the stories and hung it next to Baudelaire. I was a bit of a local celebrity and people flocked to see a real life hero. It was far from the truth, but I was no longer a failure. I was a success, just like you. I'm trying not to laugh, Andrew.

You are surrounded by killers. By serial killers and psychopaths. You don't have any friends, but your cell mate is ok. He is called Ahmed. You haven't had chance to get to know him. But you hope he will become a friend. You have been told to make yourself scarce. Something bad is going to happen to Ahmed. You have to warn Ahmed. You tell him to go to the screws and ask for help. Ask them to take him off the wing straight away. Ahmed doesn't take your advice and the next thing there are five men in your cell. Ahmed is ready for them. He has a can of beans in a sock. He puts up a fight. He is stabbed in the leg. He injures the men. Ahmed is taken away to Health Care. He has to have stitches. Ahmed is patched up but he is not moved to another wing.

You don't understand why he isn't moved. Surely that is standard procedure? But you don't understand much about prison yet. A few days later you hear a scream. It fills the corridors. You see a smackhead leave your cell with a flask in his hand. Ahmed comes crawling out. The junkie has thrown boiling oil in Ahmed's face. The oil is so hot that it melts the flask's plastic lid casing. Ahmed's face is changing colour. His skin is dripping from it. There is nothing you can do. You run down the corridor. You find a screw doing his crossword.

You never see Ahmed again. Word gets out that you informed. Now they are coming for you. You are approached by one of Ahmed's attackers. He tells you that you are going to get it. Why has he told you this? Why has he given you warning? You don't want to leave your cell, but you have to leave your cell. You are not safe in your cell. You are not safe out of your cell. There is no place of safety. You can't trust any prisoner. You can't trust any officer.

You are attacked by three men. One of them punches you in the face and you go down. They are kicking you. You curl up in a ball. They are booting you. They are stamping on you. They drag you across the room. They get you on your feet. Two of them have hold of you. They pin back your arms. You can't move. The other has a toothbrush with two razors melted into it. He approaches you. He is about to slash the flesh on your face into ribbons. There is someone else in the room. The men are backing off. They let go of you. There is only one other man in the cell now. He has a funny name. His name is Keyop.

I need to tell you something. Something which happened, that was terrible, that nearly destroyed me. It was a few weeks after re-opening the club. I was out with Ray, just past the old recreational ground, that bit of scrubland where Ray caught his first rabbit, that reminded me of the slacks in Manchester, where I'd drunk my cherry wine on the evening of my eighteenth birthday (funny how everything is connected to you, Andrew). I was heading back when I came across another dog walker. He had a staffy cross, black and white. A very playful dog. He said hello, and we got chatting.

I've got a mate with a Parsons Terrier, he said.

I nodded. It was an isolated statement.

Nice temperament, he added.

Your dog's nice, I said, just for something to say. How long have you had it for?

About two years, he said.

What's it called?

He shrugged. Dunno, he said.

This struck me as very odd but there was also something familiar about him. I tried to recollect where I'd seen him. I noticed that he had a rucksack on his back.

Best get off, I said.

It was a Friday night, and I had to open the club.

Well, nice talking to you, he said. But in a way that made me think that it hadn't been nice talking to me.

I'd walked about fifty yards or so. I don't know what it was, call it a sixth sense if you like, but something made me turn round. There he was, standing on the brow of a hillock, the sun setting behind him. He'd put on his hat, it was a military-style hat. Then I saw him take something out of the rucksack which was now beside him. I don't know why I didn't run immediately, it was as though my shoes were welded to the ground, like they were that night in 1989.

As he lifted it up, I could see the outline. It was unmistakable. It was a crossbow. It was only then that I ran. I ran as fast as I could, with Ray running beside me. I heard the 'ffsstt' of air as the bolt whizzed through the sky hurtling towards us. Then a dull thud. I stopped and turned around. There he was, my dog, my greatest companion. He was on the floor. He wasn't moving. There was a bolt through his head. His mouth was open and his tongue was lolling. His eyes stared at nothing. Dead.

I went to run after the man, but he'd disappeared. I lay down next to Ray and I wept. I clung on to his limp body. Hot tears rolled down my cheeks and onto his warm fur. I lay there until the sun had fallen out of the sky. I took Ray in my arms and carried him back to Richard's place. I buried him close to the rabbit catch the next day. I was beside myself with grief. It wasn't just Ray that had died, trust had died with him.

I had five days off work. I was a real mess. I didn't eat, I didn't drink, I didn't sleep. I couldn't smoke a cigarette. I couldn't watch the television. I couldn't even go running. Nothing gave me solace, everything amplified my loss. I spent most of my time in bed staring at the cracks in the ceiling.

On the fourth day, I decided I would get revenge on this man, whose name I didn't even know, nor his motive. It was an idle threat: I didn't have the first idea about how I would track him down. I thought of nothing else, of how I would go back to that place and find him with his dog. How I would capture him and take him into the back room of the club. How I would torture him slowly over days and weeks, keeping him alive, just. Then finally, when he was beyond the point of caring, I would end it for him.

I went to the place every day. I would sit there for hours but he never came. After a few weeks the pain of Ray's death eased and life went on. I was resigned to the fact I would never see the man again.

Then one day, I got a phone call from Pawel.

Nick.

What is it?

I see him.

I knew immediately who he meant, but asked anyway, Who?

The man with hat, the man who kill your dog.

Where?

Lidl.

When?

Just now. I am here now. They have offer on champagne again, only £10.99. We can sell for £25, is three pound cheaper than cash and carry, I don't know how they do it.

Never mind that, where is he now?

In next aisle.

Keep him there, I'll be right over.

How?

I don't know, just think of something. Say you're doing a survey.

He will know me from club?

Oh, shit, yeah. Listen. Just keep an eye on him. I mean it, Pawel. Don't let him out of your sight.

Pawel had the van, and Steve was miles away. Richard was in the club, fiddling with the PA, double checking everything for the gig tonight. I went over to him.

Richard, I need you to do me a favour.

Oh, hi Nick, what is it?

Pawel's found the man who killed Ray.

The man with the crossbow, and the hat?

That's him.

I need you to drive me to Lidl.

Lidl?

That's where the man is, the man who killed Ray, he's in Lidl. Leave that for now, come on.

They do some good offers.

Never mind that.

We set off in Richard's clapped out Peugeot. It was only ten minutes away. I rang Steve as Richard drove.

Steve, I need you, it's urgent.

I explained the situation.

That weird hat cunt with the crossbow? I'll bring my tools.

Always up for extreme violence, Steve was happy to meet me back at the club. I urged Richard to drive faster. He put his foot down. He seemed excited, thrilled even.

I've been waiting for this, he said.

I wasn't really sure what he meant. To catch Ray's killer?

For this moment. For something to happen. You know, an actual high tension event.

He started telling me about the kids who were hanging around our street. How he was convinced they were breaking into houses. How he was convinced one of them had stolen his bicycle. How he was thinking of creeping up on them at night with a bike chain. How he had planned an ambush. He was going to hide in an overgrown rhododendron and wait for the ringleader. How he was going to whip him across the face with the chain. All of this from Richard, the human dormouse. Soft, gentle, whispering Richard Digby Ebbs. To say I was shocked was an understatement.

So you're ok with this then? I said.

Nick, this is the best day of my life, he said.

We pulled up in Lidl car park and we got out.

Leave this to me, I said. Stay behind me as back-up.

He nodded. We walked into the store. We went past the fresh fruit and veg aisle and turned into the canned goods. There was no sign of him. We moved to the next aisle, past the biscuits and tea and coffee. Nothing. Then I saw Pawel.

Where is he?

He ushered me to another part of the store and pointed. I crept up to where there was a gap between some tinned goods. And there was the man who had murdered Ray, in his daft military-style hat. He was pushing a trolley and walking towards us. We ducked behind a display of boxed sweets. I watched him leave the store. Pawel and Richard were beside me.

Come on, I said.

We followed him into the car park but, before we had time to grab him, he was in his car and away. We ran to Richard's car, though it would have made more sense to use the van. Still, there was no time to think it through. We all piled in and Richard drove off in pursuit of the man in the hat.

He was already a good hundred and fifty yards in front and Richard had to put his foot down to close the gap. We were almost behind him, just one car between us, when the lights in front turned red. The man in the hat had gone through on amber but the car in front of us had come to a stop. I could see the man in the hat's car in the distance, speeding up the hill. I rang Steve.

Are you there yet?

Two minutes away.

Change of plan.

I told him where we were. Kirkstall is a long road. I described the car we were pursuing. Steve was going to come from the other end, and block him off. I wasn't sure how this would work, but Steve was very insistent. We travelled along Kirkstall, driving away from town. The man in the hat signalled right shortly after. We did the same and Richard moved into the right-hand lane. We followed the man up Greenhow Road until we came to the T junction. The man indicated left. I rang Steve.

We're on Burley Road now.

How far?

We're just opposite the park.

I'll turn up Woodside.

We stopped at another traffic light. There was still one car between us. We carried on past Haddon Road. As the man indicated left to turn down Argie Avenue, I could see Steve coming up it the other way. He spotted the man immediately, and without slowing down, drove his car into the driver's side of the man's car.

There was a loud thud. The man's car shunted sideways onto the pavement and crunched up against a stone wall. The front of

Steve's car concertina-ed. Steam was pouring from the radiator. Steve jumped out and ran over to the man's car. The man was trying to open his door, but it was wedged in. Steve yanked it hard, until it gave way. He booted the man in the face then dragged him out. The man's hat fell off and rolled into the gutter. Steve dragged him over to where we had parked. Pawel, who was in the back, opened the far door. Steve dragged him across.

I've got a delivery for you, he said. Did anyone order a dog-murdering cunt?

When we got back to the club, Steve took the man into the office. I locked and bolted the doors behind me. When I got to the room, Pawel and Richard were already there. Steve had the man on the floor and he was stamping on his head.

Hang on. Hang on.

I managed to persuade Steve to stop.

Before you give him permanent brain damage, I need to ask him a few questions.

Fair enough, Steve said. It's thirsty work this head stamping. Anyone fancy a beer?

He fetched us all Coronas from the fridge. Richard and Pawel helped me get the man onto the sofa. Blood was pouring from his mouth and both eyes were peeping out from the bruised skin.

Who are you? I asked.

He didn't say anything, just stared at the table in front of him.

What do you want with me? I tried again.

Nothing.

Steve must have thought he was helping when he picked up the steel bar from behind the sofa and smashed the man in the face with it. I could hear the man's bones crack, and saw blood burst out of his nose, spattering the white wall behind him. The man was sprawled across the sofa.

I've got a bike chain in my car, Richard said. Do you want me to get it?

The man was shaking. Then I noticed a wet patch between his legs.

He's pissing himself. Steve said. Fucking cunt is pissing all over the furniture.

The man started to cry. A congealed rope of blood and snot was swinging from his nose. His eyes were red and wet with tears. He started to make a strange animal whimper.

Listen, just stop for a minute.

I let the man come round and then asked him who he was again. There was a long pause. The man tried to speak. He put his hand to his mouth and took out two loose teeth, blood was still pouring from his mouth. He put the teeth on the table next to the ashtray.

Why did you kill my dog?

At last he managed to say something, I'm Patrick's brother, I'm Tom.

Who's Patrick?

Patrick O'Brien.

I saw the yellow spear half in and half out of Paddy's chest. Paddy wheezing, blood pouring. Paddy falling, splayed on the floor. Blood. Red. Paddy's eyes, pleading. Gasping. Fists clenching. His last breath. The light going out.

I sat Tom up and got him a beer. He had killed my dog and I had killed his brother. I explained to him how it happened. How unwell I'd been after Keyop's suicide.

Steve looked in horror. You were fucking a bloke?!

I ignored Steve, and carried on with my story, describing how mentally disturbed I was, and what Patrick had said that upset me so much. It all made sense, what Tom had been doing. Lost and found: he had lost Paddy and found me. The bar of soap. Even the noise that Madman Marz had made that night. The story I'd told Paddy. Even though I promised Keyop I hadn't told anyone else. It was a stupid lie. It hadn't mattered to me but I could see now what it had symbolised for Keyop. The one person he thought he could trust, had lied to him. He had no one else. I told Tom that killing Paddy had been a moment of madness. And I asked him for forgiveness.

He started to cry again and mutter incomprehensibly. I could see now that he had mental health problems. There are no monsters, Andrew, just pathetic mentally ill people. I tidied him up as much as I could. I helped him outside and ordered him a taxi to the hospital. Steve, Richard and Pawel went.

I sat on my own in the back room drinking my beer. I was shaking. I felt like a thread was being pulled and I was unravelling. I didn't know what to do. I needed to talk to someone with a bit more sensitivity than the three stooges I'd just dismissed.

I pulled out my phone and rang Liv. I told her what had happened. I didn't think she would come, I really didn't, but twenty minutes later there was a knock at the door. I got up, unbolted the locks and let her in. She put her arms around me and I collapsed onto her chest.

Are you all right?

He killed my dog, Liv.

I told her some of what happened. I didn't tell her about the teeth. Instead, I told her that I'd tried to stop Steve, but that he was out of control.

Why didn't you tell me about all this?

I didn't think you wanted anything to do with me. You made that clear.

I told her that I'd tried to reason with the man, but that he wouldn't talk. Then I broke down.

When Keyop died I couldn't grieve. I'd never openly admitted to our relationship. People knew, sure, but I carried this grief around me like it was a solid black weight in the middle of my heart.

I couldn't get it out ... I killed an innocent man, Liv. Patrick O'Brien. He had told a malicious lie but he hadn't deserved what he got. In my head he was mocking me. He was mocking Keyop. In my mind he had caused Keyop's death.

Maybe he did. You don't know.

Keyop caused Keyop's death. I know that now. I stabbed Paddy in the heart, Liv. I watched him bleed to death. I saw him take his final breath. Gasping on the floor, holding the spear, his eyes looking at me, pleading. I did that. I'm a murderer.

I was shaking all over. I couldn't look her in the eye. We walked into the main bar. She poured two whiskeys. She put her arms around me again and I clung on to her. She smelled sweet and warm and safe. I stroked her hair.

Then I was kissing her. First gentle kisses, then more urgent, fierce kisses. Our lips locked together. My hands round her back, my hands on her arse. Her hands all over me. She stood up and pulled the black dress she was wearing over her head. She threw it in the corner. I unbuttoned my shirt and threw it on top of her dress. I went over to her, kissing her, unclasping her bra, kissing her neck, pulling her hair, kissing her breasts, sucking the nipples. Biting them.

We moved over to the biggest table, I was pulling her knickers down, tearing them off her. I took off the rest of the clothes I was wearing. I cleared the candle holder, the menu, and the beer mats with one swipe of my arm.

She lay across the table, naked except for her shoes, clinging on to the edges. I kissed her belly, I opened her legs and kissed her inner thighs. I licked her pussy, Andrew. I licked your wife's pussy. Pushing my tongue hard against her clitoris, as though her pussy was her mouth and I was kissing it. Harder and harder. She was wet with her own juices and my saliva.

Within a few minutes she was coming. She was groaning with pleasure, jerking around, muscle spasms building. I had to cling on to her hips to keep her in one place. I dug my fingers into her arse cheeks, my tongue and lips clamped to her. She was panting and moaning.

We fucked. I picked her up, still fucking, and we lay on the rug, and we fucked and fucked and fucked, like two dogs. I was fucking her so hard I could hardly catch my breath. Her coming over and over, until eventually, I came too and collapsed on top of her, panting like a beast, beads of sweat pouring off me.

Twenty-two years I'd waited for that, Andrew. We lay in silence, Liv stroking my hair. We lay panting, getting our breath back.

Now that *was* the fuck of a lifetime, Liv said.

That's what she said, Andrew. The fuck of a lifetime. And it was for me too. We'd both had the fuck of a lifetime. No matter how many times *you* fucked her, you had never fucked her like *that*.

Don't worry, Andrew. I've saved the best till last. I suggest you have a break at this point though. Put it down for a few hours, clear your mind. You'll need all your strength.

The Shadow That Walks Behind You

"He who does not forgive, digs two graves."

Chinese proverb

HH HH HH HH II

I'm aware, Andrew, that this has been a long letter, but I'm getting to the end of it now. I'm including some photographs. I've had one of them enlarged especially. It's the one of me and Liv on top of the Rockefeller. I've had it printed double size. I thought you might want to stick it on your wall. Prison cells can be very Spartan.

Oh, I didn't tell you about New York, did I? Forgive me. You're not the only one who's been to the Big Apple. I went there with Liv in the summer. You wouldn't believe the difficulty I had getting a false passport. My Home Office licence doesn't forbid me from travelling abroad, but you know what American Customs are like. Luckily, Howler knew some people, but it wasn't cheap. You must think me mad to go to so much trouble, but I'd say it was worth every penny.

We did all the touristy things first. Liv, as you know, had already seen most of it, but it was all new to me. Forget that, I'd only come for one reason. Liv didn't want to do it. She'd already done it so it had no appeal. But I begged her and eventually she agreed.

We tried a few comedy clubs first, a few live music bars. The comedy clubs were a bit desperate for trade. The comics standing outside on the sidewalk trying to entice you in. It was free, you just had to buy a beer. Of course we were going to buy a beer, what else do you do in a bar? I liked their attitude. We sat down. Only six or seven in the audience but the comics were funny and the material was sharp. There was a ballsyness about them and a professionalism. Even though they were playing to an obviously disappointing audience they didn't let it show.

There were four Indians from New Delhi, two Spanish lesbians and me and Liv.

You know what they need? I said.

What's that?

A Café Assassin.

It was true. There were far too many places offering the same thing. There needed to be one place where it was hard to get in.

I was itching to do it, and eventually that night I did. I went to the top of the world, to topple your crown. We went to the heights where you had sat in your golden throne: the roof of the Rockefeller. First we were outside the building, looking up to the heavens, an ivory white staircase leading to the bowers. We were craning our necks to take it all in. We entered the building, the golden archway, the marble pillars, a bronze Prometheus, the bringer of fire. We read the plaque in the plaza: 'I believe that the law was made for man and not man for the law.' Are you listening, Andrew?

We were being transported, up seventy storeys, floating on a platform. We stood hand in hand, taking in the scene. The myriad lights: white, yellow, blue, green, red, orange, silver and gold. The dark oblong of Central Park. Then we looked south, down Manhattan, the Empire State Building lit up in blue and white, the flashes of cameras as the tourists at the top of that tower took pictures of us at the top of our tower.

Its entire construction was an ever-extending spire, reaching up to touch the sky. It was a visionary building, as was the Chrysler, a bit to the left, with its vast shining sunburst coronet. Times Square, the Hudson River, the Brooklyn Bridge, the Statue of Liberty. Scenes from films and television. I thought about that night, in *your* house, watching Kojak with *your* dad, *your* mum serving us drinks, pretending she was *my* mum and he was *my* dad. And this was *my* house.

It was more than pretending, it was occult thinking. I could make *them* my mum and dad, merely through an act of will. Standing on top of the Rock, I felt like a god. Hundreds of feet above the streets, surrounded by walls of clear glass: north, south, east, west. The city was beneath me. I was the city. I was above you, Andrew, and you were beneath me.

Which do you prefer? Liv said.

I'm sorry?

The Chrysler, the Empire State or the Rockefeller?

I prefer the Rockefeller.

Why?

I don't know. It's more of a radical gesture. A huge block of idealism.

Really? said Liv. I prefer the Chrysler.

I admire Joseph Rockefeller, I said, And Solomon Guggenheim.

What for?

Wealth has a different smell here. In England it stinks of rotting flesh. Here, it's a living thing. It smells of freedom.

I'm glad you're enjoying yourself, she said.

Sorry to drag you up here again.

You'll pay for it tomorrow.

Why's that?

You're taking me shopping.

Let's get a picture of us with the Empire State Building in the background.

What for?

Just because.

I hate getting my picture taken, Nick. Besides, it's weird, it's what I did with Andrew.

Please Liv, for me. It's no big deal.

I had to blot you out, I had to efface you. We asked a Japanese man to take it. Surely the world experts in taking photographs of significant tourist sites. We posed for the photograph. I was careful to make sure we were standing in the exact same spot you and Liv were standing in that photograph, with the antenna spire reaching up behind you.

Just move a bit that way, I said. That's it.

I put my arm around Liv, just as you had done with Liv, and smiled at the camera. In my mind I was smiling at you. I want you to look at that photograph now. I want you to see how happy we were. How far from a murderer I'd become. How normal, how like any other man in awe of a beautiful woman. In truth, my entire reason for being there was to take that picture. A far as I was concerned, the holiday was over.

You have just been sentenced for murdering a man you didn't murder. The man who murdered him is outside. He is free. He is going to university to study law. You look around your cell. It is bare and cold. This is your new home. You think about Andrew, about his new home, down south. All the way through the trial, you knew that he would come good. He would tell the truth. You know this because he is your best friend. You have known him all your life. You don't remember a time when you didn't know him. You became friends at the age of six over a Fascinating Facts book, but that isn't what made you best friends. What made you best friends happened a few months after, just before Christmas. It was when your Grandma died.

You don't remember your real mum. For three years, your grandma has been your mother. You have known no other. She has doted on you, picked you up from school, bought you sweets from the shop, let you watch your favourite cartoons, cooked you your favourite food. Now you are standing in a graveyard with your dad. A man you have never met before is saying things about your grandma. It is cold and his breath mists in front of his face. There is a thin layer of frost on the grass. You watch the coffin as it is lowered into the hole. That's when you notice water on your dad's face. Your dad is crying. He walks away and you follow him. He stands by a tree. He holds his hands to his eyes, but the water keeps flowing.

He is clinging to the tree. Then he is choking. Choking with grief, the tears pouring from his eyes. You have never seen your dad cry and you are shocked. You watch his whole body shake and you don't know what to do. You want to comfort him, but he seems so remote in his sorrow that you don't know how to touch him. Eventually, one of his friends comes across. He talks to him. He walks across to you and he tells you that he is going to take your dad for a drink, and that you will have to come with him.

You go to a pub. You have never been to a pub. You watch your dad pour a drink down his throat. Your dad has never drunk before. What does this mean, that he is drinking now?

Even aged six, you know it is significant. He lost his wife only three years ago, the mother you don't even remember, and now he has lost his own mother. Your dad's friend buys you a bottle of pop and you sit in the corner and watch. Your dad does not speak. He has no words. He stares at nothing and drinks.

The next day you are back at school and you are telling your new friend about what has happened. He gives you his chocolate bar. He puts his arm around you. For a mad moment, you are so grateful for this gesture that you want to embrace him and cry into his soft jumper. But you don't. When school finishes, you see him talk to his mum. Your dad is there too. Your new friend's mum is now talking to your dad. Your dad is nodding his head. He tries to give you a smile, but he can't quite manage it. Your friend's mum walks over to you. She asks you if you would like to come for tea. She tells you your dad says it is ok.

He waves at you, as you walk off in the other direction. When you get to the road, she tells you to hold her hand. Andrew is holding her right hand and you are holding her left hand. You give Andrew a look and he smiles at you. You look at Andrew's mum and she is smiling at you too. You feel bad about leaving your dad. You love your dad. But you can't help it, you feel good to be in this world of smiling faces and warm hands.

You see all this in your mind, as you sit in your new cell. The white walls, the grey floor. A world without smiles or warmth. You can't believe that, that he never came forward, that he never admitted what happened, that he lied on oath. You have no words. You are numb all over. You stare at nothing.

So there you go, and now you know, Andrew. Anyway, it's been a long letter as I've said before, and that's because I've had a lot to say and also because I know what it's like to be in prison and how nice it is to receive a letter. Mail has a magical aura. It is revered. I hope you agree and that you've enjoyed reading it. I'd like to say that I've enjoyed writing it, and to some degree that's true, but it was something that I had to do, rather than something that I wanted to do. You see, for twenty-two years I have been asking myself one question. Why did you stitch me up? I've come to the conclusion that you stitched me up for two reasons: the first is your cowardice and the second your vaulting ambition.

Of course it helps when you have two parents who are willing to lie under oath. That was quite an alibi they fabricated, and first rate acting skills too (no wonder they were so convincing as Santa and his elf helper). My dad wasn't even at the court when I was sentenced. He told me later, it was because he couldn't face it. Maybe that's true. He had a lot of upset in his life: losing his wife, losing his mum, losing his licence, losing his job. Having a murderer for a son sort of puts the cherry on the cake, don't you think?

Actually, I think there's a third reason why you stitched me up, and it's to do with that knife. The knife our custodial system was kind enough to guard for me all these years. The knife your wife gave to me for my eighteenth birthday. You won't remember my eighteenth because it largely passed without event. Unlike your extravagant affair. There was no hired room, no surprise posse of friends and family hiding behind a partition, no champagne, no cake with 'Happy 18th Birthday Son' piped on with white icing. There were no party poppers or balloons. There were no celebratory banners.

Feeling lonely, I went round to your house, but you'd gone out with your new student friends. I was no longer a part of your circle. Had you forgotten it was my birthday? Had you deliberately ignored me? I'd been excluded. I was somewhat baffled by this state of affairs. No – I was gutted. I bought a bottle of cherry wine from the off-licence and I walked across the slacks on my own, thinking about why you might have shut me out of your life. Perhaps it wasn't cool to work as an apprentice. Perhaps it wasn't cool to work. Perhaps it wasn't cool to wear blue overalls and have oil stains from the machines in the factory. I think what changed everything was that day we were excluded from school.

It was the start of the second year. I'd set off the fire extinguisher (on your say-so) so my cards were already marked. ET was the film everyone was watching and BMXs were the thing everyone wanted. We'd been to the chip shop for our dinner and we were walking past T Brooks. There it was in the window, a Raleigh Gold Burner, £160, way above our budget. I admit that it was my suggestion. I can't blame you for that. I said, 'Why don't we nick it, Andrew?' and you laughed. I was half joking but you thought this was a great idea.

You went into the shop to talk to T Brooks. I think you distracted him by asking him about a puncture that needed repairing. You were very convincing, mendacity is obviously an inherited trait. While you chatted away, I lifted the bike off its frame and carried it silently out of the shop. You glanced back, saw that I'd done the deed and you ran. Out of the shop. You jumped on the back of the bike and off we went, down the hill, quickly gaining momentum, with T Brooks running after us, his brown work coat flapping in the breeze. We soon gained distance and the gap widened. He stopped running. I looked back. He was in the middle of the road shouting at us. We were laughing.

It was stupid to bring the bike back to school with us and to put it in the bicycle sheds at the back of the school. Of course, T Brooks had recognised our school uniforms and went straight to the school. They found the bike straight away. The secretary of the school, whose office window looked onto the bike sheds, had seen us dump the bike a few minutes before. We were taken out of class less than half an hour later. Hardly the crime of the century.

We admitted it immediately, but there were to be consequences: a phone call home. Both your parents and my dad were summoned to the headmaster's office. We stood waiting for our punishment. The headmaster, Mr Sibery, said that we would have to be excluded for the rest of the year. Your parents nodded, showing solidarity with law and order. My dad shrugged, knowing full well that Sibery was flexing his muscles. Miss Cohen, the deputy, pointed out that it would be a mistake to have us both on the streets for a year, that the problem was the influence we had on each other and not how we behaved individually.

My dad was well known to the school at this point: a serial neglecter. And yet they still made the decision that I was to study at home as my dad was out of work, whereas your parents were both in full-time employment. You would sit outside the headmaster's office all year. And that was that. Everyone seemed satisfied. At the time I thought you'd drawn the short straw. My dad said I could play out as soon as I got the work done. To be fair to my dad, he made sure I did all the work. He was strict that way and I worked hard. Most days, I had it finished by twelve noon, sometimes one o'clock. I'd play out with all the other excluded kids, getting into the sort of trouble excluded kids get into.

Whereas you had to sit outside the headmaster's office at one of those folding desks they used for exams. I actually felt sorry for you, but the thing was, you thrived in this environment and when the end of the year came and we were tested to see what groups we'd be put in the following year, you were in all the top groups, whereas I was in the bottom. It was also when you probably decided that you enjoyed studying for its own sake. It wasn't until I was in prison that I could see the appeal.

So there I was, my eighteenth birthday, wandering the slacks with my bottle of cherry wine, thinking back to where it had all gone wrong. You see, I didn't really have any other friends. I found it hard to make friends: to open up, to give myself, to trust other people. Not like you, with all your trendy new student mates who were into The Smiths and The Cure, with their cardigans and quiffs and pretend NHS specs. Or their winklepicker boots, drainpipe jeans and bird nest hair. The men I was working with at the factory were much older than me. They had families. They went fishing at weekends, or to their allotments, or to football matches with their kids. We had nothing in common.

I wouldn't have stolen that bike, Andrew, without your encouragement. We were both culpable. I sensed after that incident that your mother's appraisal of me changed. Nothing on the surface, but I felt that deep down she disapproved of me, saw me as a bad influence on her precious son, and probably viewed me as a chip off the old block. My dad didn't do much to ingratiate himself that day. I'm sure she saw him for what he was: a pathetic pisshead. I realised that my pitiable dream of being adopted was never going to happen. I was not suitable material. I was shut out of your family.

I glugged down the wine. Although it was sweet tasting, it was a bitter brew. Perhaps I *was* a chip off the old block. I thought about that time, only weeks into your first term at college, when you had come home dressed like Robert Smith. I knew you were only wearing those clothes, only backcombing your hair, forcing your feet into those winklepicker boots, for one reason: to impress Liv.

You seemed foreign. A different species to me. I was in my machine-blue overalls, stinking of oil, in my scuffed steel toe-capped boots, my hands calloused, my nails chipped. I made us mugs of tea and we went into my bedroom. I put on Astral Weeks and we shared a spliff. It was a routine we performed many times. Sometimes it was Nick Drake, other times it was Bob Dylan, Lee Scratch Perry, Joy Division (never The Cure, never The Smiths). But it was Astral Weeks that time. And it was Astral Weeks that did it (such a departure from Brown Eyed Girl), particularly 'The Way Young Lovers Do'. It was the rising horn section coupled with those strings.

We both punched the air with our fists at the crescendo of the song. It was, we both agreed, not just Van Morrison's best album, but the best album of all time. I listened to Astral Weeks the other day, Andrew. I haven't played it since that night. The night when everything changed. Listening to it the other night almost killed me. You probably think I exaggerate, but you can always count on a murderer for a bit of hyperbole. I managed the title track, then Beside You, Sweet Thing, Cyprus Avenue. I turned it over and played side two. It starts with The Way Young Lovers Do.

I put my head in my hands and I wept. I was weeping for the loss of our friendship, Andrew. I was weeping for the loss of innocence. For the loss of everything I once had. I was weeping for the love I had felt for you that I would never feel again, that I could never get back. I wept and I couldn't stop.

Anyway, there I was wandering the slacks, kicked out of heaven. A wretched creature. As I finished the bottle, it started raining, not just rain but a deluge. Everything was getting darker. The sky was black with angry storm clouds. Walking up Lorn Lane, the drops plashed on the flags like liquid spikes. I chucked the empty bottle in a skip full of old crap, the glass smashing on some bricks, the fragments scattering all around me.

I wasn't that far from Liv's place. I remember seeing the attic light on, it looked so inviting, and I wondered if that was her bedroom. The rest of the house was in darkness. I didn't really know her that well, but something drew me to her that night, it may have just been the orange glow emanating from her room, who knows, it seemed so warm and normal. Soft and safe. I knocked on her door. I was soaking wet by this point and more than a little drunk. Her parents were out. She let me in and we went into her bedroom.

Nothing happened, Andrew. I didn't betray you like you betrayed me. But how I wanted her that night. She made us both coffee and we sat on the floor of her bedroom with just a candle between us. Her skin seemed impossibly smooth, and her eyes had a wicked twinkle. Her jet-black hair shimmered. I looked at her slim neck, observed the curve of it as it joined her shoulders. Her arms were bare, a light covering of hair on the forearms, her long slender fingers. She was wearing a skirt and as she folded her legs behind her, sitting by the candle, I watched the skin around her thighs tighten, watched the flesh meet in the middle and darken.

It's my birthday, I said.

There was a pause. I know, she said at last. There was another pause, but then she said, I've got you a present.

And she went to a set of drawers by her bed and pulled out a box. I couldn't believe it. I'd only met her a handful of times, chatted a bit, but not intimately.

I've not had chance to wrap it yet, she said. I hope you don't mind, and she handed over the box.

I slid off the lid of the box and there it was. That black and silver knife with the Celtic knot on the front.

I stared at it for a long time. Eventually, I said, It's beautiful.

I honestly thought it was the best present I'd ever had, better even than the boules set you bought me back from France. I held it and took out each implement one by one. I held it over the candle to examine its finery. I wanted to kiss her or at least hug her to show my gratitude. But I was sopping wet and drunk and inside I knew that it might go further if I did (see, I was thinking of you, Andrew, I was trying to do the decent thing – but where does that get you?).

We sat for a few hours. She told me about her family. Her autistic brother who had made her life so difficult when she was a kid. But she wasn't feeling sorry for herself, just being honest. Encouraged by her honesty, I opened up too. I told her everything about my own life.

Tell me a secret, she said.

I thought hard. I wanted to kill my dad, I said at last.

How do you mean?

When I was young, I wanted to kill him. I mean, I thought about how I would do it. I was going to wait for him to fall into a drunken stupor, a nightly thing, then gently place a pillow over his face, press down so he couldn't breathe. Keep it there until he was dead.

Really?

I actually got as far as walking into his room, pillow in hand.

Oh my God! What happened?

I crept up to where he was lying, sprawled out on the bed, fully dressed. He still had his coat and shoes on. I held the pillow in front of me. It was only inches away from his face. I stayed there for, I don't know, for maybe three minutes or more. But I couldn't do it. I'm not a murderer.

I know you'll appreciate the irony, Andrew.

That's mad. How old were you? She seemed to be excited by this, rather than appalled.

It wasn't just the once. I don't remember how many times I did it. I lost count.

Why did you want to kill him?

I told her about the night with you and the others, when we'd seen him stumble up Peter Street, colliding with the lamp post, falling down, lying on the pavement. My mates around me laughing. You next to me, also laughing. Not even recognising his own son. About me laughing to hide my shame. I could feel my thoughts turning melancholy. And I didn't want that. I wanted to enjoy every moment of Liv's company.

Eventually I said, Your turn.

What?

You've got to tell me your secret now.

I don't have anything. I'm a good girl, she said, and she gave me a wicked smile. God she was so sexy that night.

She paused, she was thinking. I could tell she was on the cusp of confession.

I told you mine. Fair's fair, I said.

I do have a secret … but I can't tell you.

Liv, I've just admitted to planning the murder of my own father.

Ok, I'll tell you. But you've got to promise me you'll never tell anyone, ever.

I promise, I said. Cross my heart. I was going to say, on my father's life. But, hey …

We looked at each other and laughed.

So what is it, this big secret?

I don't love him … I don't love Andrew.

I stared into her eyes. We held eye contact for a long time. The candle flickered, casting dancing shadows around the room. The light drew a daddy-long-legs. It moved haphazard, like a drunk making his way back from the pub.

He told me that he loved me, and he looked so needy. I had to lie, and say I loved him too.

Why don't you love him?

Fucking hell! How can I answer that? How can anyone answer that? It's not something you choose. I don't know. We're so different. And I know he's changed for me.

How do you mean?

The clothes he wears, the music he listens to, I know he's only doing that to impress me. I don't even like The Cure. The Cure, The Cramps, for fuck sake, how can you mix them up? They're totally different bands. I mean, I'm flattered by it. But I'm also a bit, I don't know, I don't respect him for it. I wish he had the balls to stand up to me. He never does. If we have an argument, he backs down. He's so scared of getting into a fight. When we have sex, it's nice, I mean, there's nothing wrong with it, but it's not … I don't know what I'm trying to say really, it's just not the fuck of a lifetime.

She looked at me, and I looked at her. Then she burst out laughing. We both laughed. It felt so good that laugh, like it was joining us, like we were becoming one person through that laughter. I realised that I understood Liv better than anyone ever would and that the same was true for her about me. It felt like I was shedding all the shit in my head, chucking it in that skip outside.

She told me about her friends at college, about one of the teachers coming on to her. We were quiet for a while. We watched the daddy-long-legs.

'Daddy-long-legs', she said at last. It sounds like a Harlem pimp.

A molten pool had formed. We watched it spill and trickle, slowing, cooling, to shape veins along the candle. We sat still as the daddy-long-legs flew into the candle flame. Its wings hissed and shrivelled, then it fell into the pool of wax.

What makes them do it? Liv said. Why aren't they wiped out?

We talked about so many different things. She wanted to know about me, about my dad, about my childhood. She even wanted to know about where I worked – something you had never even mentioned.

Not much to say really, it's boring. I'm not allowed to do anything yet. I just have to stand there and watch. Sometimes I get to pass the spanner or the hammer. I'm not allowed to even put my hands in my pockets.

Why not?

Don't know really, but if the foreman catches you, you get bollocked.

That's so funny, she said. So when are you allowed to do something?

Another year.

Fuck. That's harsh. There must be some characters though, she said, drawing it out of me.

I told her about the bloke I was working with.

Old Tom they call him. He has the most ridiculous hair I've ever come across. It's ginger and frizzy and he can only grow a thin line of it just above each ear. He's grown it into these massive ear flaps.

I did an impression. We laughed some more. She found my anecdotes funny. I felt myself grow and shine. I felt a weight I hadn't even known was oppressing me, lift completely off me. She was rapt by my words. I could make her smile, I could make her laugh. It was a beautiful evening and just the best way I could have spent my eighteenth. I felt like we had left the usual world and were floating above the surface of it.

Then there was a knock at the door. Loud and harsh and most unwelcome. Liv disappeared. I watched the wax melt. When she came back she was with you.

What's he doing here? you said. You were more than a little drunk too. Your ludicrous Robert Smith haircut was plastered to your face and dripping rain water.

Not 'Hello Nick, pleased to see you', or even a 'Happy birthday', just an accusatory stare.

I was just walking past, I said. I was wet.

Don't be silly, Andrew, Liv said. Listen, I'll make us all a cuppa.

Liv's bought me a present, I said. And I showed you the knife.

You snatched it off me.

What's this? you said. This is my knife.

I didn't know at the time that Liv had bought it for you, that she was just being kind by pretending it was for me. Perhaps she intended to replace it the next day.

You opened the blade and were examining it. Were you thinking of stabbing me with it?

No it's not, Andrew, it's mine.

I went to take the knife off you. You pulled away. We had a bit of a drunken tussle. I grabbed the knife off you, its new blade slicing right through the top of my finger. Blood everywhere. Gushing red blood. Liv took a towel and wrapped my hand in it, but the blood kept pumping. She fetched a second towel. I held the knife in my other hand. I wasn't going to let it go. I still have a scar where that knife cut me. *Your* knife technically, I suppose.

So here's my theory, and it doesn't put you in a very good light, Andrew: another reason you dobbed me in, the main reason you dobbed me in, the only reason you dobbed me in, is because somehow I'd managed to keep your knife and you suspected that there was something between me and Liv. Twenty-two years because I took your knife. That's heavy, Andrew, even by your standards. As you are no doubt finding out. Of course, you weren't to know I'd end up being incarcerated for twenty-two years, none of us could have suspected that. Perhaps you thought I'd do eight or nine – ten at the most. As you will if you keep your nose clean.

For the record, I did amass a dossier of evidence to prove you guilty of something. I had the video of you insufflating class A chemicals for instance, alongside a few other incriminating artefacts, although I'm not sure anything would have really stuck. Luckily, in the end, I didn't need any of the dossier. Thanks to Officer Leadbeater, who I eventually managed to track down. See what happens when you upset someone? They bear a grudge.

You probably want to know how I convinced Officer Leadbeater. It was very easy. I merely provided the opportunity for him to get even. The victim's shirt was re-examined using modern DNA profiling, not the old blood typing they did in 1989, one of the advantages of living in 2011. And would you believe it, it showed samples of your blood as well as the man's blood, but not mine. And that is how I ended up back in court. This time watching you in the dock, smelling *your* fear, feeling *your* dread.

The judge was sitting at the front of the court. He seemed a little less bored than they usually do. I wondered if you knew him. I looked at the barristers, the court clerk and the usher, and wondered if you knew them too. I'd watched each of your parents enter the witness box and lie under oath. I'd watched each of them address the prosecuting barrister, unruffled by her questions. Neither of them looked at me. The jury sat and listened. In the end they were persuaded by science rather than anecdote.

Then I watched you standing in the dock. You seemed less assured without your robe, without your wig, although you were still wearing one of your many pinstripe suits, the lapels of which you clung onto like you were clinging to the edge of a precipice – which I suppose you were.

I'd like to say I found the experience satisfying, but really I'd be lying. Unlike you, Andrew, I actually find the business of condemning a man rather depressing, even if that man is guilty of the crime he's accused of. It is hard to see prison as anything other than a waste of human life.

I will tell you about my meeting with Officer Leadbeater though. It's rather amusing. He refused to meet me in the pub, you'll see why in a minute. In the end, I went round to his house. He was very civil and we drank tea in the conservatory which overlooked his garden. He has a nice house. He has two cats he bought from a pet sanctuary. The conservatory made me think of Steve, who works for me permanently now. We've both left the world of constructing conservatories behind us, but I thought I saw in the neat handiwork – the pristine lines of filler, the perfectly fitted joints – the very stamp and signature of Steve Taylor.

Thanks for agreeing to meet with me, Paul. I hope you don't mind me calling you Paul, I said.

I didn't know if he'd prefer to be called Officer Leadbeater.

Actually, I'd prefer it if you called me Alhamdulillah.

He must have seen the surprise on my face, though I deliberately tried to conceal it.

I converted to Islam eight years ago.

I found this interesting.

Really, why's that then, if you don't mind me asking?

It was an officer I was working with. I knew he was a Muslim but I didn't really know much about it. It was during the month of Ramadan. I saw the sacrifice he would make every day. He talked to me about the Koran. Every day I was seeing the worst dregs of humanity. I suppose I'd been questioning things for a long time. He was very patient with me, really I knew nothing at all, but every day he'd go through things with me. It all made sense. There was nothing mystical about it. A lot of it was common sense. He had a sick mother who lived with him and the rest of the family. I saw how he cared for her. I thought about my own mother, who was living in a care home, being looked after by kids on the minimum wage who didn't even know her name.

He stopped talking and stared out of the window.

We used to do the weekend shifts in town together. All the drunken men and women. All the fighting we saw, the women dressed like prostitutes. I hated my own culture. It was full of sleaze and corruption. It was immoral and licentious. I was searching for another way. Do you want some more tea?

I'm fine thanks, I said. It's a nice cuppa.

One night we were called to an incident outside a club. A girl had been thrown out for giving oral sex to six men in the corridor of the club. Six men. She was so out of it. I think they'd spiked her drink with something. She was trying to get back into the club by giving oral sex to the security staff. I thought, that's it, and I accepted Islam into my heart. I took my shahada five years ago. Praise be to Allah.

He went silent for a while and we watched two male blackbirds hunt for worms on the lawn.

Please, have some more tea.

I watched the tea pour from the spout of the teapot into my cup.

Anyway, you haven't come here to listen to my story of conversion. So why have you come here?

And I told him the reason. I told him about you and me and about that night. I told him about the shirt. He listened and he nodded. He told me how mixed profiling might now be able to convict you, and he smiled.

Do you know in the Koran there is the story of Cain and Abel?

No, I didn't know that.

We Muslims call them Qabil and Habil, although they're not mentioned by name in the Koran. The story is very similar to that in the Bible. We believe that Cain slew his brother for no other reason than that of jealousy, and that this was the first sin on Earth. Not murder but jealousy.

He got up and shook my hand.

Allah works in mysterious and wondrous ways. He has brought you to me, so we can do his work. Praise be to Allah.

Don't you find that amusing, Andrew? Who says the world hasn't changed. You certainly wouldn't have got that in 1989 would you? In the end it was Officer Leadbeater, or as we should really call him, Alhamdulillah (praise be to Allah indeed), and his sense of divine justice that convicted you. I actually had nothing more to do with it.

I've been most industrious while you've been in enforced indolence. A few months after you were sentenced I opened up another Café Assassin, this one in the fashionable Northern Quarter of Manchester. If anything, it's actually doing better than the original Café Assassin. It's twice the size. We have a house band: Wanda and the White Trash. We're thinking of extending the house band idea to all the clubs eventually. We've been looking at Berlin. We went over there a few months ago to look for suitable properties. We saw some great places in East Kreuzberg. It seems significant somehow that when their wall was coming down, my walls were closing in.

We're putting Berlin on the back-burner for now. The latest venture is New York. We're opening up a Café Assassin on McDougal Street in the New Year. It's a really good spot, about halfway down, where all the bars are, not that far really from where Dylan used to play. I'm going to have a sign on the door which says: YOU CAN'T COME IN.

Here's some advice for you which will help. Try and avoid forming relationships with psychotic cellmates with suicidal inclinations. Try to avoid having a mental breakdown. Whatever you do, don't stab a fellow prisoner in the heart with a sharpened toilet brush because he said something to a person you were previously in a relationship with. If you find a man strangled by an improvised noose made of cut up bed sheets, don't blame yourself for his death. Avoid being sectioned under the Mental Health Act and being transferred to the secure unit of a mental hospital. Stay clear of class A drugs, especially any heroin substitutes, in particular Subutex. Don't, no matter how tempting it might look, cut a main vein with a broken razor blade.

The first few years are the hardest. It does get a bit easier, then it gets harder, then it gets easier again. It will be easier for you because you are forty, not eighteen. It will be easier for you because you've lived some of your life already, and it will be easier for you because you are not innocent. You are guilty.

It will also, in some ways, be harder for you. It will be harder for you because of your perceived drop in social status. It will be harder for you because you're used to the finer things in life: Jaguar cars, Savile Row pinstripe suits, vintage wines, rare ports. I'm coming round to your way of thinking on that one, by the way. You'll miss your single malts, of course, you'd got quite attached to them. You might get some of that prison hooch if you're lucky. They make it out of orange juice and sugar. An acquired taste.

It will be harder for you because you're a QC who's sent down hundreds of men for murder. It will be harder for you because you're in the same prison as Osman. You will meet Osman inside. You will meet some of the other men you've convicted, if you haven't already. Some of them will be innocent of the murder they've been convicted of. All of them will be angry. And they will direct their anger at you.

Try to befriend one of the big men. Do whatever you have to do to be his friend. He will protect you. Try and avoid being on your own at all times. Learn to take the blows. Go down straight away, there's no point fighting back unless you're a hardcase, which you're not.

Don't be fooled by convicts who tell you to stick up for yourself, this only works if you're going to see it through. If you struggle you will just prolong the beating. Make a lot of noise. Shout as loud as you can before you go down. Keep on screaming. Curl up in a ball. Protect your head. Try and make friends with the screws, they will be less likely to turn a blind eye.

Do WATCH OUT for Osman. He will be much angrier than Kareem. Avoid him at all costs. If he enters a room, leave the room. If he opts to do educational studies, opt for work. If he opts for work, opt to do educational studies. He will come for you.

Watch out for receptacles of boiling sugar water. Watch out for razors melted into toothbrushes. Watch out for sharpened toilet brushes. Don't worry about Liv – I'm taking care of her. Because you are guilty and you are admitting your guilt, you won't serve anything like the sentence I had to serve. The important thing is to survive it without too much physical or mental damage. The trick is to come to terms with it, to find the right frame of mind, to make peace with it – good luck with that.

It's Christmas Day, Andrew, and believe it or not, chestnuts are busily roasting on top of your multi-fuel stove. Correction: *my* multi-fuel stove. What's yours is mine. What's mine is yours. I can hear them hissing and we've just opened a bottle of vintage port. I had no idea how delicate the decanting process is. Luckily, Liv is something of an expert. It's a Graham's 1945. Apparently, it's one of your favourites. I can see why, the rich plum flavour, quite musky but with an aroma of roses. And what a lovely ruby colour. Magnificent. I'm wearing my new suit, made especially for me by a Savile Row tailor.

It didn't make sense in the end, for me to be staying in some shitty little room in an old hippy's house and for Liv to be on her own rattling around, for the kids to be away at boarding school. Liv's heart was never really in the boarding school idea in any case, she'd gone along with your wishes. A family should be together. And now we are – together. Even your cat seems to have taken to me. Here he is now, sharpening his claws on the leg of your unused chess table.

It took some time before Ben and Megan accepted me. It was easier with Megan. Ben wasn't rude but he was cautious. The breakthrough came when I helped him with his homework. He'd asked for help before, but I wasn't able to give it. I don't know the laws of thermodynamics, but I could help him with his English. They were studying Macbeth. I was so relieved when he asked for help. I knew I could genuinely contribute.

Let's have a look, I said. And he handed me the worksheet.

I've got to write a monologue from Lady Macbeth, between her going mad and throwing herself off the tower. I've got to imagine what she's thinking about.

That's easy, I said.

Really? Have you read it?

Not only had I read the play, I'd studied it. I'd opted for the module on Shakespeare during my OU English degree. I knew the play inside out. We talked about the regret she would feel, not regret about killing Duncan, no, but the regret of losing the person she loved, the only person she'd ever loved: her husband.

As we wrote a draft, and spoke the words together, I felt her pain as though it were my pain. The last thing we did was to turn the monologue into iambic pentameters, with Ben counting the syllables on his fingers. The final flourish was a joint effort, a rhyming couplet to end. He was absolutely thrilled a week later, when he was awarded an A star.

We all went for a walk in Moorside Park last week. Megan is a bit old for that now, practically a woman, but she came along for the ride. We broke off chunks of bread for the ducks and watched them gobble it down. It was a scene from Swiss Family Robinson. You become a father through your actions, not by your DNA.

Ben, despite resembling you physically, is such a delightful child. And Megan is turning into a very striking young woman. She's left school now. She's nearly eighteen, as you know, an interesting age.

There aren't many jobs around for eighteen year olds. Luckily, I was able to offer her a job. We'll be working closely with each other from now on. It's a practical solution. Liv's running the Leeds and Manchester bars, while I get everything ready for the grand New York opening in the New Year. Liv eventually told me about how your conduct had cost her the catering business. It was when she came back to work at the club. Late one night when we were clearing up.

She told me about the big corporate job and her car breaking down. How she had asked you to book a delivery van. How the food had never showed up. You hadn't booked the van. They were high up, big players with a lot of influence. I thought about the trouble one person can cause another person. She also told me how you'd had an argument a few hours before you were supposed to make the phone call. Surely, you wouldn't be so petty as to fuck everything up for your own wife over such a trivial argument?

Megan is helping her mum out, being trained on the job. Still too young for bar work but she can help out behind the scenes. Exciting times, Andrew. Don't you agree?

I'm sure she'll stop judging you eventually, she might even forgive you. One day. Who knows, eventually she may even pay you a visit. She's so excited about New York, she's bought a whole new wardrobe.

I have to go now, Andrew. We are going to visit Liv's brother, as a family. As you know, he's in a special home, where they can look after him. Liv has bought him a matching hat and gloves set. Ben and Megan have chipped together for some DVDs. He's a big fan of Only Fools and Horses. Then we're going round to Alun's to give out the presents and I don't want to keep Liv, Ben and Meg … I don't want to keep my family waiting.

You know Alun, you were his best man. Alun's a good friend of mine now. Your parents will be there too. I can't say it's all plain sailing there, because that would be very far from the truth. They are, and will always be, lying cunts. Don't worry, I've got plans for them.

It's been a long letter, but I think you deserve a long letter. Every man gets what he deserves, the man with blood on his face and the man with blood on his hands. My hands are clean now. It's time for you to wash yours.

Oh, before I go (I can hear those chestnuts really spitting now!), some good news: Liv says you never thought it would grow, she told me about your persistent efforts to nurture it, but in fact your mistletoe is thriving. It's creeping along the twisted bough of the oak in the corner of your garden. I'm taking some to Alun's party now. I'm cutting your mistletoe with my golden sickle.

What have I gained in royal wealth through you?
Naught worth more than love that's real and true.

Ben Honour, aged 15

Acknowledgements

I would like to thank all the wonderful people at Bluemoose Books for their dedication and expertise: Kevin Duffy, Hetha Duffy, Lin Webb, Pippa McCarthy and Leonora Rustamova (couplet queen). I'd also like to thank Jim Greenhalf, Lisa Singleton and Simon Crump for reading drafts of the book at different stages and giving invaluable advice. Special thanks to QC Paul Greaney, who helped with the legal side and was kind enough to let me shadow him in his work. Also a big thank you to Oliver Coleman for his 'insider' knowledge. Finally, a big thank you to my son, Carter Stewart, who lent me his ears when the book was forming in my head.